The Devil's Corral

North Kingstown Free Library
100 Boone Street
North Kingstown, RI 02852
(401) 294-3306

Also by Les Savage, Jr.
in Large Print:

Table Rock
Coffin Gap
Last of the Breed
The Bloody Quarter
The Shadow in Renegade Basin
In the Land of Little Sticks
Phantoms of the Night
Treasure of the Brasada
Gambler's Row: A Western Trio

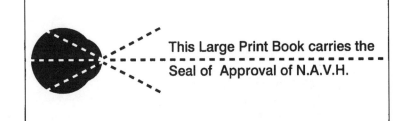

The Devil's Corral

Corral

A Western Trio

Les Savage, Jr.

WHEELER
PUBLISHING

Published in 2004 by arrangement with Golden West Literary Agency.

Wheeler Large Print Western.

The text of this Large Print edition is unabridged. Other aspects of the book may vary from the original edition.

Set in 16 pt. Plantin by Minnie B. Raven.

Printed in the United States on permanent paper.

Library of Congress Cataloging-in-Publication Data

Savage, Les.
    The devil's corral : a western trio / Les Savage, Jr.
      p. cm.
    Contents: Satan sits a big bronc — Señorita Scorpion — The devil's corral.
    ISBN 1-58724-559-0 (lg. print : sc : alk. paper)
    1. Western stories.   2. Large type books.   I. Title.
PS3569.A826D46 2004
813'.54—dc22   2003062148

The Devil's Corral

As the Founder/CEO of NAVH, the only national health agency solely devoted to those who, although not totally blind, have an eye disease which could lead to serious visual impairment, I am pleased to recognize Thorndike Press★ as one of the leading publishers in the large print field.

Founded in 1954 in San Francisco to prepare large print textbooks for partially seeing children, NAVH became the pioneer and standard setting agency in the preparation of large type.

Today, those publishers who meet our standards carry the prestigious "Seal of Approval" indicating high quality large print. We are delighted that Thorndike Press is one of the publishers whose titles meet these standards. We are also pleased to recognize the significant contribution Thorndike Press is making in this important and growing field.

Lorraine H. Marchi, L.H.D.
Founder/CEO
NAVH

★ Thorndike Press encompasses the following imprints: Thorndike, Wheeler, Walker and Large Print Press.

Table of Contents

Satan Sits a Big Bronc'   9

Señorita Scorpion   145

The Devil's Corral   218

Satan Sits a Big Bronc'

Les Savage, Jr.'s original title for this story was "Satan Sits a Big Bronc' ". It was sold to Malcolm Reiss at Fiction House. The author was paid $600.00 for the story on November 6, 1945. The title was changed upon publication to "*Señor* Black Mask — Dead or Alive" when it appeared in *Action Stories* (Winter, 46). For its first appearance in book form, the text and title of this story have been restored.

I

The shadows of the three approaching horsemen scuttled over the ground, reached the mud-walled *jacal,* and came to a halt there like a black hand clutching at the house. Renaldo Catecas must have heard the animals, for he stooped through the low door, blinking in the bright afternoon light, and then his face contorted with frightened surprise as he saw them. The horsebacker in the middle leaned forward slightly. His voice held a dark, slightly ominous timbre when he spoke.

9

"I'm Davoc Hobkirk, and I'm about fed up chasing all over Texas collecting taxes for A. J. Rhode. And if you're as sweer to give up your due as the last drowlin' straumel was, you'll find yourself walking red watshod back into that calf ward you call a house."

"¿*Qué dice?*" asked Catecas. "What did you say?"

"You'll have to forgive Captain Hobkirk," said Dallas Fenwick, tugging impatiently at his fiddling buckskin. "He's not too late from Scotland. He said, if you're as reluctant to pay up as the last crawling worm was, you'll find yourself walking in blood up to your boot tops back into that cow pen you call a house."

"Hobkirk?" Catecas said it hollowly.

Davoc Hobkirk was used to that by now. His appearance never failed to excite wonder in this land. There was probably not another horse in Texas as big as the black Clydesdale stallion that he had brought with him from Inverness. No lesser animal could have carried him comfortably.

He was closer seven feet than six, with more weight in his great gangling frame than there seemed to be. The prodigious bones of his wrists, protruding from his sleeves, were big around as an ordinary man's arms, and his big, grasping hands covered the whole front of the saddle. He had adopted the buckskin jacket and leggings of the frontier, but still wore his ancestral tartan about his waist.

"As tax assessor for Hidalgo County, I warned you I'd have to resort to Rhode's Riders if you didn't meet your bill, Catecas," said Dallas Fenwick. He was a big, florid man in a dusty fustian and black cavalry boots, and he pulled a red bandanna from beneath the coat to mop his beefy, perspiring face. "You're three months behind now, and either you make some arrangements to meet the bill, or we're here to confiscate your property in amount commensurate with what you owe."

"*Señor* Fenwick," said the Mexican, holding out filthy, gnarled hands, "you know I have no money. How can I pay Governor Rhode three percent of nothing? I am a *peón*. Like all the other *peónes* along the Río."

"Then it's poind we must," said Hobkirk in that deep, resounding voice as if he were speaking from a chasm. "What kind of stirks hae ye got?"

"Poind, *señor?*"

"Confiscate your goods, your properties," said Hobkirk impatiently. "Where are your stirks . . . your cattle, I mean . . . where do you keep the stock?"

"You have no right!" It was Catecas's woman who had shoved him away from the door so she could get out. They aged pathetically soon in this bleak land, and, although she could have been no more than twenty-four, she was already thick and sloppy through the hips and waist. Some of the fire her beauty must have once held, however, still remained in her flashing black eyes. "Three percent? Can you shake three percent of a cow, a pig? No. You'll take all of it. How can we live without our animals? What will I feed my *niños* without a goat to milk, or chickens to rob?"

"Sancha, please. . . ."

"No!" The woman thrust her husband's restraining hand away, moving on out to stand with her hands on her hips. "A. J. Rhode? What right has he to levy taxes on us like this?"

"He's the governor," said Fenwick angrily. "Now, I. . . ."

"Yes, the governor. So he declares martial law in a town that doesn't need martial law and sends ten times as many of his state militia down here as is necessary and then levies a tax on the people to pay for their keep."

"There was a dire necessity for the militia in Brownsville," said Fenwick, his voice taking on a hoarse note as it grew louder. "There had been a general uprising all over the town. . . ."

"And why?" cried the woman shrilly. "To keep your Riders from murdering one of the finest men Texas ever had."

"Eddie Pickering killed a Rider!" shouted Fenwick.

"In pure self-defense!" screamed the woman, shaking her fist at them. "We know what happened, Fenwick, we know what's happening. Everybody does, every good person in Texas. Why do you think they rose up and stormed the courthouse? You weren't going to give Eddie Pickering any trial. You were going to transfer him from Brownsville to Austin, only he would have never reached Austin, would he? He would have tried to escape on the way, like the Kelly brothers, and Orson Niles. We know, Fenwick. Maybe we can't read, but we know. I heard about that 'Poll of Horror' the *State Gazette* published. Seventeen men murdered by the state police. We know their names. We know how it happened. And Eddie Pickering would have been another. No wonder you had to bring in the state militia. . . ."

"Stop this guidwife's pibroch, Barnabas!" bellowed Davoc Hobkirk suddenly, jerking a hand at the third horseman.

"With pleasure," said Barnabas Benton, swinging off his slat-ribbed mare and tossing the reins over its head with a jerk at the end that made the ewe-necked beast wince. He wore a pair of greasy buckskin leggings over his red flannels, the long-sleeved underwear sufficing for his shirt. His great beer belly thrust itself ostentatiously forward. The sun had burned his hair to a frizzled pink, but his beard had been used so long for a napkin its dark, greasy color was indeterminate.

"Don't touch me!" screamed the woman, whirling toward him. "I'm no Eddie Pickering. You can't take me out and shoot me down in cold blood like those men. The curse of Santiago on you. . . ."

"Shut your damned mouth," snarled Benton, grabbing her shoulder, "and get back in that house."

"*Señor*," quavered Catecas, clutching at the single galus that held up Benton's leggings, "let her go. She is a woman. . . ."

"Damn you!" shouted Benton, backhanding Catecas with his free hand. It knocked the Mexican against the wall of his adobe *jacal*.

"*¡Lepero!*" screeched the woman, trying to twist free of the redhead's grip, her *camisa* ripping in his grasp. Failing to free herself this way, she bit his hand just as he was turning back.

"Well, damn you!" roared Benton. He let her go and hit her across the face, knocking her back against the wall, too, and wheeled to his mare. "Did you see that, Davoc? She bit me. The damn' trollop bit me. I'm going to blow them teeth right out of her mouth. I'm going to get my Greener and. . . ."

"Are you, Benton?"

The light of late afternoon was deceptive, and for a moment Hobkirk could not see

14

who had spoken. Then his great, narrow head turned far enough toward the sound to see the man standing at the corner of the *jacal*.

He had the appearance of a shadow, a tall, slim, wiry shadow with the long, catty legs of a man used to much riding and hips so negligible as to make the singular breadth of his shoulders almost grotesque in contrast. He was dressed all in black — black wool pants stuffed into the tops of black half boots, black shirt, black flat-topped hat, and a black mask across his lean face.

"¡El caballero fantasma!"

It came from Renaldo Catecas, still crouched at the foot of the wall where Benton's blow had sent him. Benton himself had jumped to his mare, and one of his hammy hands slapped down on the greasy oak butt of a double-barreled, sawed-off shotgun lashed behind his cantle. He stood fixed that way, staring at the man in black.

"Go ahead, Benton," said the man. His long slender fingers hung like pendant hooks above the butt of his six-shooter. "Go ahead, Benton, I thought you were going to get your Greener."

Barnabas Benton's Adam's apple moved up and down once in his thick neck. Then he dropped his hand from the shotgun.

"Does anyone else want to pull a gun?" said the man in black, turning his shadowed face toward Hobkirk. The Scotsman felt a deep, violent impulse sweep him, and his right hand closed tightly across the pommel. His whole body trembled visibly, but he controlled the impulse. The man at the corner waited another moment.

"All right," he said finally. "Get out, then. Get out and don't come back. I'll have my gun out, a second time, and I won't stop to ask stupid questions!"

The governors of Texas resided in the stately governor's mansion in Austin, on Colorado Street between West Eleventh and West Tenth, and the sumptuousness of its hushed, high-ceilinged rooms had always made Davoc Hobkirk's bleak nature squirm uncomfortably. A green-liveried Negro had ushered him into the library, along with Benton and Fenwick, and the huge Scotsman stood morosely in the center of a crimson Empire Ambusson rug, glaring dourly at the huge desk Stephen Austin had once sat behind.

He was still grimy and weary with the two days' ride from Hidalgo County, and there was a bitter rage smoldering insistently somewhere deep down in the narrow dark chasm of him. Barnabas Benton had been in Hobkirk's command long enough to know the discretion of silence when the Scotsman was in this mood. Hobkirk turned abruptly

16

toward the rustle of heavy red damask portières before the door.

Carrying his carpetbag, Alfred Johnson Rhode had come to Austin in 1869 and since that time had shocked even his most ardent supporters by his rule. He was a small man, inclined to stoop, with a nose that held inquisitiveness in its hooked beak, and a mouth so thin and small it was all but lost beneath that nose. His little blue eyes ferreted the three men in a shifty, sliding motion, and then he moved to the desk, swinging the swivel chair out to seat himself.

"Well," he said in a thin, sharp voice.

"Yure cess collectin' dinna go so well," said Hobkirk, his voice seeming to fill the room. "The people are beginning to add things up."

Rhode's head lowered and his little eyes turned up suspiciously beneath sharp brows. "Surely that didn't stop you."

"*El caballero fantasma,*" said Hobkirk.

Rhode's head rose slowly, as he grew rigid against the back of the heavy Chippendale chair. The word was barely audible. "What?"

"The Mexicans hae a quaint way of attaching names to things like that," said Hobkirk.

Rhode was looking at the other men, and his face had paled discernibly, whether with anger or fear, Hobkirk could not tell. "You all were there?"

Fenwick nodded. "A man named Renaldo

Catecas. Three months in arrears on my tax records. His woman had started making trouble, and Benton was off his horse trying to get her back in the house. This" — and perhaps the deprecating motion Fenwick made with his hand was for the name — "this Phantom Horseman appeared suddenly at the edge of the house."

"Any shooting?"

"Nobody pulled his gun," said Fenwick.

The pallor was replaced by a faint flush in Rhode's thin face. "You mean you let him chase you off? Like a bunch of coyotes, with your tails between your legs?"

There was so little flesh on Hobkirk's gaunt, bony cheeks that the small muscles were quite visible beneath the skin, twitching into taut relief with the clench of his great jaw. He walked over to lay his hands flatly upon the desk, staring at Rhode from those deep, burning eyes.

"Everyone knows what he can do wi' a gun, Rhode. I no hae any skill wi' that weapon, and I never did think a dead fule was a brave mon." He drew a heavy breath, his eyes staring past Rhode. "But someday I'll meet him on even ground, and the story will be different."

"You had him right there in front of you!" snapped Rhode, rising sharply from the chair. "You had him dead to rights and you let him chase you off like a bunch of howling prairie

18

lawyers. Rhode's Riders? You're nothing but a bunch of tramps. How many times is it now? Last month in Laredo. April south of Austin. Twice in March. And you haven't even got a good look at him." He paced across the room, bent forward in his rage, hands clasped behind his back. He threw one arm out suddenly. "And not only you. Every constituted authority in the state. Who was it broke up the confiscation of the AD herds on the Nueces last month? Who was it stopped Sheriff Giddings from evicting that tenant in Webb County?" He had come to the end of the room, and he whirled back on them, shaking his fist. "I tell you, Hobkirk, I'm fed up. At first he was only a nuisance. He's becoming a menace. The Phantom Horseman . . . !" He snorted at the end of the word. Then, with an abrupt decision, he walked back behind the desk and opened a drawer, lifting out a sheaf of papers. "You remember that list of two thousand-odd fugitives I had compiled for the one hundred and eight counties?"

Hobkirk's mouth twitched downward at one corner. "Aye."

Rhode looked up sharply at the faint mockery in the Scotsman's voice. "I've had them gone through," he said finally, "by a number of men in a position to possess facts pertaining to the case, we might say. By a process of elimination we've narrowed it down to a few names. I have them in this file, with all the existing information about each man. I'm relieving you of further duty, Hobkirk, and I want you to take these papers and put your whole company of police in the saddle and go out and don't come back till you hunt this Phantom Horseman down and kill him!"

Hobkirk took up the sheaf of papers, glancing through them, stopping at one to read it aloud. "Nicholas Carson Udell, born Austin, Texas, October Twenty-Fourth, Eighteen Thirty-Two. Height five feet seven, weight approximately one hundred fifty pounds. Last heard of with Quantrell, in Kansas." A smoldering gleam began to rise in Hobkirk's deep-set eyes. He flipped to the next sheet. "Edward Floyd Random, alias Kip Random, born January Second, Eighteen Thirty-Three, San Antonio, Texas. Five feet eleven inches, blond hair, captain of Company C, Texas Rangers, until March Eighteen Sixty-One, wanted for murder in Brownsville." The light was keener in Hobkirk's eyes now, and he went on reading off the names more swiftly. "Eddie Pickering. Him, too? Louis Tuscon Shell, alias Grandpa Shell. John. . . ." He dropped the papers abruptly, looking up. "Why these men?"

"I told you," said the governor impatiently. "We don't have the slightest idea who this crazy *fantasma* is. The Mexicans won't talk.

20

We haven't been able to get any kind of a line on him. This is the only way left. By a process of elimination. . . ."

"Ye told me that," said Hobkirk. "But why these men especially?"

"We have access to men with information pertaining, as I said, to the subject, and had them go through the files, and by a process of elimination. . . ."

"Sam Houston's plan?" said Hobkirk plainly.

Rhode stiffened as if he had been struck. For a moment he stood there without a sound, staring at Hobkirk, his face pale and taut. Finally he managed to wave his hand vaguely at the tax assessor and Benton. "I won't . . . I won't want to see you any longer."

Barnabas Benton had been lounging in one of the Queen Anne wing chairs by the fireplace, and he rose to his feet, glowering suspiciously. "What the hell. I got as much right to hear. . . ."

"Leave us," said Hobkirk, still staring at Rhode.

"The hell I will," growled Benton. "You can't shove me. . . ."

"Git out, you ree, chuffle, foul-mouthed staumrel, before I lay my claive through yure skull!" bellowed Hobkirk, whirling on him, and the room shook to the deafening echoes of his voice.

Barnabas Benton's red beard lowered against his chest with the dropping of his jaw. He turned dead white, then flushed a dirty crimson, then turned white again. He backed toward the door, through which Fenwick had already retired. When Benton had disappeared into the entrance hall, Hobkirk turned back, his great fists clenched, his whole body trembling.

"That *fantasma* really did leave you in a state, didn't he?" said Rhode, emitting a stiff, unconvincing laugh. "I'd hate to be the object of your rage."

"Ye will be, if ye dinna play square with me," said Hobkirk, when he was able to speak again. He put his hands on the desk once more, leaning forward on them. "I been taking a lot of orders from you blind, Rhode. I'm through wi' that. I always thought you took this *fantasma* business in a little larger draft than ye should. Is it mixed up with Houston's plan? Is that why ye want us to find him for ye? Maybe everything you've been doing is mixed up with it. Eddie Pickering was the bouk that caused all the trouble in Brownsville. He's on the list."

Rhode had recovered some of his composure now, and he walked to a drum table between the wing chairs, taking the stopper from a glass decanter and pouring two drinks. He brought them back to the desk, studying Hobkirk narrowly.

"I think you'll like Dramuie, Hobkirk," he said. "Heather honey and the finest old Highland malt, I understand. We just got it in last week."

There was still an angry wariness in Hobkirk, but it was dissipated by the Scotsman's love for his own brew, and finally he picked the glass up, holding it to the light. "Aye," he said, in reluctant acceptance. " 'Tis a good swats. Here's health to the sick, stilts to the lame, claise to the back, and brose to the wame."

They raised their glasses and drank together, and Rhode lowered his to let the whisky settle before he spoke. "What do you know about Sam Houston's so-called plan?"

Hobkirk licked his lips. "You know I was in Union Intelligence during the war. We got wind of what Houston was doing through a man named Anatole Tadousac. A more treacherous, conniving Lowlander I never met. But he served our purpose. Connected wi' Emperor Maximilian at the time. Naturally the French didna' want Houston diddling down there in Mexico. This Tadousac was one o' the agents they sent up to work on it. Tadousac gave us the names of the men Houston was sending to New Orleans for the money. We tried to intercept them on the train at Endytown, in Tyler County, but they shot their way out. Every one of those men is on your list here, Rhode."

"I see." A wry expression had twisted Rhode's mouth. He turned away from the desk with a heavy breath, hands clasped behind him in that characteristic pose. "All right, Hobkirk. I'll admit my desire to capture *el caballero fantasma* is mixed up with the Houston business."

"The sum spoken of was verra large," said Hobkirk.

Rhode turned to meet his narrow glance. "You'll get your share, I promise. Work with me, and you'll get your share."

"I'd better," said Hobkirk. "It wad not set well with the people to know their governor was using public officers for his own private enterprises."

"Yes," Rhode muttered, turning toward a door to one side of the room. "Yes. And now that you possess the facts, I might as well introduce you to a man you'll be working in rather close connection with from now on."

The opened door revealed a small anteroom. There was a *creak* from within, as of someone rising out of a chair, and then the sound of shuffled boots, and the man stood there. The surprise clutched Hobkirk so violently his whole body jerked with it. When the two words finally came from his mouth, they held a hollow incredulity.

"Major Edmond," he said.

II

It was a large room, but the luxury of its appointments did not match the barren simplicity of its original motif somehow. The satin-embroidered, silver-fringed hangings the Mexicans called *sabanillas* were incongruous with the plain mud of the adobe walls, and the hand-woven rugs of anil could not hide the fact that the floor was only of hard-packed earth. To one side of the open doorway stood a full-length cheval glass, framed in delicately wrought gesso. The man had been admiring himself in this mirror for a long time, turning one way and another, looking over his shoulder or facing the glass squarely, posing and strutting and grimacing.

He was dressed in the dark green coat of a captain in the Mexican army, with heavily fringed epaulets on the shoulders and embroidered frogs of gold cloth on the lapels. The Gold Cross of Honor for distinguished service in the war with Texas hung on his chest, along with a glittering array of other medals. His cream-colored trousers of moleskin were skintight, and his black jackboots were varnished till they shone like glass. His Mexican blood was evident enough, but his greenish eyes and reddish beard had always set him apart from his people.

The woman had been standing in the doorway silently, watching him, and she spoke finally, with the words dripping from her twisted lips like thick syrup.

"Juan Nepuceno Corchino."

He turned in surprise, the movement of his compact body holding a quick, catty nervousness. Then he grinned at her roguishly. "Camoa, my little sister, I did not know you were there." The grin faded, and he made a play at pouting. "*Pues,* why the sarcastic tone? You sound as if I had stolen the *chiles rellenos* again."

"Juan Nepuceno Corchino."

She said it again, bitterly, and moved on into the room, arms folded across her chest. It was a slinky, swinging walk, holding the same felinity as his motions, and her heavy skirt of blue wool worked softly against bare brown calves with each step. Her hair was jet black, as were her eyes, and a face that once must have held a singular, striking beauty was marred by a bad scar running from the tip of her left eye across the cheek to pull one corner of her full lips upward in a slight, perpetual grimace.

The soles of her leather *huaraches* made a gritty, sliding sound against the earth whenever she crossed a bare spot between the rugs, and Corchino turned with her, his puzzled eyes following her across the room till she came to a stop by the great leather

26

dower chest beneath the slot-like window.

"What is the matter, *querida?*" He frowned. "Why do you say it that way?"

Camoa took a heavy breath. "Perhaps I am disillusioned."

"*Cara mía,*" he purred, moving toward her with his hand out.

"No," she said, dipping aside to avoid him and moving down to another window, staring out of it. He stood by the dower chest, hand still held out, a speculation tempering the puzzlement. "So you had to come to Rancho del Carmen," she said at last.

He studied her a moment, the puzzlement completely gone now, a certain craft hardening the planes of his face. "*Si,*" he said in a flat, waiting tone. "And we will be ready to strike soon again, *mi hermanita.*"

"Strike what?" It came from her harshly, and she straightened, turning sharply toward him. "You've been striking all along, ever since you came here. You've been here five years, now, Juan, do you realize that? Five years, up here in the Del Carmens, five hundred miles away from your people, out of touch with them, not knowing what goes on south of the Río Grande, not even caring!"

He began to move toward her, taking each step in a careful, balancing way. "I have to gather new forces. I told you."

"New forces!" she scoffed. "A bunch of drunken, gambling, fighting professional gunmen? The most filthy, vicious, degraded *bribónes* you can find on either side of the border! What kind of forces are those? Not your people, Juan, not the people you were fighting for."

"I'm still fighting for Méjico, *mi hermanita.*" His voice held a smooth conviction. "But if a general can't change his tactics when necessity dictates, he will soon be defeated. I can't use the same men I had before the *americanos'* War of Secession. You saw what happened then. A *peón* army, a rabble of unarmed, untrained *vaqueros.* As soon as the Texas Rangers were brought against us, I started meeting defeat. I should have seen it then. That Colonel Robert Lee finished it. I should have come here then."

"No," she said, tossing her head back. "You still fought on. Because then you were what I admired, the *hermano* I was so proud of, the brother I would have died for. You were still fighting for our ideals, Juan, making a sincere effort to free the *peónes mejicanos* in Texas from political oppression."

His gray-green eyes had taken on an opacity. "It is no different now."

She whirled on him, speaking in a swift, hot stream. "It is! I know what you do with these men, Juan. You aren't a general any longer, fighting to free our people or give them liberty. You're nothing but a small-time *bandido,* taking advantage of your former reputation to raid and depredate and plunder. Perhaps the *peónes* still think you're fighting for them, and help you. Even the people in Méjico. I know what you're doing, Juan, whenever you ride out with those *léperos* of yours. You don't even bother to discriminate any more. *Mejicanos* or *americanos*. It's all the same. I know where you got that mirror. I know the *mejicano* you killed for that coat. . . ."

"No," he hissed, taking another step toward her. His face was not six inches from hers and the sensuous cruelty of his mouth was all too apparent to Camoa.

"Yes!" she said hoarsely, her whole body arching upward toward him in a wild defiance. "You can't hide it any more, Juan, from me or anybody else. Strutting around in front of that mirror. The Emperor of the Del Carmens, the Little Napoléon of the Río Grande" — she let out a disgusted breath — "I thought perhaps you would be another Santa Anna, or a Juárez. I would have done anything for you then. I did. . . ." She let her hand pass over the scar momentarily, and then shook her head as if trying to rid herself of a bad memory, and her body rose up toward him again, voice growing louder. "But I'm through with that now. I don't let you do this, not from my *rancho*, not in my house. . . ."

The sudden pain in her wrist cut her off.

It was his hand, small and hard and inexorable. The gray-green had completely gone from his eyes now, leaving them glittering and black and opaque like a snake's eyes. His broad, coarse nostrils dilated with the breath passing through them.

"You aren't opposing me, are you, *mi hermanita,* my poor, good, kind, jilted little sister?"

The last word drew a quick flush to her cheeks. "Yes," she spat at him. "I told you. I won't let you do this to our family, our people!"

"People like Colonel Jalapo Heldonia," he murmured slyly.

Pain crossed her face for the first time, and it was not from the force of his grip. "Juan. . . ."

"No, *sancha mía.*" His fingers seemed to be crushing her wrist now. "Other people have opposed me. Please, don't let. . . ."

He stopped speaking, and stood there, holding her against him for a moment. Perhaps there had been some small sound, or perhaps it was that uncanny sense of foreign presence he had. He turned his head over his shoulder, then released her, and turned completely around.

"Well, Pegoes," he said.

"Harolde said you wanted to see me as soon as I got in," said Pegoes Oporto, coming on into the room. He was a lean, sullen Portuguese with huge gold earrings in his brown ears and a dirty red bandanna tied about his head. His feet moved with the same deceptive shiftiness as his small black eyes that were never still, and his right hand hung in an endless, hooked expectancy above the wooden handle of the big Remington-Beals holstered against the greasy leg of his buckskin *chivarras*.

"*Sí, sí,* of course." Corchino smiled, executing the shift from the restrained violence of his rage into suave, smooth geniality without any visible effort. "I have a little job for you, Pegoes," he said. "As you know, I am perpetually seeking choice men to add to our forces here. I want to build an army the likes of which has never been seen on either side of the border, an army that, when I finally take the field again in the name of our noble cause" — he let a sidelong glance pass across Camoa — "will be irresistible. I have been hearing of a man for some time now. You, undoubtedly, too. It is quaint, no, the penchant our people have for applying colorful names to men. *¿El caballero fantasma?*"

A strange, fleeting smile crossed Oporto's dark face. "Who hasn't heard of that one, *senhor.* I heard that only last week he stopped Rhode's Riders from what would have probably ended in the murder of Renaldo Catecas."

Corchino nodded, studying his coat in the

mirror. "*Sí, sí.* I have been watching his movements a long time now. His name has come to symbolize a salvation for the weak and the poor and the small of the border, many of whom are the same *peónes* we seek to save. It seems to me he and I are fighting for the same thing, in reality. I think he would appreciate an alignment as much as I. And he would certainly be a welcome addition to our company here, no? That is what I want you to do. Find him and bring him to me."

"*Pues,* where, how, *senhor?* Who is he?"

"*Senhor, senhor,*" muttered Corchino irritably. "Must you always make the H sound. We are in Méjico now, not Portugal. Can't you say *señor,* like any decent *mejicano?* You have no idea how that . . ." — he caught himself, turning to Oporto, showing that disarming smile — "*perdónome,* Pegoes, a thousand pardons, what could I be thinking of? Perhaps it is this heat, no? It makes one so restless." He turned back, frowning at the mirror. "You ask who *el fantasma* is. How do I know? No one seems to know. That is your job. Do it and you will find a bonus waiting for you on your return. Now go."

Oporto allowed his eyes to touch Camoa an instant before he turned to leave. A small, hungry light seemed to kindle in them. Then he turned and stepped out the door. Camoa moved toward the other door, leading out into the *plácido* behind the house.

"Camoa." Her brother's voice stopped her. She stood there, her back to him, waiting for him to speak. He did it softly, and the tone caressed her like the velvet paws of a cat. "Perhaps it is the heat which affected you also, no? Let us hope it was. Because if it wasn't, and you persist in this attitude, there are so many ways of putting a stop to it. I know them all, and they are so very, very ugly."

III

By the course of the Río Grande, the Del Carmen Mountains were some five hundred miles north and west of Brownsville and the Gulf of Mexico, and Rancho del Carmen stood deeply within their stark fastness on the southern side of the river. There was not much vegetation in these bleak ranges, and what water was available stood in what the Mexicans called *tinajas,* natural sinks of rock in which the rainwater collected and remained through the hot months.

The ranch house had been built by Camoa's grandfather, and had been given to her when he died. Its sprawling adobe buildings rose from the floor of a valley, adjacent to one of these *tinajas* that stood protected by the rocky slope to the north.

With those vast, ageless peaks rising in un-relieved silence all about her, Camoa Corchino was filled with a sudden, awesome sense of loneliness as she stepped out into the *plácido*. She walked across the flagstone patio, past the red-roofed well beneath the gaunt summer skeletons of the poplars, to the wall at the end. Pushing open the spindled gate absently, she stepped outside. She did not see the figure there till the gate had clicked softly shut behind her.

"I thought perhaps you would be out, *senhorita*," he said. "You were having a quarrel with your brother when I came into the room. How sad. I would not quarrel with you if I were your brother. I would revere you. I would worship you like a saint."

"I thought you were riding," she said sharply.

"Alan Harolde is bringing our horses around," said the Portuguese. His voice held a guttural thickness. "*Senhorita* . . . no, I can no longer be that formal . . . Camoa, Camoa, I have been here so long, waiting, looking, longing, hoping for a glance, a look, a word, nothing more. Just the smallest something to show that you are aware that I exist."

"Pegoes," she said, trying to move back in. "Don't. . . ."

"I must," he said, shifting his body against the gate to hold it shut. "I can restrain my-self no longer. A man can wait only so long, with a woman like you. The fire, Camoa, the passion. So like your brother, so many deep terrible things in you. I've seen them."

"I asked you, please, Pegoes . . . ," she muttered, trying to twist away, but his shift had caught her partway between his body and the wall, and he grasped her about the waist with one hand.

"You need someone, Camoa. All the time I've been here, there has been no one. Alone, all the time. At night, in your room there, or out here in the patio. At day, riding the hills alone, or down by the river. All the time. You weren't made for that. Is it because of the scar?"

"No, you fool!"

"Please, Camoa," he said, struggling to turn her back farther in between himself and the wall, trying to find her lips with his. "The scar means nothing. To no one. It makes no ugliness. Your beauty haunts a man. The scar is part of it. Don't hide any longer because of it, Camoa. . . ."

"Have you ever seen what I can do with a knife?" she said sharply.

His body grew rigid against hers, as he felt the point of her belduque dig into his side below the ribs. She saw the wonder in his face at where she had gotten the weapon. He drew in a strained, hissing breath. "*Sí,*" he said. "I have seen what you can do with a knife. Is that how you got the scar?"

Her face twisted, but she did not answer, waiting to feel his body move away from her before the pressure of that long thin blade. His hand started to slide from about her waist, and she began to relax. Then she saw the expression in his eyes and heard the small, stifled sound behind, and knew her mistake. She tried to drive the blade home and twist away at the same time, but that relaxation had left her off guard, and her move was far too late.

"Get the *cuchillo,* Alan," shouted Oporto, and even as Camoa lunged forward, the elbow of her knife arm was hooked from behind, and a violent jerk twisted her away from Oporto.

Alan Harolde caught her wrist with his other hand, twisting it, and she dropped the blade with a cry of pain. She had a momentary impression of the two horses he must have led up behind them while they were struggling, and of the man himself, big and blond and stinking in a dirty wool shirt and sweat-stiffened Levi's. His teeth and the whites of his eyes gleamed from a ruddy face.

"*¡Tu lépero!*" she screamed, trying to tear free — "*¡Tu bribón!*" — and she got one hand out and had the satisfaction of hearing Harolde's roar of pain as her nails caught his cheek.

"Catch her!" he yelled. "Get her hands,

36

she's clawing me to ribbons. Oporto, grab her hands!"

She fought crazily, twisting and writhing in Harolde's sweating grip, but her screams were cut short as Oporto got one arm around her throat from behind and caught that clawing hand. For a moment she was held in that strangling grip. Then there was a hoarse, bestial scream from back of her somewhere, and she knew it was not Pegoes Oporto, because no Portuguese would know the word, or its import, and no Mexican would use it unless he were in a terrible, killing rage.

"*¡Sinvergüenza!*" bellowed the man. The arm was torn from her neck, and she heard the dull sound of a blow and the guttural cry of anguish Oporto made at the same time. Harolde's hands were still on her, but, before she could move, she was torn aside and hurled against the wall, and a small, compact figure hurtled past her into Harolde, still screaming: "*¡Sinvergüenza! ¡Sinvergüenza!*"

Harolde's shout was inarticulate. One of his great pawing hands caught an epaulet on the man's shoulder and tore it completely free of the green coat. But the man's charge carried Harolde off balance, and he stumbled and went down on his back.

The man above managed to keep his feet. He stamped a booted foot viciously into the blond man's face. Harolde shouted in pain, and caught at the leg blindly, clawing upward. The man caught one of Harolde's arms and twisted it across his thigh. Then he snapped it like a stick of wood.

Harolde emitted one piercing scream. It echoed against the cliffs behind the ranch house, and, when the echoes died, he lay there, moaning softly like a little child. Camoa had recovered herself. She stood by the wall, staring at him, as he stepped away from Harolde.

"Juan," she said simply.

"*Sí*," he said, "Juan Nepuceno Corchino."

The blood flushing his face had burned it almost black, and his chest was heaving beneath the torn green military coat. He was looking past her, and she realized he was talking to Oporto, more than her. "Juan Nepuceno Corchino, and you are Camoa Corchino. Did you hear that, Pegoes? I told you what would happen if this ever came up. She is my sister, she is of my house, she is a Corchino. I told you what it meant. You are living on borrowed time right now. Get up. You have one chance left."

Oporto rose to his feet, face still pale and set with the agony Corchino's blow caused him.

Corchino glanced at Harolde. "He won't be able to go with you. Take Jarales."

He stood there a moment, holding Oporto's eyes with his own opaque gaze, and Camoa could see him clenching his fists until he had stifled the anger. His chest was no longer heaving and his voice had dropped to that soft, lethal sibilance, like a cat purring while it sharpened its claws against a tree.

"Now understand me, Pegoes. I said you were living on borrowed time. It doesn't matter where you go. It doesn't matter what you do. You can't escape me. To the ends of the earth, you can't escape me, and you know it, and you will abide by it. So take Jarales and find *el fantasma* and bring him back here, and you had better not fail. Because if you do, I'll kill you!"

IV

My good Anatole Napoleón Maximilian Blake d'Tadousac, he told himself, sitting there Indian-fashion on the ground, a singularly obese, swarthy little man. His white marseille waistcoat was especially tailored to contain the prodigious paunch that now reposed complacently in the formation of his crossed legs. *My very* good *Anatole Napoleón Maximilian Blake d'Tadousac,* he told himself, *allow me to compliment you on your peerless perspicacity, your unfailing, unremitting, unrelenting patience, and all the rest of the various and innumerable golden talents which have brought you finally to such a highly gratifying conclusion.*

"So you know Eddie Pickering," he said

unctuously. "You cannot divine how wonderful it is to hear this, Major Edmond. You cannot guess how long and arduously I have sought someone who knew him. Ever since Pickering escaped Hobkirk's police in Brownsville."

Major H. B. Edmond's long, pale face bore no expression, but he could not hide the sharp, bright intelligence of his dark eyes. His narrow body held the same impression of keen, restrained intensity, the long tails of his black coat pulled carefully off outthrust knees that were thin without being bony beneath his broadcloth trousers. There were a few willow shoots greening with spring on the bank of the Río Grande at Edmond's back, and he had plucked one of these and was idly tracing geometrical patterns in the sand.

If that is the way his mind works, thought Tadousac, *I will be careful* — and he grinned to himself — *mais oui, very careful, indeed.*

"When your emissary contacted me in Austin," said Edmond in a thin, precise voice, "he didn't tell me what your interest was in Eddie Pickering."

"It will take a little explaining. Let us start with Houston's plan." Tadousac's sly little eyes had been on the other man's face as he said this, but they could discern no particular reaction. He gave a mental shrug. "Houston became governor of Texas just ten years and ten days ago, if you will remember, on De-

40

cember Twenty-First, Eighteen Fifty-Nine, and it is now known, to a few privileged men, that Houston had already begun his plan for the conquest of Mexico."

"That was just a wild story put up by his political opponents," said Edmond carefully.

"On the contrary, there is proof." Tadousac had lifted a worn briefcase and pulled a key from beneath his waistcoat to unlock it, ruffling through the vast, motley collection of papers within. "You might call me a man of letters," — he muttered in a sort of rueful apology — "ah, the one I wanted. This is a set of letters written from one A. M. Lea to Governor Houston, and two missives from Colonel Robert E. Lee to this A. M. Lea, revealing beyond any doubt that A. M. Lea was an emissary for Houston trying to interest Colonel Lee in joining Houston's plan, either in his official Army capacity, or as a private citizen.

"Here, too" — he began fishing again — "are transcripts of authorization from Governor Houston for the raising of three new companies of Texas Rangers, and orders issued to the chief justices of twenty-three border counties to organize minute companies of twenty-five men per county. The dates, as you can see, are only five days after Houston's inauguration. Six months after the inauguration, he had over a thousand Rangers on active duty, more than Texas ever had in the field before, and had written the Secretary of War requesting that the government furnish Texas with two thousand percussion rifles, three thousand Colt revolvers, and one thousand cavalry accouterments. All this on the excuse of the Corchino war, which was to all intents and purposes at an end, even when Colonel Lee arrived to take command of the Department of Texas."

Edmond was studying the A. M. Lea letters. "This is fantastic."

"Not as fantastic as it may seem," said Tadousac. "Houston was a dreamer, but he was also a hard-headed soldier and a very clever, brilliant politician. It was his dream to lead ten thousand Rangers into Mexico on the greatest filibustering expedition the Southwest had ever seen. He had done it before, had he not? He had taken Texas bodily from Mexico in Eighteen Thirty-Six. He was one of the primary influences that annexed Texas to the United States, an act which led to the Mexican War and the acquisition of all the Southwest. And had not his rewards for this raised him to the highest offices in the land, save one? Twice president of the republic he helped create, governor of the state afterwards, United States senator. Why not President of the United States, for the annexation of Mexico? That was his dream, Major, and it had greater chance for fruition than the few people who knew of it would admit.

He had planned carefully. If the South had not chosen that precise time to secede from the Union, his plans would have gone into effect with far-reaching results."

Edmond had handed back the papers, and taken up his stick again, drawing a square. "It's hard to believe."

"Ah, well, perhaps it takes a dreamer to appreciate a dream," said Tadousac, shrugging plump shoulders and glancing at the square. "And perhaps you are not a dreamer, *hein? Voilà.* Houston also had another very good reason for faith in his dream. He had obtained very sound financial backing. Due to the Corchino war, the value of Mexican bonds had depreciated alarmingly. Houston had interested certain English bondholders in his scheme, and they had agreed to back his filibustering expedition to the tune of a hundred thousand dollars. Their representative arrived in New Orleans with the bank draft in January of Eighteen Sixty-One. Houston sent three of his most trusted Rangers to get the money . . . Kip Random, Louis Shell, and Eddie Pickering. Federal Intelligence agents intercepted the three Rangers at Endytown, on their way back to Houston with the money. All three of them escaped, however, and, as there is no record of the federal government obtaining the money, it is assumed that one of these men, or the three of them, possess it, or know of its whereabouts."

"Anatole Napoleón Maximilian Blake d'Tadousac," meditated Edmond aloud, drawing a circle in the sand. "A strange mixture."

"A whim of mine." Tadousac's shrug held a deprecation. "In my profession, a man works for many masters. A soldier wears his medals. Why not I? Napoleón the Third employed me, you might say, in a political capacity in Mexico in Eighteen Fifty-Eight. While there, the Emperor Maximilian. . . ."

"Blake," murmured Edmond, breaking in, "isn't there an English banking firm by that name, with offices in New York?"

This chuckle flowed from Tadousac's thick lips like oil. "Major Edmond, you are a man after my own heart. That is correct. I am working for the House of Blake. They were one of the bondholders who supplied the major part of that hundred thousand and have a natural interest in regaining their money." He hesitated a moment, fat cheeks puffed out by his bland smile till they almost hid his twinkling eyes. "Now that we have exhausted the possibilities of my name, shall we discuss yours? Kip Random was one of the three Rangers transferring that money. January Fifth, of Eighteen Sixty-One, a military order for his arrest was issued from Brownsville barracks on the charge of murder. But he had already left for New Orleans with the other two men, and the order had not caught up with him yet when his party was intercepted by Federals at Endytown. Unless he was killed there, his motive for not appearing since is obvious enough. He is still wanted for the murders of those two men, a Lieutenant Steele, and a Major Howard Benton Edmond!"

Edmond had drawn another cube. "What a striking coincidence."

Tadousac dropped his glance to the sand. "Isn't it an unfortunate failing of plane geometry that, when a solid is depicted on a flat surface, all of its sides cannot be seen in their true light?"

"You have a point," said Edmond.

"The fewer sides one sees, the more difficult it makes things," Tadousac murmured.

"Perhaps you would like to draw the other sides," said Edmond.

"I will draw them," said Tadousac. "I cannot believe your motive for coming all this way to meet me was purely altruistic. The fact that I sought information on Eddie Pickering implied I, also, had some on him. Some, perhaps, which you do not possess."

Edmond threw his stick away. "What is your pleasure?"

Tadousac nodded in a pleasant way. "Eddie Pickering was another one of those Rangers that Houston sent. Since Endytown, he had not been heard of until two months ago when he showed up in Brownsville in the custody of the Rhode's Riders. The uprising there was instigated by old friends of Pickering's who thought the police meant to kill him *en route* to Brownsville, the way they had Orson Niles and the Kelly brothers and so many others on the Roll of Horror. But, in the light of Pickering's connection with the Houston plan, I considered another possibility. Perhaps the police meant him to reach Austin alive. Perhaps Rhode wanted to see him. A hundred thousand dollars is a large sum of money, even to a governor. Do you know Governor Rhode, Major?"

"I met him once," said Edmond.

"You are dealing in that plane geometry again."

"No," said Edmond. "I told you. What do you want to know about Pickering?"

Tadousac nodded with a satisfied smile. "Perhaps you could tell me where a Carlotta Mateo can be found."

Edmond thought a moment. "There's a Mateo in Webb County, but I think his wife's Concepción, and he had no daughters. Perhaps Pablo Mateo. He has two daughters."

"Near here?"

Edmond shook his head. "Up near Zapata. Never saw his place."

"It could be found?" asked Tadousac.

"With time, I suppose," said Edmond. "Does it have a bearing?"

"You have thrown your stick away," said

Tadousac. "I will cast mine after it, and we shall deal from here on in the light of complete, mutual trust and honesty, *hein?* I have here a letter" — he began rattling through those papers again — "hmm, *non.* Ah? *Non.* Ah. *Oui.* See. December Twenty-Third, Eighteen Sixty-One. A rather significant date, *non?*"

"Where did you get all those papers?" said Edmond.

"A man in my profession, Major. . . ." Tadousac's shrug was vaguely apologetic. "Certain connections, you might say. You know. *Voilà.* December of Eighteen Sixty-One, from Austin, Texas, written by Eddie Pickering to Carlotta Mateo. Allow me. 'Dear Carlotta, I am being sent on a very important mission by Governor Houston but hope to return in time to marry you this April. . . .' " He stopped reading to raise his glance.

Edmond stared at him a moment, then made a faint gesture with his slim hand. "Zapata," he said, "would be several days' ride from here."

The sun-baked buildings of Zapata stood at the upper end of the lower Río Grande valley, and its small plaza was visible from the rolling hills surrounding the town. Dropping down the river road from these hills, his fat hams bruised and protesting from such a long time in the saddle, Anatole Tadousac heaved a profound sigh of relief.

"Under any other circumstances, Major," he said, "I would wish that this was not the end of our journey. It is so rare one has the honor to discourse with a noble intellect. But I fear the vast possibilities of discussion on subjects on which we seem so mutually well informed would far outlast the very narrow and limited possibilities of my posterior."

They turned into a rutted wagon road that finally became the main street of the town. Chickens cackled and scratched for worms behind a sagging mesquite fence, and a pair of squawking naked children darted across in front of the horses. An irate woman howled at her husband from a low doorway.

There were half a dozen men dozing in the sun against the adobe wall of a *tienda* that passed for a general store. They seemed indifferent to the riders approaching, but Tadousac caught the white gleam of suspicious eyes from the shadows of their huge straw sombreros. Major Edmond started to rein his horse toward them, but Tadousac caught at his coattail.

"*Non,* Major. Too many of them to ask questions. The *peónes* of these villages are extremely suspicious of outsiders. I think that right front shoe on your roan should be replaced anyway, *hein?* He seemed to be troubled with it through the hills."

Edmond glanced at the twinkling brown eyes, and shrugged. They walked their animals on down the street to where a great-bellied smith sat on a bench outside his ramshackle, half-frame, half-adobe barn.

He opened a miscreant eye to squint at them, and his voice held a gruff hostility. "I hope you do not have any work for me today, *señores*. It is too hot for work. In fact, it is always too hot for work. Except in the winter, when it is too cold for work."

Edmond swung down off his horse. "We are looking for a man named. . . ."

"*Oui, oui,*" broke in Tadousac, climbing from his wheybellied Billy horse with amazing alacrity. "We are looking for a man with just such sentiments. I have some papers here which you might be interested in, *oui*, some papers." He unlocked the briefcase and fumbled inside again, speaking in a slurred undertone from the side of his mouth while he did so: "You cannot do it that way, Major, two strangers coming up and asking . . . is this it, *non* . . . you must use a little oil in the machinery . . . could this be, *non* . . . before you start it up . . . ah, *oui* . . . see."

"I cannot read, *señor,*" said the smith, a puzzled look crossing his face as Tadousac pulled a tattered, leather-bound book out.

"You do not have to read," said Tadousac. "I think you know which page your name is on. Let us see now. Page twenty-three. Zapata. The smith, the smith, ah, yes, here. Cabo Pedro Alimente de Vargas."

The blood drained from the man's coarse brown face, and he made a strained, wheezing sound with the effort it caused him to rise. He stared at the book Tadousac had opened, speaking, finally, in an awed whisper.

"Corchino?"

"*Oui*." Tadousac smiled. "When he sent us, he said, seek the smith in Zapata. He was once a *cabo* in *los* Corchinos. There was no more faithful or courageous corporal in my whole army. He will surely give you aid in my mission. Now, perhaps, you will put a shoe on the roan, here."

The man turned from one side to the other, half pleased, half fearful. Then he headed for his rusty tools piled before the barn. "*Sí, sí*, Corchino, *por Dios, sí.* . . ."

There was something almost impatient in the way Major Edmond took the book from Tadousac's hands, leafing through it. "What is it?"

"I told you." Tadousac chuckled in a pleasant way. "A man of letters, Major Edmond. A letter for every occasion. In effect, at least. Corchino still lives for these people. He was a god to them, and there are the usual legends passing around about a man such as he. One, which is given wide credence, is that he is still alive, somewhere up in the Del Carmens where his sister once had a ranch, and is gathering another army with which to liberate the oppressed *peónes*. This is his GREAT BOOK, printed in Eighteen Fifty-Nine when he was at his peak and had formed the secret society of his followers known as *los* Corchinos. In this GREAT BOOK, he put forth his plans of conquest, and listed the names of all those in *los* Corchinos. No man save a member of the society, of course, would possess this book."

"Don't tell me you belonged."

Tadousac shrugged with that deprecating smile. "Not exactly. But as I said, a man in my profession. . . ."

It was the first time Tadousac had seen Edmond smile. It was a fleeting upward movement at the corners of the man's thin mouth, coming with a vague reluctance. It disappeared almost as swiftly as it had come. Edmond handed back the book.

"You amaze me, Tadousac. I would give a pretty penny to see all the papers you have in that case."

"Many men would," said Tadousac. "Yet, if everything I possess here were to come to light, half the men in Texas would be incriminated, and perhaps more than half of those would be sent to the gallows. Ah, *m'sieu* . . ."

— he turned to the smith, who was lighting a fire — "now, perhaps, we can get down to the real business. Corchino is interested in a . . . Mateo."

The man had started to work his bellows, but their huff stopped abruptly. "Mateo is not in the GREAT BOOK."

"To be sure, to be sure," said Tadousac, "yet he is worthy of a place in the new GREAT BOOK. There are going to be many additions, Pedro."

"It is true, then." An excitement had lit the man's dull eyes. "Corchino will ride again." The man led Edmond's roan near the bellows, hitching her to the bench. "Mateo is in some kind of danger from the Riders. It is mixed up with that business in Brownsville. He was in town only last week and told us. So far no *gringo* knows where his *rancho* is. It would be unfortunate if the wrong ones should discover it."

"*Oui, oui,* it would be well for us to hurry and reach him first."

The smith took up his clinch cutter and began cutting the ends of the nails off the shoe. Applying the pincers under the heel of the shoe, he moved them slowly forward and downward to loosen the nails. The shoe dropped into the dirt with a dim thud.

"Rancho Mateo is difficult to find," he said. "It is about thirty-five miles due north of here in the Reynosa hills. There is no road. You have to reach the hills at sunset. Turn toward the setting sun as you top the first ridge, and you will see twin peaks silhouetted before you. Ride through these twin peaks into a dry riverbed that will lead you up a gorge. At the other end, this gorge opens into a small valley. That is Vallejo Mateo."

"If it is that far, perhaps you had better put new shoes on both those front hoofs, ah, to make it even?"

"*Sí*," said the smith, cutting the nails of the other shoe.

"And water," added Tadousac, waddling over to the wooden water butt and dropping a bucket in. He came back, and removed the bridle from the roan. "Yours first, Major. Never let it be said that even Tadousac's horse is not a gentleman." He moved between the animals and threw the roan's bridle across the withers of his Billy horse. Then he mounted and turned the animal away. "While you are working, I will go down to the *tienda* for a drink, *non?*"

"Tadousac!" called Edmond.

But Tadousac had already lifted his animal into a trot. He heard Edmond curse behind him and call something to the smith, then he clapped his boots into the sleek flanks of the Billy horse. It was not far to the edge of town, and he was past the *tienda* and the surprised, staring faces of the men there, before he turned to look back.

It had taken Edmond that long to find a

53

length of rope and he was just knotting it around his roan's lower jaw to make a crude hackamore. The animal shied when he tried to mount, and his mouth worked in a curse Tadousac could not hear. The major swung the roan about, and spurred it brutally. Without shoes on its front hoofs, the animal stumbled in the wheel ruts and went to her knees, almost pitching Edmond.

The major yanked her up again, but the animal was spooked, and wheeled aside. This carried them into a mesquite fence. The fence gave way, and the roan plunged over the collapsed picketing into a bunch of cackling chickens and squalling children. A woman ran from the door, screaming at Edmond.

How unfortunate, Major, thought Tadousac, *how unfortunate. And when you extricate yourself from that situation, how long do you think your roan will last at top speed across this rough ground, without any front shoes?* He giggled to himself, and allowed his boot heels to touch the Billy horse again, urging it up the first rise into the purple-clad foothills. He reached the top, seeking a trail or a game trace that would take him northward, and found it on the other slope, a clearly discernible track that led into the sage. The purple brush crackled against the legs of his animal.

"Hein?" he said, and his fat face turned to the ridge on his right, but the movement that

had drawn his glance had ceased. A buck, perhaps, or a coyote. Perhaps. Yet, he had a strange apprehensive sense at the pit of his stomach. The trace dropped into a shallow valley between two spur ridges. He passed through a grove of cottonwoods budding white with spring. A third ridge met the valley, parting it, and the trail led down the western section. He was a few yards down this when the brush crashed from ahead.

A rider trotted into view, a big, black-bearded man in a pair of greasy *chivarras* and a pair of long-sleeved red flannels that sufficed for a shirt. He held an ugly, sawed-off Greener across the pommel of his saddle.

"The better part of valor, General Díaz," Tadousac told his horse, and wheeled it back down the valley toward the fork. He was only a moment's gallop up this fork, when another man appeared, a huge, gangling rider mounted on an unbelievably prodigious Clydesdale stallion.

"*Sacre nom,*" gasped Tadousac, and whirled his animal back once more. He passed the fork of the valley only a few yards ahead of the man with the Greener coming in from the other section, and kicked his Billy horse madly up the trail he had come in on from the road. He could hear them behind, crashing through the brush in voiceless pursuit that filled him with a strange fear.

If they would only shout, or something, he

thought, and then brought his horse up short at sight of the third man coming toward him from ahead. It was Edmond, the roan fighting and stumbling down the trail in a wild run that could not possibly have lasted much longer with her hoofs in that condition.

Tadousac tried to wheel his mount up the slope to the side, but the man on the Clydesdale quartered up above him, cutting him off. Tadousac wheeled back the other way, but only to face the one in the red flannels. There were others now, behind these first, half a dozen riders bursting up the trail, and Tadousac drew up his horse. Major Edmond brought his roan to a stumbling halt in front of Tadousac, speaking to the singularly tall one on the Clydesdale.

"It's damn' good you stopped him when you did. My roan's about finished."

"We followed you all the way up," said the other. "When we spied him comin' back alone, we kenned he gave you the slip somehow."

"Clydesdale?" said Tadousac, looking at the huge man's black stallion. "Burr? Not Captain Hobkirk of Rhode's Riders, surely?"

"Aye," said the man. "Surely."

"You *do* know Governor Rhode, then," Tadousac told Edmond.

"Did you find out where Pickering is?" Hobkirk asked Edmond.

"Tadousac has a letter from Pickering to Carlotta Mateo which might mean Pickering is holed up at the Mateos'," said Edmond. "He thought I knew where the Mateo place was."

"Did you?"

"Not exactly," said Edmond. "But I do now."

"Then we don't need him any more, do we?" said the black-bearded man, lifting his Greener till Tadousac could look down those twin barrels.

My good Anatole Napoléon Maximilian Blake d'Tadousac, he told himself bitterly, *allow me to compliment you on your peerless perspicacity, and all the rest of the various and innumerable golden talents which have brought you finally to this highly gratifying conclusion.*

V

The Spanish land grants, the *porciónes* of the early 18th Century, were theoretically of the same size, but the grants had been measured with rawhide chains, and some of the early settlers had contrived to have their *porciónes* measured on wet days, when the chains would stretch far beyond their usual length. It was a legend of the house that when the royal agent had overseen the measuring of the Mateo *porción,* it was raining so heavily that the chain had stretched around the whole valley before the allotment was used up. It was a well-timbered valley, with post oak and blackjack on the slopes. At dusk, *chachalacas* filled the bear grass with small soft bird sounds and an early coyote had started to complain.

The man seemed incongruous, somehow, in this scene, leading his horse slowly and carefully down through the scrubby timber just below the ridge. He was dressed in black half boots and black wool pants, black shirt, black hat. Blond hair, bleached almost white by the sun, grew down the back of his neck in a shaggy mane. The blond stubble on his lean chin had a rough, hacked appearance, as if he might have prevented it becoming a full beard with his Bowie knife. His face was hollowed hungrily beneath the cheek bones, and his eyes, their slate blue barely visible behind the narrowed wind-wrinkled lids, held a driven, feverish light.

The square yellow rectangles of three lighted windows glowed in the ranch house, the corrals forming a dim pattern about the main, tile-roofed buildings. A slight sound from down there stopped the man. Then more sound, and he stepped back, reaching up to grasp the rawhide bridle on his black Morgan, drawing the nose band tightly to prevent its whinnying. He stiffened at a shot, started forward, then caught himself. One hand dropped instinctively to his gun, but the horse began fiddling, trying to free its head, and he reached up again to hold it down.

There was the sound of running animals, and more shots thrust their sharp detonation into the velvet silence of dusk. He stood there with his body against the quivering Morgan. Someone shouted down in the valley, and it came dimly to him. Then he saw the figure of a man staggering through an open space in timber on the lower slopes.

He swung aboard the horse, and broke down through the blackjack, dipping into a swale full of the scrubby, matted oak. He was almost to the ridge, breaking into a meadow of curly red mesquite grass, when the figure silhouetted itself. The man in black dropped his hand to his gun again before he saw the other was unarmed. The one on the ridge had seemed suspended there, staring blankly. Finally an unbelieving voice said hollowly: "Kip. Kip Random."

"Pickering!" said the man in black. He spurred his horse across the meadow, and caught Eddie Pickering as he started to fall. He lowered Pickering to the ground, fumbling at the blood-soaked front of his shirt.

"No, no. . . ." Pickering shoved his hand away feebly. "It's my last bet. You're looking at the hole card." Breathing shallowly, he stared up at Random. *El caballero fantasma.*

I might have known it would be you."

"It's the only way I could fight, Eddie," said Random. "Think I could stand by and let Rhode's police ride their big horses over every friend I had and not do anything about it?"

"But why didn't you contact us?" said Pickering. "Everybody thought you had been killed in that shuffle at Endytown."

"How could I come out in the open with that murder charge hanging over me?" asked Random. "How could I know you'd ever want to see me? Edmond was almost as good a friend to you and Grandpa as he was to me. We shouldn't have separated at Endytown."

"Those Union agents would have caught us all if we hadn't, and got the money, too. What happened to you?"

"I tried to make my way back to Sam, but before I reached Austin, I heard there was a court-martial waiting for me for Edmond's murder," said Random. "I ran north till the war was over, and then I couldn't stay away any longer. How about Grandpa?"

"I think Grandpa Shell is up in New Mexico some place," said Pickering. "We've all had to keep under cover pretty much, Kip. They want that money."

"Who?"

"I don't know . . . I don't know." Pickering's head moved from side to side. "There must be a dozen different parties. Maybe even that damn' Governor Rhode. You saw how they nabbed me as soon as I showed up in Brownsville. Hadn't been for Mateo and his friends, Hobkirk and his killers would have taken me to Austin. I don't know whether they planned to kill me on the way or not. Either way, I think it was hitched up with the hundred thousand!" He was growing weaker, and there was a delirious light entering his eyes. He looked up at Random. "What were you doing here, anyway?"

"I heard Hobkirk was out after you with a whole company," said Random. "And Renaldo Catecas told me he'd got word there was a Creole named Tadousac, or something, asking around for the location of Rancho Mateo. I figured he knew about you and Carlotta, and, if he and Hobkirk ever got together, they'd be on your neck. I guess I got here too late."

"It was lucky you did," said Pickering, and his head started moving back and forth again, eyes growing wilder. "Get out of it before they nab you, Kip. You'll get it, too, the minute you show your nose. It's an awful big pot, and there's so many sitting in on the game you can't count them. They'll be on you from a dozen different directions."

"Who, Eddie?" asked Random hoarsely. "Who was it here tonight?"

"Get out, Kip," said Pickering, heaving up

against him in a last burst of violence. "Get out. They'll be on you like a bunch of vultures picking at a coyote. Get out. . . ."

"Perhaps it is too late to get out now, *senhor*," said the man who had just topped the ridge.

A cricket was chirping from the curly red mesquite. The coyote must have been traveling away, for his complaint had grown dimmer. These were the only sounds for a moment after the man had spoken from the ridge.

Random had not been conscious of the motion, but now he felt the walnut grips of his big Walker Colt moist and sticky against the palm of his hand. His arm was still stiff with the impulse to draw, but what he saw in the man's right hand stifled that.

"I am glad you did not do it, *senhor*," said the man, coming on down with his gun still pointed at Random. "I would not even have had time to introduce myself, would I? Allow me. Pegoes Oporto, late of Lisbon, Portugal, later of Rancho del Carmen, Mexico. And you, as I have overheard, are Kip Random."

Random spoke in a strained voice. "You did it?"

Oporto allowed the muzzle of his Remington-Beals to wave at Pickering. "That? I assure you I am capable. Do not make me prove it, *senhor*. I have come to act as an escort, you might say, for *el caballero*

62

fantasma. Juan Nepuceno Corchino wants to see you."

"Corchino?"

"Yes," said Oporto, approaching till he stood above them. "There is more truth than fiction about Corchino's being alive and raising another army to fight for the same people which you now defend. For a long time he has heard of the war you waged against Rhode's Riders. He would like you to join him."

"Join him?" replied Random. "He's crazy. I fought against him during the Corchino war. I was with Rip Ford when Corchino tried to sink the *ranchero* on the Río Grande. Why should he think I'd want to join him now?"

"Because even then you were fighting for the same thing," said Oporto. "You rode in the Rangers when Houston was governor, no?"

"Yeah," said Random warily.

"Houston was one of Corchino's friends," said Oporto. "You may recall that, although Houston called out many new Ranger companies as soon as he was inaugurated, he made no effort to remove Corchino from Texas, and even withdrew much of the regular army from the border. The whole cause of the Corchino war was the way the *peónes* had been treated by Texas *prior* to Houston's election. Corchino was only defending the same people you are trying to help now.

Didn't you prevent Hobkirk from what would probably have resulted in murder at Renaldo Catecas? Wasn't it the Mateos who saved your friend here from the Riders?"

"Maybe Corchino wants a crack at that money, too," said Random.

"What money?" said Oporto.

"You know what money," said Random. "He knows, doesn't he, Eddie? Was he the one . . . ?"

For the first time since Oporto had appeared, Random felt how limply Eddie Pickering was leaning against him. He looked down and saw the man's eyes were no longer open. Something closed around his heart momentarily, like the clutch of a great fist. He let the dead man drop backward onto the ground. He looked up at Oporto again.

"If I don't get you for that," he said, "there are a couple of others who will."

"I'm afraid," mocked Oporto. Then he started to whirl at a sound from over the ridge, but he turned back before the noise had carried him completely around. Kip Random's spasmodic movement stopped again, the way it had the first time. He watched Oporto move down the slope behind him, and then turn toward the ridge, waiting silently.

It was almost dark, and the man coming up over the top in a puffing, waddling run through the curling reddish grass did not form such a sharply defined silhouette as Oporto had. He took a couple of steps down the slope toward them before his eyes made out the shadowy bulk of the horse, and then the three men. He started to wheel back the way he had come, but Oporto's voice stopped him.

"I have a gun on you, *senhor.* Stay right where you are."

Still panting, the fat little man stopped, and turned slowly back, glancing stupidly at the great rip on the front of his coat.

"A great boor of a Scotchman and a major with mathematics for a mind and a black-bearded fool who wears red underwear for a shirt . . . they desired the edification of my company longer than I cared to share it with them." He shrugged, pawing at the rip, then spread his hands in an apologetic gesture.

"Anatole Napoleón Maximilian d'Tadousac," said Oporto.

"Blake d'Tadousac," supplied the little man.

"Well," said Oporto. "You have taken on another employer since I rode for Díaz. Then you were only spying on Maximilian for Napoleón III, and spying on Houston for Maximilian."

"Díaz?" said Tadousac, bending forward to peer at the Portuguese. "Oporto."

"That's right," said Oporto. "You spoke of a Scotchman. Are the police here, too?"

"In the valley," said Tadousac. "They sought Eddie Pickering. Barnabas Benton wanted to kill me at Zapata, but Hobkirk would not allow that until we finally located Pickering."

"You have," said Oporto, indicating the dead man.

"*Non,*" said Tadousac, taking an involuntary step toward them, staring down at Pickering. There was disappointment in his voice. "After all this labor, after all this ceaseless, arduous, tireless labor. What an atrocity."

For the first time he was close enough to see the man in black, and he straightened very slowly once more. "*¡El caballero fantasma!*"

"A stupid habit of the Mexicans, attaching names like that to people," said Oporto. "In reality, Kip Random."

The smile that spread across Tadousac's fat brown face drew his cheeks up till they almost hid his little eyes. "Well." He giggled. "*Voilà!* What auspicious circumstances to meet under, *M'sieu* Random. And how is Major Edmond?"

Random stiffened, his face twisting faintly in the gloom, but it was Oporto who spoke. "I mistrust your great pleasure, Tadousac. It is hard for me to decide whether to leave you alive here or not. Killing a man is so drab."

"Going somewhere?" said Tadousac, unperturbed. He looked at the gun. "You mean to take *M'sieu* Random somewhere."

"Corchino," said Random, watching Tadousac's face narrowly for the effect. He heard Oporto's abortive shift behind him, too late to stop him.

"Now I will have to kill him, *Senhor* Random," said Oporto.

"*Non,*" said Tadousac. "Not that murderer. Random, you should not allow him to take you to Corchino. I should not allow it. I *will* not!"

"You have nothing to say about it," said Oporto.

"On the contrary," said Tadousac, and a briefcase appeared in his hands. "Oh, *m'sieu,*" he protested as Oporto twitched the tip of his gun up, "it is only filled with papers, I assure you. See, you could surely shoot me before I did anything. I have in here a paper, which will be of singular interest to you, in light of your service with Corchino."

"I don't want to see any papers," said Oporto, but the forward motion of his body might have meant something else.

"Here, here," said Tadousac, fishing a sheet from the case. "You can read, *non?* The moon will be over those trees in another instant. It provides amazing light at this time of year. *Oui.* Here. Take it. A letter from Juan Corchino to one Frank Fullerton in Santa Fé. Dated the Fifth of last month. It will show you what a precarious path we ride."

The first light of the rising moon spilled into the clearing, sending the scene into striking contrasts of black shadow and yellowish illumination. One side of Oporto's face was lit like a bizarre mask as he reached for the paper. He took short little glances at the letter, raising his eyes in between to look narrowly at Tadousac.

" '*Señor* Frank'," he read. " 'It has been so long since we rode together on the border before the days of the Corchino war. But then we were the great *amigos*, no? And since friendships such as we knew never die, I am contacting you now in what I know will be your greatest interests. You have undoubtedly heard the rumors that I am gathering another army. It is true. Not an army of rabble such as I had before. I am picking my men carefully. I am combing the border for the best. That is why I write you. I have a lieutenant now, Pegoes Oporto. Perhaps you remember him from former days, but he is disloyal and untrustworthy, and I need a man upon whom I can rely. I will remove him from command upon your arrival . . . perhaps it will be necessary to eliminate him completely . . . and you will occupy . . .'."

Tadousac had let but one glance reach Random, during one of those intervals while Oporto's eyes were on the paper. Now, as the first flush of anger darkened the illuminated side of Oporto's face, and each interval in which his eyes rested on the paper became longer, Random felt his whole body stiffening. Once more, Oporto's eyes raised to Tadousac, filled with a mixture of disbelief and baffled rage, and then dropped to the letter again.

Kip Random's long body made an indistinguishable blur, rising off the ground smoothly, and struck Oporto with a dull, fleshy *thud*. One of his hands had streaked out while he was in mid-air, and it met Oporto's gun hand, ramming it aside as the Remington bellowed.

He felt the hot silk of Oporto's shirt against his head and heard the man scream as one of his clawing hands caught an earring. Oporto twisted beneath Random even as he went down. He shoved a shoulder against Random's chest, and threw him on over with his own momentum. Random rolled over the man, and Oporto was on his feet first. The Portuguese had dropped his Remington, and, without trying to recover it, he jumped quickly uphill at Tadousac.

Oporto struck the fat man's legs, and knocked Tadousac across Eddie Pickering's body. Random was on his feet with his Walker out.

"Oporto!" he shouted. "Get off! I've got a gun out, and, if you don't get off, I'll shoot!"

Oporto did not seem to hear him. Face contorted and bloody, he lurched up above

Tadousac, striking at him savagely. Random resisted the impulse to fire and jumped at them, slashing the gun across the back of Oporto's neck.

The Portuguese groaned with the blow, pawed blindly at Random's legs, and Random struck him again. Tadousac's flailing legs got between Random's feet, tripping him. Random went down, slashing at Oporto a third time.

Oporto went limp, still clinging to Random's thighs, and his weight came over, bearing them both downhill to Eddie Pickering's body.

Random squirmed from beneath the Portuguese, and got to his hands and knees. Then he saw what Tadousac had been trying to get from under his coat when Oporto jumped him. The moonlight revealed a ponderous French saloon pistol with the magazine on top. Tadousac held it in both fat hands, a bland, unctuous smile on his swarthy face.

"*Voilà*," he said. "At last the wheel has stopped, the little ball has come up on the right number, and I find myself in command of the situation."

"On the contrary," muttered Pegoes Oporto, raising his head with a great, painful effort. "If you will look at the ridge behind you, you will see a Mexican Indian whose name is Jarales, and *he* is in command of the situation."

VI

The old days had seen fabulous names troop through the banquet hall of Rancho del Carmen. Santa Anna had eaten from the heavy Corchino silver service. The great, hand-carved master's chair shipped from Andalusia by Camoa's grandfather had been occupied by none other than the Emperor Maximilian. It was said that Porfirio Díaz, when he was a mere captain, had gotten drunk on the Corchino *mescal* and pulled the *tápalo de matrimonio* from the wall above the pier table.

Most of the people of the border country had heard these traditions of Rancho del Carmen, and it seemed to Kip Random, as he was ushered into the great hall, that the glory it had known was past. There was something tawdry about the innovations Juan Corchino had instigated. The glittering glass chandelier, capable of holding a hundred candles, the Turkish ottomans covered with sleazy damask, the cheap pile carpeting, already soiled and torn from boot heels. There were a dozen men eating and drinking noisily at the great table, and two or three women.

"Indita!" shouted Corchino, beating on the table. "Where is that *chorizo con frijoles?* And more *vino*. The bottles are empty. . . ." He saw who had come in the door, and shoved back the master's chair to rise. He moved carefully around behind the line of chairs, peering at Random with a strange expression on his face. "I am glad to see you did your duty so well, Pegoes," he said, still looking at Random. "And you are *el fantasma*, Kip Random." He said the name slowly, meditatively. "Kip Random. It is hard for me to believe."

"He rode for Houston," said Pegoes Oporto.

"I know, I know, it only gives us more reason for an alliance. Sam Houston was my friend." Corchino seemed to become aware of Tadousac for the first time, standing behind Random, and waved his hand at the fat little man. "And what is this?"

"Anatole d'Tadousac," said Oporto. "He stumbled in when I had found Random, and found out about you. I didn't think you'd want him free with the knowledge."

Corchino turned slowly toward the Portuguese, something passing across his face as he saw how strangely Oporto was watching him. "What's the matter, Pegoes, are you getting squeamish?"

"I was going to kill him," said Oporto. "But he was such an interesting fellow and knew so many interesting things."

"What things?" said Corchino.

"Has Frank Fullerton gotten here yet?" asked Oporto.

"*Sí,* he came last Sunday, while you. . . ." Corchino trailed off, his eyes growing narrow. "How did you know Frank was coming?"

"Tadousac told me," said Oporto, his black eyes glittering.

"Did he, now?" murmured Corchino. His voice was a purring sibilance. "Did he now? Well, *Señor* Tadousac, you *are* an interesting fellow. We must hear more. You will dine with us, no? You will dine with us and tell us how you know such things."

He stared at Tadousac intently. The fat man held up his hand, opening his mouth to say something, but Corchino turned abruptly to Random. "You have not spoken."

Random was dusty and weary from the long ride, and it came from him thinly: "What would you like me to say?"

"*Señor, señor,*" Corchino told him expansively, reaching out to put a hand on his shoulder, "you seem so suspicious, so wary. Did Pegoes have to use force? I'm sorry. It was only that I wanted to see you so badly. You come as a friend, not a prisoner. Your welcome to Rancho del Carmen is the traditional welcome it has always extended to guests. The house is yours . . . everything we have is yours. And now, allow me to introduce you to our company."

He turned toward the table, his arm about Random's shoulder, his voice rising. "*Compadres,* meet a new member of our household.

Señor Kip Random. . . ." Corchino broke off as half a dozen men at the table stiffened, one or two allowing their hands to drop toward their guns. Corchino laughed, and went on. ". . . *late* of the Texas Rangers, gentlemen, but no longer."

The men relaxed somewhat, but still continued to watch warily as Corchino led Random over, indicating a beefy, blond man with his arm in a sling. "This is Alan Harolde, Random. And you must know Cookie Keith."

"Ever since Laredo State was robbed in Eighteen Fifty-Eight," said Random.

Cookie Keith was a sloppy, unshaven man with a soiled vest and pants of brown broadcloth that must have once been part of a suit. He wore a black patch over one eye and picked absently at his teeth with the blade of a long, shining Barlow knife. "Yeah," he said dryly. "Yeah. It wasn't till a long time later that I figured out that must have been you sticking to my tail when the rest of the posse had quit. You wore a black hat even then."

"You haven't been active lately," said Random.

"Most of the men here haven't been active lately." Corchino laughed. "And this is *el cojo*."

El cojo was a short, top-heavy man with great shoulders and a barrel chest set grotesquely on spindly legs. His small eyes regarded Random without expression from the brown enigma of his face. He had a carefully tended goatee that he stroked habitually with hands almost womanish in their small, supple motion. "I cannot say it is a pleasure," he said finally.

Corchino went on introducing them to Random, one by one. Some he had known before, or had heard of. A few were strangers to him, exotic, bizarre names, coming from Corchino's smiling lips — Bogus Bill Halderman, who played with a deck of cards and had invited Random to a poker game sometime, Ellie Watts, who carried a pair of short-barreled Bisleys, Jesús Santiago, Frank Fullerton, and Little George the Baptist. . . .

Random did not know the exact moment he stopped consciously taking in the names, and the faces, and the reactions, for the simple reason that he did not know the exact moment he had become aware of the woman. The fireplace occupied almost the whole south wall, with only enough room at the far end for a door leading into the south wing of the house. There was a two-foot hearth containing ash-filled depressions for several small pot fires in front of the main fireplace and a chimney hood that extended from the ceiling over the entire end of the room. She had been standing in that doorway, hidden partly by this hood.

Perhaps it was her motion, as she took a

step out into the room, which first drew Random's attention. She had on a dark blue wool skirt of close Indian weave and a *camisa* that hung loosely, leaving one shoulder bare. He felt a vague, instinctive repulsion at the sight of the scar on her face, drawing her full, ripe lips up at one side faintly. But as he continued to stare, not knowing why, at first, the repulsion died before another indefinable emotion. There was something haunting about the delicate, brooding planes of brow and cheek and jaw.

"And now, *Señor* Random," Corchino's voice broke in on him, "perhaps you would like to wash up before eating. Jarales, will you conduct our guests to their room? The one at the end of the south wing will do."

Jarales was the man who had been with Oporto back in Vallejo Mateo. He moved with the soundless, feline tread of the full-blooded Indian, despite his great, square bulk. He wore nothing but a vest made from the hide of a white horse, and, as he moved around to lead Random and Tadousac toward the door, the skin of his beefy, sloping shoulders and smooth hairless arms was polished bronze in the firelight. Jarales's shift blocked the woman off from Random's sight for a moment, and, when he could see the door again, she was gone.

Jarales led them down a long adobe-walled hall from which a line of doors led to rooms on either side. The last chamber was a large bedroom with *jerga*-patterned Chimayo blankets on the floor and a pair of single beds and some sand-rubbed pine chairs pegged together. There were half a dozen tin *candeleros* about the chamber. Jarales lit a punk from flint and steel, and moved around the room, lighting the candles. Then, without a word, he slipped out the door, and Random had the eerie feeling that the man had never actually been with them.

"*M'sieu* Random," said Tadousac, and the tone of his voice drew a wariness across Random's face as he turned toward the man. "It is the first chance I've had to talk with you alone."

"Why were you looking for Pickering?" asked Random.

"That is what I wish to discuss with you," said Tadousac. "There were three men at one time, but now there are only two, if you know what I mean."

Random's gaunt face bore no expression. "I'm afraid I don't. Why do you always keep testing the rigging, instead of just stepping on the horse, Tadousac?"

The man chuckled appreciatively. "A quaint analogy. Perhaps it is my nature, *m'sieu*. I have, in the past, come close to being trapped in many quagmires for failing to inspect the ground carefully beforehand. Perhaps, if I gave you a name . . . Endytown. . . ." His twinkling little eyes watched Random's face carefully, narrowing as he saw the word had failed to elicit any expression. He drew a small breath. "Ah, *m'sieu,* you are so uncooperative. Major Edmond was far more entertaining. He was quite willing to take up the verbal foil. . . ."

"Edmond." It came out of Random explosively. He took a step toward Tadousac, but Tadousac jumped back with surprising agility for such a fat man.

"Oui." He giggled slyly. "Not Endytown, *hein?* But Edmond. Now, *m'sieu,* perhaps we are on better ground. You have something I want. I have something you want."

Candlelight glinted across the blond hair on the backs of Random's sinewy hands. "What do you mean . . . something I want? Edmond? What do you know about Edmond?"

"I have here. . . ." Tadousac unlocked the inevitable briefcase, and rattled through its contents, mumbling to himself. He extracted a yellowed sheet of paper, stained darkly at the lower edge. ". . . A letter, *m'sieu.* Dated January First, Eighteen Sixty-One. Written on the stationery of Fort Taylor, now known as the Brownsville Barracks. Shall I read it?"

The inquiry in his eyes held a sly innocence. Random dropped his hands. The blood drained from his cheeks beneath the blond beard. His voice was hoarse and trembled with the strain of control. "Where did you get this letter?"

Tadousac shrugged. "It was in the files of the Provost Marshal's office at Brownsville Barracks. There is a sergeant in the Provost Marshal's office who had some rather pressing debts, and I had some money. Rather similar to our situation, *hein?* A fair exchange. Shall I read it?" He cleared his throat, eyes filled with that veiled craft, and began: " 'Dear Eddie . . . I have at last found the murderer of Lieutenant Steele. It was such a terrible blow that I could not bring myself to believe it at first. But now I must. I know it will be as big a shock to you when I tell you his name, since we have for so long considered him our closest friend. But tell you I must. Kip Random. I know you will find this as hard to accept as I did, but the evidence continues to pile up, and it is irrefutable. Kip came back from Brownsville drunk last Tuesday, and I had to get his bedroll from his horse. In it I found Steele's watch, wallet, gun, and the exact amount of money in gold he was known to be carrying at the time of his death. I confronted Kip. He left me in a drunken rage, swearing he would kill me if I betrayed him. But betray him I must. The evidence is in the hands of the Provost Marshal now. You know I am not a coward, but I was never one to overestimate my own capacities, and if Kip should ever reach me. . . .' " Tadousac stopped, raising his head with a faint smile. "It breaks off here. They say the stain is blood. The letter was found in Major Howard Benton Edmond's quarters on his desk, and on the floor was his coat, with two bullet holes in it. The body was never found. The implication was murder. That meant two counts the Provost Marshal's office sought Kip Random on. But he had disappeared. Isn't it a precarious path we follow, *m'sieu?*"

"Tadousac. . . ."

"Oui." The man smiled. "Perhaps you see now, what I mean. You have something for me, I have something for you."

"What good will that letter do me?" said Random. "It was what convicted me in the first place."

"I wasn't thinking of the letter," said Tadousac. He cocked his head to one side, slipping the sheet of paper back into the case. "Just what did happen to Major Edmond, *m'sieu?* How did his coat come off? Did you overlook that, in removing his body? The whole thing seems rather a careless job to me."

Random did not answer. His breathing made a harsh sound in the room. One of the candles guttered faintly.

"Did it ever occur to you," said Tadousac, "that Major Edmond was the sole instrument of your conviction, and by the same token

Major Edmond is the only man who could clear you?"

"*Is* the only person?"

Tadousac chuckled complacently. "Perhaps, now, *m'sieu,* you will admit the possibility of an exchange here. As I said before, there were three men on that train to Endytown, and now, with Pickering dead, there are only two. Some, you know, think that the men divided what I seek equally among themselves before they separated. I, however, possess certain knowledge and information leading me to believe that only one of the men has it, or knows of its whereabouts."

Random could control himself no longer, and this time Tadousac's surprising alacrity failed to serve him. Random's lunge carried Tadousac against the wall. Random's sinewy fingers dug into the swarthy flesh of the man's neck.

"What are you getting at, you fork-tongued, double-dealing, conniving Creole?" he shouted. "I'm tired of riding through the brush this way. If you don't come out in the open. . . ."

"Frenchman, please, *m'sieu,* not Creole," gasped Tadousac, struggling vainly in his grasp. "And if you choke me to death, how can I impart anything?" Random slackened his grip. Tadousac reached up, trying to get those hands off, but Random's fingers closed again. "All right," gasped Tadousac, dropping

81

his hands. "All right. What would it mean to you if Major Howard Benton Edmond were alive now, and I could lead you to him?"

Random's hand tightened spasmodically on his throat. "You couldn't . . . you couldn't . . . he's dead!"

"Who is dead, *señores?*"

The woman stood in the open doorway. The guttering light cast her face into shadow, and the scar was not so perceptible. She pursed her lips around the name. "Camoa Corchino. It is a sad day when a woman has to introduce herself in this household, but my brother has lost some of his manners, among other things. I wanted to see . . ." — she hesitated a moment, an indefinable edge entering her voice — *"el fantasma?"*

Random had dropped his hands from Tadousac's throat. The little man regained his composure instantly. "Ah, do I detect a hint of sarcasm?"

Camoa Corchino was still looking at Random, and the brooding planes of her face seemed to draw taut and hard. "It is hard to believe you are The Phantom Horseman. I had conceived you as such a different type, a crusader, a man with a certain nobility. But then one is so often disappointed, no?"

A trace of bitterness entered her voice. "Kip Random. When was it, January of Eighteen Sixty-One? We were in Matamoras at the time and heard about it. How can you reconcile it with what you are doing now? Don't they come to you, sometimes, in the night . . . Major Edmond, or Lieutenant Steele? Don't they come to you and ask you . . . how can you do it this way . . . ?"

"Shut up!" said Random hoarsely, his face twisted.

"It *does* touch you." She took a step aside, standing against the heavy beam forming the support of the door frame, her head thrown back against it. "Perhaps it frightens you, too. Are you a coward, as well? A coward, but not a complete coward, because you have faced brave men without revealing your fear sometimes. I could almost admire a man who murdered well. . . ."

"Shut up!" His hands were opening and closing viciously, and her eyes dropped to them.

"Would you throttle me, too, *Señor* Random?"

Her glance raised once more, seeming to look for something in his face. A sharp, decisive breath raised her bosom, beneath the white, pleated *camisa*. "It doesn't matter. I can't let you do this, anyway. No matter what you are. Even a coward. You are dangerous. You are still one of the most dangerous men in Texas, by the admission of all who know you. And with you joined to all the men already here. . . ." Something desperate had entered her voice, and she stepped toward him, her face lifted pleadingly. "Random, you *did* stop Hobkirk from what he was doing at the Catecas place. And all those other times, you have been fighting Rhode's Riders. There must be some good in you, something I can appeal to. Can't you see it? To join my brother would not help Catecas, or Mateo, or any of the others who need help so badly. He is no longer fighting for the thing you are."

"Then what is he fighting for, *sancha mía?*" Random watched Corchino step into the room. Camoa's eyes widened, and Random saw the expression in them before she turned. Corchino's mouth was smiling at his sister, but his voice held no humor. "Now that you have welcomed our guests, perhaps you will allow us a word alone."

She stepped around him, casting a last glance at Random. The fear was still in her eyes. Corchino watched her go, that smile still fixed on his face. When she had disappeared in the hall, he turned to Random, shrugging.

"You will have to forgive my sister. It is the misfortune of our family. A betrothal, an accident" — he made a vague gesture toward the side of his face with one hand — "a change of heart in the young man. . . ." He shrugged sadly. "You know how those things are with a woman. Sometimes she must not be taken too seriously . . . oh. . . ." He seemed to remember what he held in his hand. "I have brought your gun back. It is too bad Pegoes had to take it. One of the original Walker Colts, no?"

"I went with Sam Walker when he showed Colt what kind of gun the Rangers wanted," said Random.

"I was relieved of my weapon, also," ventured Tadousac.

"And will remain relieved of it," said Corchino. "What happened between you and Oporto? He keeps looking at me. Something about Frank Fullerton?"

Tadousac shrugged. "How could I know? I was injected into this by the greatest of force. It was not my desire. I did not care about you or what you were doing or anything. I am only a harmless little professional man."

"*¡Punta en boca!*" said Corchino. He still held the Walker in its scabbard, with the gun belt wrapped about it, and he jerked it violently toward the door. "Shut your mouth! Jarales, Watts, remove this *pordiosero*, and let me have that briefcase."

"Briefcase?" said Tadousac. "Are you saying . . . ?"

"That I don't want you any more," said Corchino. "Take him, Jarales!"

The Indian must have stayed out in the hall, and Ellie Watts had come with Corchino. Both of them moved into the room now.

"No!" cried Tadousac, stepping backward. "You cannot dismiss me like that. You cannot kill me like that. Not Anatole Napoleón Maximilian Blake d'Tadousac, not the man who has been in the service of emperors. Greater men than you have tried it, *m'sieu*. I will not allow this. *Voilà*, I have here a paper" — he had begun fumbling in the case — "which, I am sure. . . ."

"If he won't shut his mouth, shut it for him," snarled Corchino in a growing rage. "And get him out of here!"

"Hold it!" said Random.

"Random!" said Corchino, whirling toward him. "Don't anger me now. Don't you understand? This Creole, this . . . parasite . . . I want him gone. I'm tired of his fat, sneering face in my presence. Oporto had no right bringing him here in the first place. For anyone not belonging to *los* Corchinos to know where we are and remain alive. . . ."

"Take your hands off me!" cried Tadousac, his voice raising, as Jarales reached for him.

"Tell them to stop, Corchino," said Random. "Tadousac's with me."

"No!" bellowed Corchino. "Get him out, Jarales. Get him out!"

"He's with me, Corchino, I tell you," said Random, then saw Ellie Watts reach for one of those Bisleys in his pocket, and moved. His boots made a swift, shuffling sound and the movement was so fast Ellie had not yet freed the gun when Random caught him. He hooked one hand through the elbow of the gun arm, whirling Ellie around, and heaved him violently in the direction of a heavy chair. Then Random wheeled toward Jarales, who was still struggling with Tadousac against the wall. He caught the Indian by his thick ankles and jerked backward and up-ward.

Jarales tried to maintain his grip on Tadousac, but the Creole twisted aside, and with his feet pulled from beneath him the Indian fell flat on his face. Random was aware of a movement behind him, and whirled to face it. The old-style gunman started a throw-down, lifting his weapon back over one shoulder, but the motion was never completed.

"No, Ellie!" bellowed Corchino. "I don't want him shot." He charged full tilt from the other side of the room. His hard body crashed into Random, knocking him into the wall so hard the *viga*-poles raftering the room trembled. Corchino still had Random's holstered gun, and he struck at Random viciously, his dark face contorted.

Random threw up one arm to block the blow, but the gun caught him on the forearm, stunning him to the shoulder. With his other arm he gave Corchino a kidney punch that caused the man to shout in agony.

The movement gave Random a chance to slip from between the man and the wall. As he wheeled around to face Corchino from the outside, he was dimly aware of Ellie Watts coming in, Bisley clubbed. Corchino raised the holstered gun for another blow, and Random ducked in under the arm to butt Corchino fully in the belly.

"Sagrado nombre," gasped the man, bending double. Carried backward, he tripped over Jarales and fell heavily onto his back. Still bent over, Random whirled to meet Watts as the man came into him and threw up both arms to catch the clubbed gun. With his face down, he couldn't see much, but he heard the *thud* of boots dimly in the hall, and the swelling sound of moving bodies and shouting men in the room.

He booted Watts in the shin and tried to whirl around, lashing out wildly. His arm was caught from another direction and twisted with a force that brought a hoarse yell from his lips. He turned back into the sweating, beefy face of Bogus Bill Halderman. With his free arm he punched blindly and felt flesh and bone crunch beneath the blow.

They were on all sides of him now, and a blow behind his neck drove his head down. Random jerked up violently and butted a man who had gotten too close. He heard the groan of agony, and twisted, lashing out with his free fist.

"He's crazy!" Frank Fullerton shouted. "He's crazy! Corchino, we've got to shoot him. . . ."

"Shoot him and you'll pay with your own life!" roared Corchino from somewhere.

Random finally pulled his arm free of Bogus Bill. Blinded by sweat and blood, he almost succeeded in getting to his feet again when another blow on his head sent him back down. This time it was onto his belly. Someone kicked him in the ribs, and a terrible suffocating weight descended on his back. A man caught his hair, beating his face into the earth.

"¡Basta!" he heard Corchino yell, dimly, from somewhere far above. "Enough, enough!"

The weight was gone from Random's back. It seemed he lay there a long time before he could get enough strength to roll over. But it must have been only a moment, for when he had pawed the dirt and blood off his face and could finally see from one aching eye, he made out the ring of men spreading away from him.

Bogus Bill Halderman was holding a bloody bandanna to his nose. Little George the Baptist sat over against the wall, face contorted with agony. Jarales stood stiffly against the wall. His face was enigmatic and his mouth was closed, but his black eyes held unblinkingly on Random's face, filled with smoldering hate. Finally Random saw Corchino.

The man still held that holstered Walker and Random expected to see him pull it free. But a strange, small movement was twitching at the man's lips. Suddenly his mouth spread in a grin. Finally he threw his head back and laughed. It was a spontaneous, roaring, infectious laugh that caught at every man in the room. Even Random felt his lips twitch with an involuntary smile.

"*Sacramento*," shouted Corchino, "*barba del diablo, que un tigre* . . . did you ever see such a tiger? All right, Random, if that's the way you want it, if Tadousac means that much to you, he bears a sacred immunity from now on, and the man who touches him will have to answer to me. But only on one condition."

"Yeah?" said Random gutturally.

"*Si.*" Corchino laughed. "That you ride with us. With a man like you in our ranks, how could we lose?"

VII

A faint breeze swept in on the Gulf Coast and up the Río Grande, and it held a mournful plaint through the timber on the river side of the little adobe ranch house. The snort of a horse made a vagrant, somber impression on the sighing wind. It set the other animals to stamping and shifting nervously where the line of them stood in the boggy motte of post oaks.

Davoc Hobkirk pawed irritably at a blowfly buzzing around his face, and leaned forward to peer through the night-shrouded trees at the open compound Renaldo Catecas had cleared about his house.

"Are ye sure this is nae a trop?" he asked Major Edmond suspiciously.

"That's the chance we'll have to take," said Edmond, sitting his roan beside the Scot. "That *peón* wasn't fooling, at least. He really did come from Tadousac. The Creole was waiting for me in Matamoras, as I told you. Tadousac said Kip Random would meet me here at ten tonight."

"It's natural Random should want to clear himself of that murder charge," said the Scot. "But what could Tadousac gain from this? Ye said he was hunting the three men who had Houston's money. Why should he put Random in our hands?"

"Trying to divine Tadousac's motives in anything is like trying to play poker without looking at your cards," said Edmond. "It's patent he's playing Random off against us. Maybe he made a deal with Random to effect this meeting, if Random would reveal what happened to all that money."

"Aye, the Creole is an auldfarren conspirator," said Hobkirk, and his saddle creaked as he turned to stare at Edmond's face. "But he is nae the only one who plays a many-sided game. How is it they came to think Random had murdered you, Edmond?"

"I don't know. One of those mix-ups you get in war time," said Edmond.

"Ye were in the Army then," said Hobkirk. "Are ye in the Army now?"

Edmond must have sensed Hobkirk's direction for he met the Scot's eyes squarely. "What are you getting at, Davoc?"

"I heard from Rhode while you were awa'," said Hobkirk. "There's a rumor of an agent for the federal government working on this, somewhere down here."

Edmond bent toward him, also, until their faces were very close. "And by what devious Gaelic channels did your towering intellect connect me with that?"

Hobkirk felt a dark rage rising within him, and a small glint of it lit his eyes momentarily.

"There was too meikle mystery about what ye choose to call a war time mix-up, Major. Yure connections wi' this whole affair are not as clear as they seemed when ye first came. Then I thought ye were Rhode's mon, wi' no hidden interest o' yure own in it. Gin I thought ye were playhin' the same kind o' game Tadousac is. . . ." Hobkirk leaned forward as he spoke till their faces were not an inch apart, and let one great hand drop to the hilt of his knife. "I'd put my whinger through ye mair times than Bothwell ever whingered Little Jock Elliot."

Edmond's sharp face did not change expression, and he spoke with a careful, passionless deliberation: "Do you think you can cow me like you do the rest of your crow-bait police force, Davoc? The only leads you've gotten in this whole *el fantasma* goose chase have been through me. I was a close friend to every one of the three men you seek, and without my knowledge of them you'd be through with this whole thing. But don't make the mistake of thinking I depend on my position. Don't make the mistake of thinking anything except this . . . anytime you want to do some whingering, come right ahead, because I've got a blade of my own in my boot, and there was a man in Texas named James Bowie who'd make your Earl of Bothwell look like a kid with a dull Barlow when it came to carving the turkey!"

Hobkirk's hands tightened on the horn of his saddle till the tendons stood out in great bluish ridges across the massive bones of his wrist. He felt a terrible impulse to tear them off the horn and use them on Edmond. He wanted to drive that keen, unflinching light from the man's eyes and see them filled with agony and fear. Finally he got control over himself, and took a heavy breath.

"Maybe ye'll get a chance to try and prove that, Major. Sooner than ye expect," said Hobkirk.

He held the man's gaze a moment longer, then turned away to give his men their orders. He sent Barnabas Benton and six others around the house to the hills on the other side, leaving Sergeant Peterson and the rest. He dismounted from his own horse, and pulled a bolt-action Ward-Burton from beneath the stirrup leather, turning to indicate Edmond should precede him out.

It was not a long walk to the house. Edmond dismounted and pushed open the door without bothering to knock. Renaldo Catecas knocked over the three-legged stool he had been sitting on as he jumped to his feet in surprise.

"Hobkirk!" he gasped, and cringed back against the wall, holding the half-filled tin cup in one trembling hand.

"Where's your guid wife?" asked Hobkirk, swinging into the room.

"In Brown . . . Brownsville," quavered Catecas. "Her family. . . ."

"All right," said the Scot. "I'm goin' in the back room, Catecas. We're waiting for Kip Random. When he comes, you act natural. Just remember I have this gun at yure back."

He stepped into the rear room, drawing the dirty woolen curtain almost shut. He found another stool, and placed it by the door where he could look through the crack in the curtain. Edmond had sat down at the table, made Catecas pour him a cup of coffee.

After that, the Mexican dropped weakly to his hams in the corner, watching Edmond with wide, fearful eyes, like a dog, waiting to be kicked.

Without action to occupy him, the narrow, dark thoughts began to move through Hobkirk's narrow, dark mind. *A hundred thousand dollars,* he thought, *a hundred thousand dollars to take back to Braemar and build a castle as great as Balmoral and drink as a laird at the Highland Gathering. No more of this steaming heat, no more of these strange soft tongues. Davoc Hobkirk, standing in the tartan and kilts of his clan, with his back to a fire of good Highland oak and lifting up his beaker of Banffshire. Here's health to the sick, stilts to the lame, claise to. . . .*

"Edmond."

It was a low, tense voice, breaking in on his turgid thoughts, and the first moment it had come Hobkirk did not comprehend its significance.

"Kip," said Edmond, rising from the stool, and then the man who had spoken first moved into view from where Hobkirk looked through the crack between curtain and doorway. He was tall and lean through the hips, like a man much used to riding. There was a short growth of blond beard on his jaw, and his blue eyes held an icy lucidity. He was dressed completely in black.

"You haven't changed, have you, Kip? I

95

didn't even hear the door open," said Edmond, and for the first time took in the outfit. He waved a vague, surprised hand. "Tadousac didn't tell me. . . ."

"That I was *el caballero fantasma*," finished Kip Random.

"He-he." At the insane giggle Hobkirk went taut with the irritation Tadousac always raised in him. "Forgive the omission, gentlemen," said the Creole. "In a thing like this, there are so many detai. . . ."

"What was it, Edmond?" Random burst out. "What was it?"

Edmond frowned. "What was what, Random, I don't. . . ."

"Yes you do," said Random, taking a vicious step toward him. "Ten years, Edmond. That's a long time. That's a long time to run and hide and run again. And eat cold mostly because you're afraid to build a fire and never see any of your friends because you're afraid it will be a trap. And never go into a town and never have your gun off sleeping or waking. . . ."

"Of course, of course, Kip," said Edmond. "Take it easy. That's what we came here to straighten out. It was just one of those mix-ups you get in war time."

"No!" Random grabbed him by the arms. "I want the truth now, Edmond. I've had enough conniving and going around the barn, and, damn it, if you don't. . . ."

"All right, Kip, all right." It was the first time Hobkirk had seen Edmond perturbed, and it gave the Scot a certain satisfaction. Edmond twisted free of Random, indicating the table. "Let's sit down. Catecas has coffee."

"I'd rather not," said Random. "You can tell me standing up."

Edmond looked at him, shrugged resignedly. "All right, Kip. My federal service in Eighteen Sixty didn't extend merely to my commission in the regular Army. I was actually working with Intelligence, along with Lieutenant Steele. They had the wind up about Houston's plan, and sent us down here . . . to find out what was going on. In a way, it was unfortunate that you and I should have become such great friends, Kip. It was Steele who discovered Houston was sending you and Pickering and Shell to New Orleans to get the British money. Steele contacted Washington, and they sent out agents to intercept you *en route*. Under any other circumstances, it wouldn't have been so bad. But with the South about to secede, I knew they would shoot you as traitors. I couldn't let you go into that. Steele was probably killed by one of Corchino's men on patrol, but his death, and the fact that I had been recalled to Washington, gave me only one chance to keep you out of it. I had been recalled by Intelligence, rather than the regular Army, so the Army itself didn't know what happened to me. I left that letter in my quarters, along with the bloody coat, knowing that even if they did arrest you, your release was almost certain as soon as the South seceded. They would never have held you for shooting Union officers. They would probably have given you a medal."

Random studied his face narrowly. "That sounds a little too good for me."

"Kip, I swear it's the truth," said Edmond. "I had no idea it would end like this. How could I foresee carpetbaggers like Rhode getting in the saddle here after the war and resurrecting every old charge they could find against ex-Confederates in order to keep themselves in power? My only thought at the time was to keep you out of the trap I knew Houston's agents were headed for."

"You can clear me then?" said Random.

"We'll have to go to Austin to do it officially," said Edmond, shrugging.

Renaldo had been shifting nervously behind Edmond, face white, and Random turned to him. "What's the matter, Renaldo?"

"*Nada, Señor* Kip, nothing," protested the Mexican, "*sagrado nombre*, everything is all right, I swear it."

"Where's your wife?" said Random, but before Catecas could answer, the outer door was flung open and a woman burst in. The only impression Hobkirk had was of a scarred, strangely haunting face and fierce, flashing black eyes.

"Get out, Random, the Riders have surrounded the place and are closing in on all. . . ."

Hobkirk did not think he had ever seen a man move so fast. Before the woman had gotten her first half dozen words out, Random leaped toward the table. His action was so swift, Hobkirk lost it, but he must have swept the oil lamp off the table, for the whole room was suddenly plunged into darkness.

The Scot tore the curtain aside, and plunged through. He crashed into someone, caught a flailing arm. A scream of pain in his ear almost deafened him.

"*Brazo mío, brazo mío,* Hobkirk, you've broken my arm," howled Catecas.

With a disgusted oath, Hobkirk flung the Mexican aside, tripped on an overturned chair, went to his hands and knees. He was aware of a last figure blocking out the dim rectangle of the door momentarily. He tried to get his Ward-Burton up in time as he rose, but the doorway was empty before he could fire. He crashed against the table, kicked it aside, and stumbled out the door.

Edmond's horse had been tethered at the doorway, but it was gone now. The rickety cottonwood corrals extended from the south end of the house toward the river and from these a group of riders was breaking into a gallop toward the post oaks. A last man was trying to swing aboard a wheeling animal, and Hobkirk caught a dim impression of a fat, short little figure lifting one foot into the stirrup of a short little Billy horse as it spun.

Hobkirk opened fire on Tadousac, but it was dark and the violent shift of movement made a poor target. Not till his third shot, when Tadousac was in full gallop after the others, did Hobkirk see the Billy horse rear into the air, screaming in agony. But the Creole fought the animal down, and booted it back into its run.

"Peterson!" roared Hobkirk, emptying his gun at the fleeing riders. "Peterson, where in the Queen's name are ye? They're comin' toward the river. Stop them, ye crowlin' Lowlander. . . ."

Peterson erupted from the post oaks, barely visible in the darkness. But before he had cleared the trees with his men, another bunch of horsebackers came into view from the timber on his left flank, opening fire.

With Random's group racing at their head and the others closing in on their flank, Peterson's men began to veer and mill wildly, not knowing which to face. Hobkirk could hear the sergeant shouting orders. Then the police broke completely and fled back into the timber.

"Oh, ye filthy mid staumrels!" roared

Hobkirk, and flung his empty gun after them, almost crying in rage. "Ye crowlin' bluntie blae mid staumrels. . . ."

Random's group turned to meet the other horsemen that had appeared on Peterson's flank. They joined them at the edge of timber, and together the whole cavalcade disappeared into the timber after Peterson. There was a sporadic volley of gunfire, drowning the crash of brush. It was not a long stretch of timber, and Hobkirk reached it before the firing had ceased.

"You didn't think I'd come alone, did you, Hobkirk?" he heard Random shout, from somewhere deep in the motte of oaks. Then there was another flurry of shots, and a man's yell of pain.

In a blind rage, Hobkirk crashed into the timber toward the sounds, hoping against hope he would find his horse where he had left it. Salt grass whipped at his booted legs and Spanish moss caught wetly across his face. His feet slopped through a strip of bog. But when he reached the trio of giant live oaks not far within the fringe of timber, his animal was not there.

The sounds were all about him, slowly dying — a single shot far away, a man's shouting, the crash of a running horse nearby, another shot. Face contorted with that awful rage, he wheeled back and forth, not knowing which way to head, swept with a primal desire to get his hands on someone, something.

The other sounds had died momentarily, and, as he whirled and started back toward the open compound, the crash of his passage was startlingly loud. He had only taken a few steps when he stumbled over a body. The man was dead from a bullet through his chest, and the size of his torso looked grotesque above the sprawled, spindly legs.

Hobkirk heard a sound off to his right. It was only a faint swish of salt grass, but it stopped him. He stood there, above the dead man, listening. It came again, nearer. It struck him, abruptly, that the moon had finally broken through the scudding clouds and was dropping its light vagrantly through the trees. A streak of it splashed across him, and he stepped carefully into the black shadow beneath a live oak.

The other sounds had died completely now, and he realized his passage a moment before had been the only noise. Could they have heard? Aye, it was possible. It was probable. And that's what they were coming after.

Then his eyes caught something out in the timber. It was just a momentary glimpse — a brief flash of moonlight running like a strip of glittering quicksilver across its surface. *There was a man in Texas named James Bowie who'd make your Earl of Bothwell look like a kid with a dull Barlow when it came to carving* the turkey. *All right,* he thought, pulling his knife, *gin this is where ye want it, here's my whinger, and ye'll get it.*

The sound came once more. The softest swish of salt grass. The faintest squish of feet in the soggy earth. Hobkirk tried to keep a rigid control over his breathing. But there was something deadly about waiting here in this blackness with the moonlight filtering wanly through the warped oaks, something that clutched at things over which a man had no control. He felt his palm sticky against the leather-wrapped hilt of his knife and realized he was sweating. A bullfrog boomed suddenly to his left, whirling him that way in a violent reaction. He turned back, his whole great body tense and rigid. *Come ahead, ye clootie, come ahead.*

With the noise of the fight gone, the small animals had begun their nocturnal sounds again. More frogs joined in with the first one. A mockingbird began to sing. Blowflies congregated about Hobkirk's perspiring face. His hand jerked instinctively to paw at them, and then he realized the slightest movement might give him away. The flies buzzed dismally about the blood clotting on the dead man's chest.

Finally he could stand it no longer. The smallest movement, hell! He jumped into the stretch of moonlight, his great voice sounding through the timber like the rumble of raging thunder. "Here I be, Edmond, if that's what ye followed me from the house for! Here I be with my whinger, so quit tittling around like a giglet at a rockin and come out. . . ."

Before he had finished shouting, the body struck him, and, as he was carried backward by the animal violence of the charge, he felt the sharp bite of steel in his side. He was knocked from his feet, and, as they rolled into the black shadow, he felt the blade pulled from him. The earth jarred the breath from him, and he tried to jerk aside from that next thrust. But the movement came faster than he could match, and the steel bit deeply into him again. With a hoarse groan, he flung up one arm as a lever and rolled himself over on top.

Even as they rolled, he felt that blade drawn from him for another thrust. He had never met with such blinding speed before, and, knowing he could not hope to thwart the third lunge with any orthodox block, he simply threw the whole weight of his body flat and pulled his whinger far out to the side for his own thrust. The blade caught him in the shoulder. Then, with the steel still in him and his own knife held out to the side, ready to drive home, he saw for the first time who it was.

The woman's scarred face stared up at him, red lips writhing back across white teeth, great black eyes flashing wildly. He barely held his knife arm back. In the next moment, something went through him he had never felt before, something so poignant it blotted out the pain of his wounds. It must have shown in his face, for the woman ceased her struggles and stared up at him in a strange, dazed surprise. Then she started fighting again, trying to jerk her blade free. He twisted over so her arm was pinned beneath his shoulder. She reached up, and clawed his face from brow to chin. He reared back, and she squirmed from beneath him and leaped to her feet.

"*¡Escoces diablo!*" she spat at him, "Scot devil!" — and whirled, and was gone before he could get up.

He sank back to his knees, staring after her dully. Finally he found the strength to pull her knife from his shoulder. His shirt was soggy with blood from the other two wounds, and dimly he realized how weak he was from this bleeding. But, somehow, the pain and the weakness did not hold the significance it should.

He heard the sound of movement off to his left, but did not turn. He was still staring off in the direction the woman had taken, when Edmond and Barnabas Benton rode fretting, lathered horses into sight.

"Davoc!" called Edmond, swinging down, and then he saw the blood.

"A woman," said Hobkirk dully. "A woman

with a scarred face."

"A what?" said Edmond, stepping across the dead man to go on one knee beside Hobkirk. "You don't mean Camoa Corchino? How bad is it?"

"Camoa Corchino?" said Hobkirk.

"Yes." Edmond was trying to strip off his bloody shirt. "That was some of Corchino's men with Random tonight. This dead one here is *el cojo*. The Lame One. Ridden with Corchino for years. I had no idea Corchino's sister rode with him on things like this."

"Ye never saw the like," said Hobkirk, pushing him away. "With a whinger. I thought it was you. That was funny, wasn't it? With a whinger. Like lightning. So fast I couldn't see. A tiger. I never knew a woman could be . . . like that."

"He's delirious," growled Barnabas Benton, dismounting.

"Where did Tadousac say Corchino was?" asked Hobkirk. "The Del Carmens?"

Edmond caught at him again. "Now, wait a minute. . . ."

"Gather up the men, Barnabas," said Hobkirk. "We're going there."

"No, Davoc, don't be crazy," said Edmond. "You're in no state for such a ride . . . you're. . . ."

Hobkirk whirled on the man, and his voice crashed like thunder. "I said gather up the men. We're riding to the Del Carmens!"

VIII

Random was sitting behind the saddle on his Morgan, with Camoa in the kak, his arms about her to hold the reins. He pulled up on the black horse as they dropped down the road toward town, speaking in a muted voice. "You still haven't given me a real explanation of why you followed us to Catecas's."

The impatient movement of her head brought her black hair against his cheek, and despite the dust of the long ride it still held a faint perfume. "I just didn't trust Tadousac, that's all. He always has so many reasons for doing anything. I couldn't believe his only motive in getting you and Edmond together was to help you clear yourself."

"So you followed us all the way from Rancho del Carmen," he said. "That doesn't quite jibe with your attitude toward me when we first met."

Her ribs lifted against him with a breath. "Maybe my attitude changed since then."

"When did that happen?"

"I called you a coward," she muttered. "But no coward would fight the way you did when those men jumped you at the *rancho*. Like my brother said. A *tigre*? Perhaps that's why I followed you down here."

"That doesn't seem a very strong reason," he said.

"They say it is a short step from hate to love," said Tadousac from behind them. Random turned in surprise, not realizing the man had been so close. Tadousac sat, leaning back in the saddle on his Billy horse with fat legs flapped out wide in the stirrups to ease the cramp of the long ride. The girl had turned toward him, also, a strange anger in her face.

"Don't be loco," she said.

"Your denial is so vehement." Tadousac grinned. She turned to the front with an exasperated sound, and the Creole giggled. "You called him a murderer, too, and a hypocrite. Don't you want to apologize for that now, in the light of Edmond's revelations?"

"I do, I do," she said impatiently.

"He-he," giggled the Creole. "What say we reach Vargas's place by the rear? It would be safer."

There was a motte of willows behind the blacksmith's barn, and Pedro de Vargas was waiting in their shade, an old-fashioned, smooth-bore *escopeta* in his gnarled hand.

"*Señores,*" he muttered, shuffling forward as they swung in to dismount, "my wife has food and drink inside and there is enough room in the loft for you all to sleep, but you had better wait till I get rid of the man out front. He asked me if there has been any news of *el caballero fantasma* here, and other very suspicious questions."

"Might be one of Hobkirk's men," said Random, helping Camoa off. "What does he look like?"

"An old coyote of a man," said Vargas, "with no hair on his head and the dirtiest buffalo coat I have ever . . . *señor!*"

But Random, as tired as he was, had already broken into a run toward the barn, tearing open the wooden door at the rear that led into the aisle on one side, running past a line of stalls. He could see the oldster out front, rising from where he had been seated on an upturned barrel.

"Grandpa," called Random, "Grandpa Shell!"

"Kip." The old man cackled, running toward him. "Where in Davie Crockett's name'd you come from . . . ?" — and then he stopped, staring at Random as he burst into the light. Random halted, too, and they stood there staring at each other, Grandpa Shell's eyes taking in the black boots, the black pants, the black shirt. *"El fantasma,"* he said finally in a strange, hollow tone.

"Yeah," said Random, feeling something small and cold touch him. "What is it, Grandpa?"

Grandpa Shell drew a heavy breath. "This is a helluva way to meet, after ten years. After we separated at Endytown, I tried to come back to Austin, but several attempts were made on my life, and I realized it was because of that hundred thousand. I was too old to join the Army, so I went up into New Mexico. They knowed I'd been in the Rangers, and I finally got herded into acting as sheriff for Lincoln County under the territorial legislature. I figured it was far enough away to be safe from this Houston business, and I hadn't been able to contact either you or Eddie in so long I finally gave you up for dead. Last April a prominent rancher was murdered in Fort Stanton by a man three witnesses swore was *el fantasma*. Nobody knowing his true identity, I was given a warrant and extradition papers for John Doe."

Random stood silently a moment, aware that Camoa and Pegoes and the others had moved in behind. "How did you figure I'd be here?" he said finally.

"Word's been going around that *el fantasma* was at Catecas's place a couple of days ago, and *el cojo* was found dead in the timber by the river," said Shell. "I figured that might have meant *el fantasma* was hitched in with Corchino's old crowd. I knew Corchino's sister was supposed to have had a place in the Del Carmens. From Catecas's to the Del Carmens goes right up the river. I been hitting every town in between."

"You were always a good officer, Grandpa,"

said Random. "You going to serve that warrant?"

"This *el fantasma* has become some sort of a legendary figure," said Grandpa Shell. "I remember it was the same way with Corchino. You'd hear about him raiding half a dozen places at the same time, or someone would see him in Brownsville on the same day another jasper was willing to swear on a stack of Bibles he saw him in Santa Fé. It happens with a man like that. I'd just like to ask you one question, Kip. When were you last in Fort Stanton?"

"I haven't been west of El Paso in fifteen years, Grandpa," said Kip.

"That's good enough for me," said Grandpa, stepping to his gaunted bay and opening one of the *alforjas* behind the cantle. From these saddlebags he drew the warrant and extradition papers, turning to lay them on the fire beneath Vargas's bellows.

Pedro de Vargas had laid a pair of planks across two sawbucks to form a long table in the barn, and his wife had loaded this down with platters of the succulent corn tortillas and a huge tin pot of coffee. They had all come into the barn and were just sitting down to eat, when a muted shout came from the west end of town, and then another, and a man ran by the door.

"When a *hombre* hurries in Zapata," said Vargas, turning to go outside, "it is time for me to see what has happened."

Random watched the huge, heavy-shouldered man shuffle down the aisle, and stop just outside the door, turning to look up the street. There was more shouting from that way, and Random saw the smith straighten abruptly.

"Corchino," he said hollowly, taking an involuntary step on out. Then he whirled back to them, his face shining with excitement. "He's come, *es verdad,* Corchino! He's here. He's come for me. We're riding again. *Los* Corchinos! Where is my *escopeta,* woman, get me my shotgun, get me my horse, he's here, Corchino. . . ."

Camoa was sitting beside Random, and, as he rose, he saw a pallor seep through her face. He did not stop, caught up, somehow, by Vargas's excitement. The others seemed to be excited, also, for the whole bunch of them were running by the time they reached the door. Vargas was jumping up and down, his beefy, swarthy face dripping sweat.

There was a great cavalcade of horses trotting down the street, and at their head, like a conqueror, rode Juan Nepuceno Corchino. He was dressed in a gaudy, glazed sombrero with tinkling silver pendants all around the edge of its brim with rows of medals across the chest. The gold-chased handles of twin Colts protruded from thonged-down holsters. He forked a double-rigged Mexican tree saddle heavy with silver plating, hung with ancient shoe stirrups of solid bronze. His horse was a high-stepping, deep-chested beast, prancing nervously from side to side toward them.

"Corchino!" shouted Vargas, catching at the man as he tried to swing down. "You've come for me. I will ride with you again. You have come for me."

"*Sí, sí,* of course, Pedro, of course," said Corchino impatiently brushing the man off. He turned toward Camoa, smiling with his mouth. "So you had to follow my *amigo* down here. I am sorry if she caused you any trouble, Random" — and then he made that gesture toward his face, shrugging — "you know. . . ."

"She saved my life," said Random.

Corchino's satanic brows raised. "Did she? Good for my little *hermana!* What happened?"

"Hobkirk was there with his men," said Random.

Corchino's face darkened, and he turned toward Tadousac, but the Creole threw out fat, defensive hands. "Must you blame me for everything that happens? How was I to know Edmond was connected with Hobkirk?"

"*Sí,*" said Corchino. "How *were* you to know? Where is *el cojo?*"

"Barnabas Benton killed him," said Random. "Jarales and Pegoes didn't find out

113

the others were there in time to warn me, and I would have been trapped in the house if Camoa hadn't come. We all headed for the river timber. That's where *el cojo* got it. Camoa had her horse shot, and Hobkirk almost got her. I found her down on the shore."

"*El cojo* was an old *bravo* of mine," said Corchino, his lips writhing over the words with a terrible, barely audible intensity, his smoldering eyes holding Tadousac's. "I will find out who is responsible, and, if it is you, *Señor* Anatole Napoleón Maximilian Blake d'Tadousac, your death will be as certain as the rising of the sun, and much, much uglier."

"*M'sieu* . . . ," bleated Tadousac.

Corchino turned aside, breaking in on the Creole with a wave of his hand at Shell. "Who is this?"

"Louis Shell," said Random. "A *compadre*."

"Not Grandpa Shell?" said Corchino. "Not Daniel Parker's *amigo*?"

"That's right," said Shell. "I was sitting on the council in Eighteen Thirty-Five when old Dan got up and offered a resolution, creating a corps of Texas Rangers."

"And you have brought him to ride with us." Corchino grinned at Random. "This is a day. How can they stand up to us, with such *bravos* as these along? Kip Random . . . *el caballero fantasma* . . . and Grandpa Shell, the

114

only. . . ." He broke off suddenly, turning slowly to Pegoes Oporto. "Why do you watch me like that, Pegoes?"

"I am just waiting, *senhor*," said Oporto.

"*Senhor, senhor*, will you ever learn how to say it right. This is Mexico, not. . . ." Corchino stopped, the muscles about his mouth working. Finally he spoke again. "Waiting for what, Pegoes?"

"Is Frank Fullerton along?" asked Pegoes.

"*Pues,* of course," Corchino told him. "All the *bravos* are here. What has that got to do with it? What do you mean . . . you are waiting?"

"I'm just waiting."

Corchino stared at him a moment. "Perhaps we are all waiting," he said, after another pause. Then he turned to Random. "*Sí,* we are all waiting, *Señor* Kip. Let us ride."

Camoa caught his arm. "Kip. . . ."

"*¡Punta en boca!*" snarled Corchino, whirling on her. "What have you been telling him?" He turned back to Random, seeing suspicion in the blond man's eyes. "What has she been telling you? I told you it had no significance, Random. I told you how it was with her. Aren't you convinced yet? Let me prove it to you, then? What do you think I brought my army for? What do you think I rode *el almagre* for? This is it, Kip, what we have been working for and planning for all this time, *both* you and I. We will see Texas rid of Rhode and his carpetbaggers and his assassins for good. I have heard the rumors of Hobkirk's presence hereabouts. He won't be able to stand up against us, Kip. Together we will be irresistible. Are you going to hide because a poor, frustrated, cheated woman has some warped idea in her brain? Are you going to let that keep you from joining in on the culmination of what you've been fighting for so many years?"

Random studied the man's face a long moment, then drew a heavy breath. "All right. Let's ride!"

IX

The road led down the flat surface of the upper Río Grande valley south of Zapata like an unrolling ribbon in the dusk. The silence of a long ride had settled over them. This unremitting pace could be kept up indefinitely by a horse in good condition, and covered much more ground than a cantering animal, although it took a man inured to the saddle to sit the steady, jarring beat.

Random and Grandpa Shell had taken up their position directly behind Corchino, who was flanked on one side by Pegoes Oporto, and on the other by tall, dour Frank Fullerton. Grandpa Shell cast a look over his shoulder at the men behind him, then sidled his horse in close to Random.

"Corchino's right about Houston's being his friend," he muttered. "Sam always said Corchino was fighting for the same thing we were, though nobody realized it. If he means to break Rhode in this state, I'm with him till the last dally's thrown. But there's something wrong here, Kip. This bunch doesn't seem to be the crusading type."

"If you'll remember, the Rangers were pretty rough in the beginning, too, Grandpa," said Random. "You have to have men like this to battle the thing Rhode has built up here."

"What was this about the girl?"

"Camoa?" Random's face darkened. "I don't know, Grandpa. She is a little strange."

"You mean you can't figure her out?" said Grandpa. "Or maybe can't figure yourself out?" Random turned sharply toward him, and the old man showed yellowed teeth in his grin. "I seed it, Kip. I know when a man's been struck." He sobered. "I wish Corchino hadn't made her stay behind with that smith's wife. I'd like to hear what she has to say before we go into this."

"She's got some idea Corchino's changed," said Random. "But he's backed his word to the hilt so far. Did all he could to help me find Edmond and try to clear myself, even sent some men along with me. Without them I'd never have gotten free of Hobkirk."

They were approaching a crossroads, and Corchino raised one gauntleted hand, turning back to Random. "We turn here, *amigos*. The first *rancho* we strike tonight is that of Rhode's most ardent supporters."

They wheeled northward, the dust from their myriad horses rising like white mist in the lowering night. The moon was up by the time they sighted the low hills ahead of them. There was something familiar about the landscape that caught at Random, and he kept looking from side to side in a puzzled way.

They rose into slopes timbered with oak and blackjack and topped the crest, dropping down into a meadow of mesquite grass. At the bottom, Corchino turned up a shallow valley. The twin peaks were not visible at night till the cavalcade had ridden into the gorge between them. Up this sandy gorge, choked with chaparral and mesquite, they forced their way.

"Corchino!" called Random. "These are the Reynosas. You're not hitting the Mateo outfit?"

"*Sí,*" said Corchino.

Random tore up through the thickening brush, clutching at the man's arm. "Don't be loco, Mateo. . . ."

"Is one of Rhode's most ardent sup-porters," said Corchino, turning on him. "You were there when Eddie Pickering was killed. Who do you think betrayed him? After he escaped from Brownsville, he fled here, because Carlotta Mateo was his wife. How do you think Hobkirk ever found this place?"

"Tadousac and Edmond got together. . . ."

"And who do you think brought them together, and told them Pickering was here?" asked Corchino.

"Listen. . . ."

"Don't argue with me!" The man's face had darkened, and there was a glint in his greenish eyes. "How can we ever accomplish anything if you oppose every move I make, Random? The whole fate of any army lies in the degree of its ability to move swiftly and decisively. *¡Halo, compadres!*"

This last was shouted past Random to the others. They had broken free of the brush-choked gorge into the round bowl of Vallejo Mateo, with the ranch buildings ahead of them. The riders spread out and swept down on the outfit at a gallop. Frank Fullerton veered away, and Ellie Watts and a dozen other men followed him in a running file toward the dim shift of cattle in the moonlight on the other side of the valley.

The thunder of hoofs surrounded Random, and he could see Pegoes Oporto ahead, turning to look at Corchino every once in a while. The valley was shaking with their pounding charge now. A rectangle of yellow light appeared in the center of the main building, and a figure was silhouetted there momentarily. A dim shout reached Random. Then someone started shooting from behind him. The figure took a step outward and fell.

"Corchino!" screamed a woman's voice from inside. "¡Esta Corchino!"

A gun began banging from one of the windows. The big roan Bogus Bill Halderman was riding screamed, and reared up beside Random. Cursing, Bogus Bill slammed his flat hand into the beast's neck again and again, knocking it back down, and then stepped off before it fell.

More guns began to make their cherry blasts from the dark bulk of the house. A figure formed its shadowy, flitting motion through the pattern of corrals. Corchino whirled his Barb ahead of Random, pulling one of those gold-chased Colts to fire into the corrals. On the third shot, Random heard the scream, and there was no more of that dim motion within the cottonwood bars.

"Take Little George and some others around the back!" Corchino shouted at Cookie Keith, and the sloppy man spurred toward a motte of willows sighing over one end of the long front porch, waving a string of others after him. Random's Morgan had been too tired to take right out again, and Vargas had given him a little bay pacer from his barn. It stumbled suddenly, and a hollow, sick groaning sound passed through its body.

Random kicked free of the stirrups, and dove head foremost, rolling over and over on the hard-packed ground, coming up against something with a solid, stunning force. He lay there a moment, the screaming horses and shouting men and rocking gunfire enveloping him dimly. Then he felt someone shake him.

"You hit, Kip?" shouted Grandpa Shell, above the noise.

"No." Kip tried to sit up, but Grandpa shoved him back down.

"Play snake, 'less you wanna be sent to hell on a shutter. You rolled into the corrals right across from the house."

There were a dozen horses in the three corrals, running the fence and fighting one another in their frenzied effort to escape. Not ten paces from Random was the body of the man Corchino had shot. Grandpa and Random could look past the undressed cottonwood post Random had rolled into and see the house.

Cookie Keith and his riders had gotten around back and were charging into the *plácido* between the two wings, their guns blazing. Corchino had ridden his Barb right up to the porch, followed by Jesús Santiago and half a dozen more of his most reckless *bravos*. Their guns formed a continuous, deafening din as they swept the windows with their fire.

Corchino dropped from his horse, a gold-chased six-gun in each hand, and shot the hammered silver lock from the door, lifting a boot to kick the portal open. "I'm coming in, Mateo," he shouted, "see if you can stop me now!"

He disappeared into the lighted doorway, gray smoke swimming giddily about the figures following him. There was a renewed crash of gunfire within the house. More Corchinos clattered up to the porch, dismounted, and went through the windows now as well as the door. Random got up.

"I don't like this, Grandpa, at all," he said, and ran for the door, skinning his big Walker Colt. Men were still coming in on horseback, and there was a crazy confusion of dismounting Corchinos and whinnying, rearing, empty horses about the front porch. Random ran into Corchino's Barb, shoved himself away, and went head first into another dismounting person.

He caught hold to keep from falling. A clawing hand raked his face, and he straightened up, grasping the writhing, kicking body. Then he saw who it was.

"How did you get here?" he gasped.

"Did you think the cow Vargas calls his wife could keep me from it?" panted Camoa Corchino. She pulled free of him, eyes flashing. "Are you satisfied now? Do you still think Corchino is interested in freeing the *peónes?* Look at them, murdering, plundering, killing . . . !"

The firing had stopped inside, and Jesús Santiago reeled through the smoke-filled doorway, holding a pair of gold candlesticks in his grimy hands. "Look, Vargas!" he shouted at the smith. "These will bring two hundred *pesos* in Durango at least."

"*Viva.*" Vargas laughed, firing his gun. "Corchino is on the march again. *Viva* Corchino."

"*Sí,*" said Camoa bitterly. "*Viva* Corchino. Long live Corchino. Long murder Corchino."

"Is that the way you feel, *hermanita?*"

He had an uncanny faculty for appearing like that. Random turned to face the man, taking a heavy breath before he could control his voice. It shook a little anyway.

"Maybe that's the way I feel, too, Corchino," he said.

The low of cattle came through the shouting, and Ellie Watts swung in on a lathered horse, wiping sweat from his face. "It's a good fat herd, Juan. We got 'em all on the move without much trouble. Bogus Bill wants to know where we head them."

Another *vaquero* climbed from a window, holding a wine bottle above his head, and a woman screamed from within the house. Corchino spoke to Ellie Watts without taking his eyes from Camoa's face.

"Drive the herd to the Del Carmens. Take

only the men you'll need for it. Leave the rest with me." As Ellie swung away, Corchino held out his hand. "Now, Camoa, my little sister, I think you had better come with me."

Camoa stiffened against Random. "No!"

"Yes." Corchino's words slipped from his thin lips with that soft felinity, and his mouth was smiling, but his eyes were not. "Yes. I grow weary of you, Camoa. I grow weary of your obsession about me. I told you what would happen if you persisted. Let us take a walk. Let us go out in the trees, just you and I, Camoa. . . ."

Random's whole body had grown taut, and Grandpa, standing behind him, must have seen it, because his palm came against Random's back, flat and calloused, and his voice formed a slurred mutter in Random's ear. "Don't do anything, boy. You wouldn't stand a chance with the whole outfit around you."

Corchino took a step toward the woman, reaching for her hand. "Camoa."

"No, no!" screamed the woman, wheeling away into Random.

"Yes!" said Corchino, in a hard, flat voice, and caught her by the arm and whirled her back, those green eyes blazing.

"No!" said Random. It struck Corchino like a slap. Both Corchino's Colts were leathered, but Random held his gun in his hand. He went on, something deadly in the

124

utter lack of vehemence of his words. "I've got this Walker pointed right at your belly, Corchino. Make one move and I'll blow your lantern out for good. Now get back on your horse, Camoa. Round up some nags for us, too, Grandpa."

There was still shouting and yelling from within the house, but many of the Corchinos had surrounded them now, Cookie Keith behind Corchino, Vargas and Jesús Santiago over at the end of the porch, Ellie Watts sitting his horse amid the other unridden animals. Random heard Grandpa move behind him. There was the faint beginning of a shift among the men.

"Any of you got ideas, forget them," said Random, and his voice carried to every one. "Shooting me won't stop Corchino's hide from being hung up. I can get one slug out of this flame pusher no matter how many holes you put in me. And that's all it will take."

The movement stopped, and a palpable tension dropped over them. Corchino's face was black with diffused blood. The greenish tint had completely left his eyes. Random heard the creak of saddle leather behind him. He shoved Camoa to one side, and heard her mount.

"All right, son," said Grandpa Shell. "I'm up, and my iron's looking right down his belly button."

It happened when Random turned to mount the animal Grandpa had gotten for him. The movement caused the excited horse to shift into Grandpa's horse. Grandpa was mounted and had covered Corchino, but the animal, shying into him, threw his gun off just an instant.

"*¡Hola!*" shouted Corchino, and there was some violent movement behind Random. He grabbed the saddle horn and swung aboard without waiting to get a foot in the stirrups. Grandpa's gun went off above his head as he hit the saddle. Corchino jumped aside, and the other men jerked into movement, hauling at their guns.

"Let's go, Grandpa!" shouted Random, emptying his gun. The three riders plunged into the darkness. Random turned in the saddle to see Corchino run toward his horse.

"*¡Vámonos, sus perros!*" he shouted at his men. "If you let one of them escape with his life, ten of you shall pay with yours!"

X

Allow me to express my apologies, thought Anatole d'Tadousac, standing there on the Texas side of the Río Grande and staring blankly across the turgid river toward the Del Carmens, *allow me to express my humblest apologies that you should come to such an ignoble, ignominious end, after such long and faithful service.*

"You have killed my Billy horse," he said finally, turning to Corchino. "Your own Barb is dying on its feet. The other animals will drop with their next step. How can you expect us to go any farther?"

There was a gaunt, ravening look to Corchino's face, and he spat contemptuously at the dead Billy horse that had fallen in the sand. "My *almagre* is no coon-footed Quarter animal. It's your own misfortune. I should have had you killed long before this."

Tadousac took a moment to realize what Corchino meant. The blood drained from his fat, swarthy face. "You aren't leaving me here afoot!"

"I'm not wearing down anybody's horse riding you double," said Corchino. "We've followed Random three days now, and I'm not losing him because some fat, greasy, little Creole didn't. . . ."

"Frenchman, *m'sieu*, Frenchman," said Tadousac, drawing himself up. Then he caught himself, and began to make small, conciliatory motions with one hand. "Please, *m'sieu*, you would not do this to anyone. A man would die out here. A man would have no chance. It is hundreds of miles to civilization. Wild Indians. Savage animals. How could you possibly . . . ?"

"It is not hard," said Corchino wearily,

turning in his saddle. *"Andale, compadres, andale."*

His Barb thrust its head forward and started moving, and the other horses broke into motion. Tadousac turned to fumble in his saddlebags, bringing out the briefcase, and started to waddle after them, sweat rolling down his pale face.

"Please, *m'sieu,* you cannot do this, please!" he cried. "I have here a paper, *oui,* a paper which I am sure. . . ."

"¡Hola!" said Corchino, and the harsh restraint of his voice stopped Tadousac. The Mexican was staring ahead.

For the last day they had been riding into the wild desolation of the Santiagos, and now they stood in a valley with the barren, forbidding peaks towering all about them. Corchino's face was turned toward a ridge ahead of them. Tadousac saw it then. One. Two. Three. Like that. Three silhouettes skylighted on the crest, one after the other, barely perceptible.

"They are making for the river," said Corchino in a hoarse, vicious tone. "Bear to the left and cut them off. We'll have them then, *amigos.*"

"No, please, *m'sieu,* you can't leave me like this, I won't allow it," babbled Tadousac, running toward them as they lifted their animals into a trot, "not the man who has served emperors, not the man who was the

128

bosom friend of the great Nap . . . ol. . . ."

He trailed off, and stopped running, to stand there, coughing in the rising dust. Tears formed gleaming, translucent streaks through the grime of his face. *You* meurtriers, he thought, *you assassins, you. . . .*

He stopped, lifting his plump shoulders in a shrug. The tears had stopped, and he giggled suddenly. How droll. Anatole Napoleón Maximilian Blake d'Tadousac left to die by the little Napoleón of Tamualipas, the Red Robber of the Río Grande. How exceedingly droll. He started on the trail they had left.

He started to cross the ridge between two great stones, then ducked back abruptly. He stooped down behind one stone, lifting his head only high enough to see over the top. The slope dropping away from him on the opposite side formed a rugged, channeled pattern of deep gullies and broken spur ridges, and not twenty feet off the ridge, in one of these gullies, was gathered Corchino and a group of his men. Corchino's voice floated up to Tadousac.

"This ridge and the next one point right into that box cañon you can see from here. If we can drive them into that, we'll have them trapped. Frank, you take Little George and six or seven other men and cross to that other ridge to keep Random from crossing to there. Vargas, you stay here and keep them from getting through to the river if they turn back. Pegoes and I will follow this ridge down and keep them from coming back across it. *Andale*."

They broke into the three groups, and Tadousac whirled to start scrambling down the slope on one side as Corchino came up the other with Oporto. The Creole found a shallow gully, and dropped into it, seeking the screen of sparse mesquite as he slid on down toward the sandy bottom. He stopped himself abruptly as Corchino topped the ridge, and crouched there, staring up.

Pegoes followed Corchino, and they turned up along the ridge in the direction Random had taken, dropping down far enough on this slope so they would not be skylighted. Then Corchino halted his Barb, and they were close enough for Tadousac to hear it.

"All right, Pegoes," said Corchino.

"All right what, *senhor?*"

"*Senhor, Senhor,*" snarled Corchino. "You know what," he said, after a moment. "You have been watching me ever since you brought Random in. You said you were waiting. You are through waiting."

"*Sí.*" Oporto's lean body had stiffened a little in the saddle. "Perhaps I am. Perhaps this is what I was waiting for. It is the first time we have been alone since I brought Random back, is it not?"

"So?" said Corchino.

" '*Señor* Frank'," quoted Oporto, in a

bitter, mocking tone, " 'it has been so long since we rode together on the border before the days of the Corchino war. But then we were great *amigos,* no? And since friendship . . .'."

"Where did you get that?" Corchino had bent forward in his silver-mounted saddle, face twisted, staring at the Portuguese.

" 'That is why I write you'," continued Oporto, relentlessly quoting that letter. " 'I have a lieutenant now, Pegoes Oporto. Perhaps you remember him from former days, but he is disloyal and untrustworthy, and I need a man upon whom . . .'."

Corchino straightened again in his saddle, flapping those ancient bronze shoe stirrups out wide in order to straighten his legs fully. The movement caused the sun to glint on the gold-chased butts of his Colts. He had both hands on the reins of his horse now, just above the saddle horn.

"I see what you mean," he said in that soft, purring tone. "All right, Frank Fullerton is here now. I'm glad you didn't wait any longer. I wouldn't have waited much longer myself."

"You *carbón!*" shouted Oporto, his face turning livid, and he must have been the first to go for his gun, but Corchino's hands moved so soon afterward that it seemed both men drew at the same time. The crash of guns seemed to rock Tadousac's head, but he did not see the men, because another sound had come just before the shots, turning him.

The mesquite below Tadousac was so thick it choked the whole gully, and it was in this growth Major Edmond appeared. He stood there for an instant, a tall slender fox of a man, eyes flashing.

"Tadousac," he said, with the echoes of the gunfire still rolling about them, "I might have known it." His elbow swept the tail of his black frock coat away from the gun holstered on his hip. "This is the last pie you'll put those greasy fingers of yours into!"

Tadousac had never been too skillful with a gun. The first shot came and there was a terrible, shocking blow against his chest, knocking him backward. He stumbled and went down, fumbling to tear the French saloon pistol from its shoulder harness beneath his coat. Edmond took a vicious step forward, lean face twisting above his buckling, smoking gun, and fired again. But Tadousac was going over backward, and the second bullet passed above his face.

His back struck the ground so hard his breath left him in a grunt. But the gun was out, and his thumb brought the hammer back. Edmond took yet another step forward, his lips pulling away from his teeth, the muzzle of his gun dropping toward Tadousac in a little jerk. The saloon pistol's hammer clicked on full cock and the breech dropped shut. The gun bucked so hard in Tadousac's hand it flew loose.

Edmond stood there for a moment, staring at Tadousac. Slowly the hand with his gun dropped, till it was pointing at the ground by his feet. Then all the keen intelligence fled from his eyes, and he toppled over backward into the mesquite.

"You were wrong, Edmond," gasped Tadousac, holding his precious briefcase against his chest. "It is not a pie. It is a square. It is the sixth and last side, Edmond, of a square."

When the gunshots began coming from the ridge above him, Davoc Hobkirk halted his gaunted Clydesdale, staring up the gully at the mesquite into which Edmond had disappeared ahead of him. Riding north from Brownsville, they had heard at Zapata of Corchino's raid on Rancho Mateo, and had struck the broad trail he had left into the Santiagos.

As the last shot died, Hobkirk pulled his Ward-Burton from its scabbard beneath his stirrup leather. "It's Corchino, Willie," he said to the man behind him. "Ride for camp and bring the rest of the clan back here. The rest of you will follow me up."

Wee Willie Porter turned his horse laterally up the slope, and Hobkirk shot the bolt on his gun, and heeled the Clydesdale through the mesquite choking the draw. A little within the thicket, he came across Edmond's mare, tethered to a bush. He urged the Clydesdale on, and burst free, reining the animal aside to avoid stepping on the body of a man in the sand of the gully.

"Well, Major," murmured Hobkirk, staring down at the man, "it looks like ye'll nae be able to show me how much better that James Bowie mon was at whingering than Lord Bothwell, after all."

Farther on was Tadousac, lying on his back. Hobkirk thought he discerned a shallow breathing, but he pushed on toward the crest.

Just below the ridge lay the body of another man. Hobkirk passed him, and topped the ridge, and there below him, gathered in the draws and coulées of the slope, were too many horsemen for him to count. Another group, farther below, looked as if they had started to cross the valley, but had stopped at the sound of the shots, and were milling about indecisively. In between Hobkirk and the riders was a lone man, dropping toward the main group, stirrups gleaming brazenly in the afternoon sun.

"It's Corchino!" shouted Hobkirk. "We've got him as sure as Wallace had Surrey at Stirling Bridge. Down on them, ye crowlin' mid staumrels, the pibrochs are playin' and the claymores are out and it's Thig Ris for the last time!"

His great voice boomed out over the desolate silence like roaring thunder, and the file of weary Riders behind him seemed caught up by its clarion call, for they spread out with a new eagerness, urging their horses over the ridge into a sliding, stumbling gallop. The man with the bronze stirrups had reached his men and turned his horse, shouting to them in Spanish. They wheeled to meet the oncoming governor's men.

Barnabas Benton was the first to fire. His double-barreled Greener roared, and a big, crop-haired blond in the forefront of *los* Corchinos reeled off his horse with his chest shot apart. Another Corchino urged his jaded horse into a gallop upslope and yanked twin Bisleys from his hip pockets.

Sergeant Peterson screamed from behind Hobkirk, and a moment later his empty horse went past the Scot in a headlong gallop. Hobkirk whirled toward the man with his Ward-Burton, but that left-hand Bisley had risen and fallen. The Clydesdale whinnied shrilly, rearing up. With both hands on his rifle, Hobkirk was thrown clear of the wounded horse.

He lit rolling and came up on his knees, the bolt-action still in his hand. He was in the midst of a battle that had spread out across the whole slope. The little man with the Bisleys had gone on past Hobkirk, guns rising and falling alternately. Barnabas

Benton reeled into view, running crazily through the carnage.

The man with the Bisleys wheeled toward him, left-hand gun rising. Benton's Greener boomed, and the Bisleys dropped from the man's hands one by one, and he slumped off his horse. Benton whirled to meet another rider coming in on him, letting go his other barrel. The man was right on top of Benton, and, as he screamed and leaped from his horse right into the blasting gun, Hobkirk recognized the smith from Zapata who had been in the GREAT BOOK.

The Scot rose to his feet, firing at the wheeling, cavorting riders about him. He had spilled two from their saddles, and was jamming a fresh load into the breech, when a third came charging in from his flank. He whirled to meet the man and caught the brazen gleam of those shoe stirrups and the glitter of the saddle.

"Corchino?" he shouted, snapping his bolt shut.

"Juan Nepuceno Corchino!" screamed the man, and then the blast of both their weapons drowned him out.

Kip Random pulled his jaded animal into a halt when Grandpa Shell came toiling back up the slope, and sat there to wait beside Camoa for the old man. Both their faces were haggard and the gray dust they had been driven through these last days lay thickly over their clothing. Grandpa drew his puffing horse to a halt, shaking his head at them.

"We're blocked off from the front. There's a camp of Rhode's Riders at the end of this cañon, and that Wee Willie Porter just came down over the hill and told them something that's put them all in the saddle and headed them up the valley this way."

"Hobkirk?" Random shook his head in a dull incredulity, then jerked it back over his shoulder. "Is that what the shooting's about down the line?"

"Might be the Riders have run into Corchino," said the old man.

Camoa drew a hopeless breath, her eyes on Random. "We can't just stay here and wait for them."

"They'll spot us if we break for either slope," said Grandpa. He sat there a moment, studying them. "Unless one of us made a show up this near side and drew them on him. The other two might make it over the ridge after they'd passed."

It took a moment for Random to define the expression on the man's face, and he leaned forward sharply. "Grandpa, no."

"I'm an old man, son," said Shell.

"No . . . we've been through too much together. . . ."

"All the more reason. You owe it to the

girl. Turn loose your horses. You'll be able to take cover better without them and those nags are so dead on their feet right now they couldn't go as fast as you could on foot. Stay here in this mesquite till the police are past you, and then move across the valley to that opposite slope. Reach the river and you might make it."

"Grandpa. . . ."

"See you where the grass is greener, Kip."

The old man booted his horse upslope. Kip tried to spur his animal after, but the beast stumbled and went to its knees. He swung off and started running, then stopped to look back at Camoa. Owe it to the girl? For a moment he knew a poignant desire to go out with the old man. Then he moved wearily back to Camoa. She stepped off, and he saw the pinched whiteness of her lips. It was natural for his arms to slip around her.

"OK, OK," he said. "We'll make it." He held her a moment, feeling all the fear and weariness in her lithe, trembling body. Then he realized how her face was strained up to him and the expression in it. He could only half read it. "That time you came after us when we went to Catecas," he said. "You never did explain clearly what made you do it."

"Don't you know?" she said, lowering her face to his chest. "Even when I thought you were a murderer. . . ." Suddenly, as she trailed off, he did know, and slipped a grimy, sweaty hand beneath her chin, lifting it. His fingers crossed the scar, and he knew what she meant when she whispered: "Does it matter?"

"No," he said. The utter simplicity of it must have touched something deeply within her, for tears crept down her cheeks.

It was the yell that jerked his head up. A long, eerie Texas yell from the slope above, from Grandpa Shell, standing up in his stirrups halfway to the ridge. Then the Riders broke into view, forcing their horses laterally up through gullies and draws toward the old man. At first, Random thought the gunfire came from them. Then he realized it was on the other side of Grandpa.

The battle was sweeping toward them. A riderless horse appeared. Then a running, staggering man in a red undershirt, loading a double-barreled shotgun. Behind him a swarthy Mexican in *charro* trousers quirted a horse up out of a gully and began to fire with a six-gun. The man with the shotgun jerked, went to his knees, then turned to squeeze both triggers of his sawed-off weapon.

More Corchinos appeared, riding past the man in the red undershirt as he sagged to the ground, and the police after Grandpa were forced to wheel their line to meet Corchino's men. Then, very close to the mesquite thicket in which Random and the girl crouched, a horse ran by. Fading sunlight caught the bronze glint of flapping shoe stirrups. Before the animal had passed, the crash of mesquite from behind whirled Random, and with the girl still in his arms he heard her hoarse mutter.

"Juan. . . ."

Random released her, taking a step toward the sound, pulling at his Walker. He had it free as the man crashed into the open, a rifle swinging in one arm.

"Guid," said the man, bringing his rifle around — "Good." — and Random recovered enough to pull his trigger.

A thin whine followed the explosion of his shot, and he saw the rifle jerk upward and heard Davoc Hobkirk's scream of pain. Random fired again, and saw one of the Scot's legs buckle. But Hobkirk was coming forward with such great impetus that he crashed into Random anyway, clawing at the gun, carrying him to the ground. Gasping blindly, he felt his gun hand pinned to the ground, and then, the bite of steel into his side. Every wiry muscle in his lithe body contracted in a violent, convulsive effort that twisted him away from that knife before it had gone in very deep, and felt the man draw back his arm for another lunge.

Random wriggled in one last, desperate effort to free his gun. But the Scot's grip on that wrist seemed to be crushing the bones. Face twisted in agony, Random brought his knee up into Hobkirk's stomach. Hobkirk groaned with the pain, his great body twisting as he drove in with the blade again. With his free hand, Random caught the knife arm, pumping up with his knee again, and again, and again. Finally, unable to stand the pain, Hobkirk tried to twist aside from that knee. It put him off balance a moment, and Random kicked out one leg and rolled them over.

He had to drop the gun and release his grip on the knife arm to get up. Hobkirk strove to follow him up, but his wounded leg buckled. He caught Random before the blond man had risen completely, pulling him back. Random felt the Scot's awesome strength and knew there was no fighting it. He let himself go right down on Hobkirk, his whole concentration on blocking the thrust.

He was bleeding all over the Scot and blinded by his own sweat and blood. His body was a savage, twisting thing in Hobkirk's grasp, never still an instant, blocking the Scot's lunges or jerking away from them, and at every thrust Random clawed desperately for that knife arm, trying to get it in the position he wanted. Finally Hobkirk came up with a bent elbow, and Random saw his chance. He lashed out for the arm with both hands.

Hobkirk saw it and tried to abort his lunge, but too late. Random caught the bent arm at the elbow and wrist, and threw the whole weight of his body on that side, twisting the arm inward. The Scot tried to stop the motion, but he couldn't hold against Random's rolling weight. All at once Hobkirk was a terrible, dead weight, dropping on him.

Panting, clutching at the shallow, bloody wound in his side, Random squirmed out from beneath Hobkirk. "Little different than whingering women, I guess, Hobkirk," said Random feebly.

Camoa tore part of her skirt off and started sopping at his side. She was still doing it when Grandpa Shell broke through the mesquite, driving a man before him.

"I let them Corchinos fight the Riders," the old man said. "They're wiping each other out, though Corchino himself is down. I picked up this weasel, coming off the ridge."

"He-he," giggled Tadousac, holding his briefcase up in front of him. "How fortunate I am to be among such good, good friends again. Everyone wanted to kill me. You have no idea . . . Corchino, Hobkirk, all of them. And finally Edmond. His bullet struck my briefcase, or I would not be here now. . . ."

He trailed off as he saw Hobkirk sprawled out on the ground with the knife in him.

"With his own whinger, too," said Tadousac. "I'll wager he never dreamed of that."

"Edmond," said Random, staring emptily at Tadousac. "You . . . you . . . ?"

"Yes." The Creole grinned. "But do not look so hopeless, Random."

"He was the only one who could have cleared me of those murders."

"Exactly why I got a signed confession from him before he died," chuckled the Creole, opening the case. "He was your friend, to the last. It must have torn him constantly to be working against you that way. But this written confession will absolve you completely of the murders." A bland, shy smile spread Tadousac's lips. "And now, surely, after all this labor I have done in your behalf, all this utterly altruistic service I have rendered you. . . ."

"Yeah," said Random. "Sure, I'll tell you. You can get Sam Houston's hundred thousand if you want. It's in a trunk buried near Endytown. But it won't do you any good. When we cashed that British draft in New Orleans, it was into Confederate money."

Tadousac gazed blankly at Random a moment. Then the blood began to drain from his face, leaving it a putty color. "All this . . ." — he waved his fat hand in a vaguely inclusive gesture — "all this, and for . . . that . . . ? I think I'd better sit down," said Tadousac, and stumbled over to a mesquite tree.

Camoa sat there a moment, gazing soberly

at Random. "Where will you go," she said finally, "now that you are free?"

"Funny." He stared at the ground. "Funny, I've fought so long against this thing. . . . Now that it's done, I don't know. . . ."

"Rancho del Carmen was a beautiful place at one time," she said. "If Juan's gone, and *los* Corchinos with him, I think it could be that way again."

Grandpa Shell was smiling benignly. "I always wanted to get hitched with a Mexican gal. The closest I ever got was standing up with Eddie Pickering when he married the Mateo filly."

"Maybe you'll get a chance to do that again, Grandpa," said Random, looking into Camoa's wide, darkly shining eyes.

"My good Anatole Napoleón Maximilian Blake d'Tadousac," muttered the fat little Creole dismally, "allow me to compliment you on your peerless perspicacity, your unfailing, unremitting patience, and all the rest of the various and innumerable golden talents which have brought us finally to such a highly gratifying conclusion."

Señorita Scorpion

Les Savage, Jr., narrated the adventures of Elgera Douglas, better known as *Señorita* Scorpion, in a series of seven short novels that originally appeared in *Action Stories*, published by Fiction House. She was, by far, the most popular literary series character to appear in this magazine in the nearly thirty years of its publication history. The fifth short novel in this series, "The Brand of Penasco", is included in *The Shadow in Renegade Basin: A Western Trio* (Five Star Westerns, 2000). The seventh, and last, story in the series, "The Sting of Señorita Scorpion", is collected in the eponymous *The Sting of Señorita Scorpion: A Western Trio* (Five Star Westerns, 2000). The short novel that follows, which was actually the first story in the saga, was titled "Death 'Rods the Big Thicket Bunch" by the author. It was bought for $150.00. Malcolm Reiss, the general manager at Fiction House, changed its title to "*Señorita* Scorpion" when it appeared in *Action Stories* (Spring, 44). He wanted another story about her for the very next issue, and so the series began.

I

Chisos Owens stepped off his horse in front of Anse Hawkman's big frame hotel, and the *creak* of his Porter saddle was the only sound in the strange hush that hung over Boquillos. He dropped his reins over the animal's head and onto the sagging cottonwood hitch rack and stood there for a moment, feeling the physical weight of the silence press in on him.

A hawk-faced Apache stood barefooted between two adobe hovels, hands hitched into the big silver *conchas* of his Navajo belt. As Owens watched, a pair of gaudily garbed Mexicans trotted dusty horses in from the north end of the border town. They slowed to a walk going by the Apache. For a moment their sombrero-shadowed faces turned toward him, and a glance passed between the three men. The door of the *cantina* across the street opened to emit a drunken *peón*. Owens caught the noise of the usual Saturday afternoon revelry from within. Then the door closed again, and once more there was that silence. The two riders had halted their horses without dismounting. One spoke softly to the other, glanced toward Owens. Another horseman appeared at the opposite end of the street, halted there. He wore a fancy suit, too.

146

Owens shrugged and walked around the hitch rack before the hotel porch. He bent forward slightly in his sure-footed stride, like a man who might be hard to stop, and his blue denim jumper covered the square, ungiving block of his torso. Beneath a Texas-creased Stetson, his eyes had the slitted, wind-wrinkled look that comes to a man spending his life in the open. The long ride had grimed the flat, strong planes of his face with dust and thinned his lips with weariness, but his chin held a certain stubborn tenacity in its bulldog jut.

Bick Bickford had been waiting on the porch, a man taller than Chisos, heavy about the waist. The boards creaked beneath his weight as he moved forward, big freckled hands tucked into a cartridge belt.

"Began to think you weren't coming, Chisos."

"What," said Owens in his deliberate voice, "is the matter with this town?"

"Same thing that's wrong with the whole border around the Big Bend," said Bick heavily. "Same thing Anse Hawkman brought you down here for."

Owens's lips twisted at the name as if he had tasted rotten *frijoles*. He hadn't thought he would ever be coming back to this border town — much less be working for Anse Hawkman.

He spat. "Let's go in."

The door creaked on dry hinges and closed behind them. They crossed a faded flowered carpet in front of the desk. A bowlegged man in slick apron chaps blocked their way to the stairs, his rope-scarred right hand slipping to his Colt.

"It's all right," said Bick. "Chisos Owens."

The man stood aside and watched Bick and Chisos all the way up the stairs. At the head of the banister on the second floor was a Mexican *vaquero* wearing the tails of his white cotton shirt outside his buckskin leggings and a pair of .45s buckled around outside that. He turned his head sharply.

"Chisos!"

"Don't tell me you're working for Anse too, Ramón," said Owens.

Something sullen crept into the boy's face. "You been away four years, Chisos. Everybody down this way works for Anse now."

Chisos followed Bick on past Ramón Delcazar and down the hall, and, when they were out of earshot, he asked the big man: "Anse has enough gunnies around to start a small war. Somebody finally catch up with the old buzzard?"

Bick didn't answer. He stopped before Number 3 and opened the door, indicating Chisos should precede him in. It was a shabby room with a cheap white pitcher reflecting itself in the cracked mirror above a rickety washstand. Springs squeaked as Anse

Hawkman rose swiftly from one of his own beds. He was a tall man, gray beginning to show at his bony temples. His cold blue eyes were set deeply beneath craggy brows, and they wanted all the land and all the cattle they had ever seen, and his great, questing beak of a nose was always looking for more. The black frock coat, though, hung loosely from his shoulders, as if he had lost weight, and there was a haggard, almost haunted, look to his face. Owens had never been one to hide his feelings. Hawkman saw the first momentary expression slide over his features and spoke a little warily.

"Four years, Chisos. I didn't think you'd still hold the Smoky Blue against me."

"Why not?" asked Owens, a heavy bitterness in his tone. "It was my land, and you forced me out. I can't help the way I feel."

"Can't you understand . . . the Big Bend isn't a place for small spreads," said Hawkman. "I did it legally."

"You always do it legal," said Owens. "A man like you don't have to step outside the law. But I didn't come down here to talk about that. I made two or three false starts after the Smoky Blue, and I'm just low enough and broke enough to swallow what pride I have left and come to you for the job. When Bick found me up Santa Helena way, he said there was a thousand dollars in it. What is it?"

Hawkman's face paled visibly. "The Scorpion."

"The Scorpion?" muttered Owens. "What or who is he?"

"A woman," said Hawkman swiftly. "The Mexicans call her *Señorita* Scorpion. She's a devil. They say she's lightning with a knife or a whip or a gun. Tall, blonde, rides like fury. She's. . . ."

Anse stopped, breathing heavily. Chisos waited, watching him get control over himself. Finally Hawkman spoke again, holding himself in like a man bunching his reins tightly on a spooked horse.

"If it keeps up much longer, Chisos, I'll go crazy. I've been robbed and rustled and threatened and shot by that blonde witch till I don't know which way my saddle's on. Every trail herd I try to shape up this *Señorita* Scorpion stampedes. My line camps in the Chisos and the San Vincentes have been raided and burned to the ground. She held up my bank at Santa Helena last week and cleaned it out. Nothing in the Big Bend is safe from her. You saw the town when you came in . . . dead as boothill, doors all shut, nobody on the streets."

"A woman," mused Owens. "How did you get hold of her spread, Anse?"

"It isn't anything like that, Chisos. I swear, I never saw the girl in my life. . . ." He cut off, and began to pace back and forth.

Owens's eyes were drawn to his deep, painful limp. Hawkman saw the glance and snapped: "I told you she threatened to kill me. That's why I met you here instead of in my own house. She hit my home spread two weeks ago, burned the barn, ran off the saddle stock. I was lucky to escape with a slug through the leg."

"Why bring me in?"

"Why bring you in?" asked Hawkman. "Why bring in Chisos Owens? Because that's where she's holed up, Chisos, somewhere up in your mountains, the Chisos, the Rosillos. You were born and raised there. You know the land better than anyone else . . . know the people. I've tried to follow her. I've set traps for her. Bick can tell you. He followed her farthest."

"After she took Anse's bank in Santa Helena," said Bick heavily, "I got some Comanche trackers and tailed her as far as the Dead Horses. You know what kind of country that is. They lost the trail, and they gave up finally . . . even the Indians."

"The Dead Horses," mused Owens. "Ain't the Lost Santiago supposed to be somewhere in those mountains?"

"I'm not interested in mines," snapped Hawkman.

"For over two hundred years," persisted Owens, "nobody's been able to find the Lost Santiago. And now nobody can find this blonde bandit. Sort of harnesses up like a matched buggy team."

The veined hand that Anse Hawkman gripped onto the iron bedstead was made to grab what he wanted and hold on with all the bitter, grasping, greedy strength in him. He stood that way, face pale, mouth thin with control.

"Will you forget the mine, Chisos," he said tensely. "It's just another wild story like the Lost Adams Diggings or the Tayopa. All I care about is the girl. I'll give you a thousand dollars to bring her in . . . dead or alive!"

"Hell, Anse," said Owens, "a man can't go gunning after a woman like that. . . ."

"What does it matter whether it's a man or a woman?" snarled Anse, spinning around. "She's a cattle rustler. You catch a man running off stock and you string him up. Why should it be any different with a woman?"

His voice again cut off suddenly, anger-fired eyes sweeping past Chisos Owens to the sound of running feet coming down the hall outside. Bick stepped away from the door, turned, pulled it open. Ramón Delcazar stopped there, panting.

"She's here," he gasped. "*Señorita* Scorpion!"

Through the window Owens heard the sharp, flat sound of shots in the street below. Someone shouted. Chisos shoved out past

152

Bick and knocked Ramón partly aside to run down the hall. The stairs splintered and popped beneath his boots, and behind him he heard Bick's heavy stride.

In the moment he took to run out across the hotel porch and down the steps into the dusty street, the whole blurred picture appeared before him. The Apache still stood between the two adobe houses on the same side as the hotel, his bare feet spread a little wider. His dark hands were no longer hitched into the big silver *conchas* of his Navajo belt. They held a gleaming Winchester. Farther down the pair of Mexicans still forked their mounts, and they had guns out. In front of the *cantina* was a sharp-faced *hombre,* a blue serape draped over a shoulder, who stood holding two horses — a palomino stallion and a huge bronze-and-white pinto that kept lunging on the reins.

Then Owens was in the street, and he could see the girl. She was backing from the *cantina*'s open door. In one hand she held a big Army Model Colt, firing backward into the Mexican saloon with it. In the other hand, by each of its four corners, she gripped a blue bandanna bulging with gold pieces and greenbacks. The tall, slim roundness of her body was accentuated by her tight yellow blouse caught in a broad red sash and her clinging leggings of buckskin with bright flowers sewn down the seams.

At the sound of Owens's pounding boots she turned her head sharply, and he could see a flash of blue eyes behind a narrow black mask and her long blonde hair cascading around, shimmering in the sun, stunning and unbelievable against the high color of her face. Bick had reached the porch behind Chisos then, and he shouted.

"That's her, that's the Scorpion . . . !"

The girl's Colt was already coming up. Owens tried to halt his headlong run and throw himself aside. He didn't think of her as a woman when he went for his gun, because if he had, he wouldn't have pulled it. But his .44 was no more than half out of leather when he saw the girl's rich red mouth twist with the upward jar of the big Army Model in her hand, and he felt the bullet smash his fingers off the butt of his gun.

Without a weapon now he didn't try to halt his lurching sideways motion, and he fell and rolled in the dust, beneath the line of fire. Bick was shooting from the hotel porch. Owens saw the man's first slug kick adobe out of the *cantina*'s wall a foot from the girl's head.

Then the Apache stepped from between the buildings on the same side as the hotel, and, holding his Winchester across the silver *conchas* of his Navajo belt, he shot through the supports of the porch railing, and Bick Bickford fell forward down the steps, a plank collapsing beneath his great weight.

Ramón must have gone down the back stairs of Anse Hawkman's frame building. He appeared suddenly from the opposite corner of the porch, the bowlegged man in slick apron chaps with him.

The Apache moved out into the street, and drove a couple of shots toward Ramón, and the two Mexicans began throwing lead. Ramón and the bowlegged man ducked back around the hotel. While this was happening, Owens had risen to his hands and knees, clawing with his good hand for the Bisley .44 he had dropped. But already the girl was swinging into the saddle of her great palomino. Slung in front of the pommel were Mexican saddlebags, and she leaned forward and stuffed the bandanna full of money into one pocket of these *morrales,* digging spurs into her horse at the same time. With a reckless grin the man who had held the two horses swung onto his own paint stallion and pounded down the street after the Scorpion. Blinded by that dust, choking in it, Owens lurched to his feet and raised the Bisley left-handed.

Then he lowered it without firing. They were already gone, the Apache, the gaudy riders, all of them — and coming back, warped on the breeze, was *Señorita* Scorpion's laugh, as feminine as a cat screaming through the swamp on a moonless night, as wild as the howl of a wolf signaling its kill.

Now that it was over, Owens felt the knifing pain in his bullet-smashed fingers. He holstered his gun awkwardly. Bick Bickford had twisted around on the steps and was trying to sit up. His face was bleeding where he had fallen on it, but apparently his only real wound was the bullet hole in his thick upper leg. Owens's buckskin had run halfway northward along the street, spooked by the gunfire.

"General!" called Owens, almost angrily.

The buckskin turned, cocked an ear, then trotted back hesitantly, reins trailing. The hotel door squeaked, and Anse Hawkman limped out. Only then did Chisos Owens realize how swiftly the whole thing had taken place — all in the time it had taken Anse to limp from the upstairs room to the porch. Maybe he hadn't hurried. His haggard face was flushed from anger, but there was something in it besides anger. His voice was harsh, yet it held a tremor he couldn't hide.

"That was fine," he said acridly. "Fine. You had her right on the end of your guns, and you let her get away."

"She had her gunnies spotted all over town," spat Bick. "You can't just walk out and rope that wildcat like you'd dally a buggy mare, Anse."

Hawkman's voice had a shrill note. "Don't you think I know that . . . by now?"

Ramón had come from around the side of the hotel, white shirt tails flopping around his buckskin leggings. His dark face was angry, sullen. A fat Mexican dealer in a green eyeshade and striped shirt sleeves came from the *cantina*. He stood in the doorway a moment, then walked swiftly across the street. One by one others followed him out the door. There were a dozen Mexican cowhands in flapping pantaloons or buckskin ducking britches, a girl with black pumps and a short skirt, a scattering of tall-hatted Texans. They spread into the street, some following the dealer over.

"Well, Faro . . . ?" said Anse Hawkman thinly.

"Nobody hurt," said the dealer. "The Scorpion threw a lot of lead but just to keep us beneath the tables."

"I wasn't talking about that," snapped Anse.

"If you mean the take, she got it all," said Faro. "Cleaned out the cash boxes . . . monte table, chusa, roulette. She's out for your hide, Anse."

Chisos glanced sharply at Anse. "What's your hide got to do with the local *cantina?*"

Anse didn't answer. Chisos turned back to Faro. The fat Mexican dealer wouldn't meet his eyes. The other men began shifting uncomfortably. Owens took a weary breath.

"Don't tell me you own that, too."

Anse shrugged. "Why not? My cattle practically built this town, the hotel, the barns. . . ."

"And the bank in Santa Helena, and the wells up in the Smoky Blue," said Chisos harshly. "You've spread out since I left, Anse."

"What's that got to do with it?" snapped Anse sullenly. "Will you take my offer now?"

Chisos looked away, lips twisting down. If he had realized how much dislike for Anse was still in him, he wouldn't have come down here. Yet there were other emotions, now, beneath that dislike for Anse, emotions he couldn't explain or name. It seemed he could still hear the blonde girl's laugh, taunting, challenging.

"I'll take it," he said deliberately. "One thousand dollars for bringing her back. . . ."

"Dead or alive," finished Anse Hawkman.

II

There were some *viejos* among the Mexicans who declared the Chisos Mountains derived their name from the Comanche word for echo, and then there were others who held the derivation was from the Apache name for ghostly. Born and raised in those mountains, Chisos Owens always leaned toward the latter — for they did look ghostly, somehow,

158

rearing up darkly red or blue or yellow, like bizarre spirits cloaked mysteriously by the pale atmospheric haze that hung over them most of the time.

A week's riding was behind Chisos Owens as he dropped down through the talus toward the valley of Smoky Blue Creek below him. He had traveled westward from Boquillos, through Chilicoatl Basin, hunting out the *peónes* who had been his friends and from them trying to get a lead on the blonde girl. So far, he had gotten nothing but vague rumors. Either the *peónes* didn't know, or they weren't telling. They gave him nothing.

General's buckskin-colored hide was whitened with the alkali of the basin, and the scabbard of the .45-90 Winchester tucked beneath the left stirrup leather was turned dark with sweat. Owens sat humped forward in his saddle, free-bitting his horse as a weary man will, one rope-scarred hand holding the reins and resting on the pommel, the other hitched in his old apron chaps slung around the horn. From somewhere below him came the creak of a windmill, and it was almost painful to hear it.

Six years ago people in the Big Bend had identified the Smoky Blue with Chisos Owens. He had built himself a house at the headwaters of the stream, was running a sizable herd of Angus in the valley below, and had plans for a future. But already Anse

Hawkman was spreading his grasping hands over the Big Bend, and he had seen the Smoky Blue, and that was enough for him.

When the Smoky Blue began to dry up, Owens saw the beginning of the end. For two years he fought. He tried to raise the capital to dig wells, but the men who would have lent it gladly to him suddenly decided it was a bad investment, and Owens knew Hawkman had brought pressure to bear on them. Finally there was no more water in the creek, and Owens sold his herd, and even that didn't bring him the required cash for the wells.

Chisos shrugged sullenly. It was over now. He had finally been forced to sell, at Anse's own price practically, and Anse had turned around and sunk the wells, and the valley was now a line camp for his two-year-olds. Owens knew he had no cause for bitterness really, but a man became close to his land, and it was his feeling for the Smoky Blue that had drawn him back here, although it was a detour in his search for the Scorpion. Riding down the slope toward the two-room cottonwood cabin he had built, Owens felt a growing nostalgia.

General slid down through some slick rock, shoes striking sparks. Then they were into the first clumps of grama grass on the lower slopes. He could see the windmill now, creaking, pumping water up for the AH cattle. He struck the first bunch of cows a little beyond it and stopped his buckskin suddenly. A steer raised its head to look at him with bovine indifference. He rode closer, saddle creaking as he bent forward, eyes slitted with the eerie feeling that had come over him.

For twenty, thirty years now the cattlemen had been breeding out the old scalawag string-beefed longhorn strain and breeding in the sleek fat shorthorned Herefords and Angus. Yet these cattle all had the huge curving scimitar-like spreads of the old longhorns, and it was like meeting a memory out of the past.

Frowning, Owens quartered in closer to squint at the brand. A heifer bawled at him. Then he caught the mark. It was like none he had ever seen before — a fancy-tailed S inside a big circle. He rubbed his stubble-bearded jaw, neck-reining General to ride off a way and look the cattle over from there. The whole thing just didn't make sense, somehow. Cattle like this hadn't run the Chisos since he was a kid.

At last he turned the buckskin up toward the cottonwood cabin that Anse had turned into his line camp shack. He passed another bunch of cattle on the way, but they were fat whitefaces with the AH big and bold on their flanks. In front of the house, in the dappled shadows cast beneath the cottonwoods by the

161

late afternoon sun, sat a pair of horsemen, one of them Ramón Delcazar.

He greeted Chisos Owens without a smile. "Hawkman sent me over ahead of you to ride extra guard on these two-year-olds. The Scorpion's hit his line camp over by Crown Mountain. She hasn't been here yet. He thinks it'll be soon now."

Owens climbed stiffly off General, turned to the old man who had been standing beside the two riders. "Ain't you glad to see me again, Delcazar?"

Pedro Delcazar was Ramón's father, a bent old Mexican in buckskin *chaparejos* that had seen better days, rawhide *huaraches* on his feet. He wouldn't meet Owens's eyes. He snuffled, wiped at his nose.

"Sure, Chisos, sure, I'm glad to see you. Like the old days, eh?"

Owens began untying his latigo, wondering at the old man's strange withdrawal. "Not exactly like the old days, Del. You didn't work for Anse then."

Ramón wheeled his horse with a sudden, vicious jerk on the Spanish bit, spitting his words out. "Anse Hawkman got our spread up Rosillos way. What else did you expect? And what else could we do but work for him? You're working for him, I notice. I'm nighthawking the herd. I'll see you in the morning."

He spurred his animal off in a hard, angry

gallop, the other rider following. Owens looked after them, then he turned and slipped his freed latigo from the cinch ring.

"Sorry to hear you lost Rosillos," he said softly.

Delcazar didn't answer. He was scuffling about, gathering wood for the fire. He had aged since Owens had seen him last, hair pure white now, veined hands trembling a little once in a while.

"Where'd you get those Circle S longhorns down the valley, Del?" asked Owens, heaving the double-rigged, sweat-soaked Porter from his horse. "Anse taken up the sticky loop?"

"You know Anse don't have to rustle his cattle," mumbled the old man. "It's a loco thing about those longhorns, though. About four months ago some *peón* named Natividad came to Anse down in Boquillos. He was a go-between for an *hombre* named Douglas who wanted to sell Anse a big herd of beef. Anse made arrangements with this Natividad to have Douglas drive his cattle here to the Smoky Blue. Anse and Bick came up the night they were supposed to arrive. We were all down by the cabin. There was a shot up on the ridge. Before we could get our horses, there came a whole herd of longhorns stampeding down the valley, no point rider, no swing, nobody. We finally stopped the cattle down below. This Douglas never showed up. Nobody else showed up. It leaves Anse with a bunch of steers that shouldn't even be alive, and he has no bill of sale. He doesn't know what to do with them."

Owens slipped off his bridle. "I didn't think there were any critters like that left this side of cow heaven. How about the brand?"

The silence before Delcazar answered was noticeable. He glanced almost sullenly at Owens from beneath shaggy white brows. "The *Circulo* S was registered in the county book about fifteen years ago by Douglas. Nobody knows where his spread is. The brand itself looks like the old Mexican brands that date back to the Moorish *rúbricas*."

Owens nodded meditatively. "Ever see it before?"

The old man set a coffee pot deliberately on two stones over the fire. He took his time about stirring up a pan of *frijoles*. Owens stepped around his horse.

"What's the matter, Del? Why're you being like this?"

Delcazar stood suddenly, turned toward him, eyes accusing. "Ramón told me you were up this way, and why you had come, Chisos. I wouldn't believe him until I saw you riding down from the ridge. I wouldn't believe you're the kind to go gunning after a woman."

Owens's face relaxed. He grinned faintly. Using his rawhide dally for a hackamore, he

164

led his horse around beside the cabin, staked it there, then came back toward the fire.

"So that's it," he said. "I should have guessed the *peónes* were pulling for this *Señorita* Scorpion."

"If I was ten years younger," said Delcazar tensely, "I'd be riding with her against Hawkman myself. You're a fool to go out after her for that thousand dollars. Before you get much further, some *peón* will shoot you and save her the trouble. But I guess you'll go ahead. You were always such a stubborn *burro*."

He broke off, shaggy white head raising a little as he turned to gaze past Owens, mouth opening slightly with the concentration of listening. Chisos could hear it then — a familiar sound on the border. In their half-breed bits many of the *vaqueros* put metal crickets set to emit a singular eerie clicking sound when the horse spun it with his tongue, the noise magnified by big hollow *conchas* on the outside of the bit itself. The two men stood there, hearing that noise a long time before horse and rider appeared, looming up like somber shadows from beneath the stunted cottonwoods banding the dry Smoky Blue.

The animal was a pinto, white and tan. The rider sat a silver-plated, cactus-tree saddle with a jaguar skin slung on behind for show, and the reins and headstall dripped red tassels of horsehair. The pinto was five-gaited, and the horsebacker put it through all five as he turned around the fire and stopped without using the reins or his feet or saying a word. Chisos Owens knew he had seen an exhibition.

"Buenas tardes, señores," said the man, dismounting and bowing low to remove his glazed sombrero with a flourish. "I am *Don* Veneno Castellano Porveara del Santiago Morrow, and I am at your service."

His black spade beard and small mustache accentuated the chalky white of his teeth. His sombrero was of black *vicuña* skin with a band of gold *pesos,* and his leggings were slick and shiny. Owens was trying to remember where he had seen the horse before.

"Santiago," he said. "Any connections with the Lost Santiago?"

"Señor," said the man grandiloquently, "I am a direct descendant of *Don* Simeón Santiago who discovered the Santiago Mine in Sixteen Eighty-One!"

"I've heard all the versions," said Owens, "but never a *hombre* who claimed to be a direct descendant."

Sudden anger flared in Santiago's sharp face, flushing it, and his hard bright eyes dilated as he stepped forward jerkily, spitting words at Owens. "You doubt me, *señor?* That is an insult. You insult the House of Santiago!"

"Please, *señores,* please," begged Delcazar,

166

coming between them, turning to the *don*. "I'm sure Chisos did not mean the insult, *Don* Santiago. It is rare we have such a *caballero* as you in this country any more, such a gentleman of the old school. We are honored by your presence."

The flush left Santiago's cheeks. With a startling change of mood, he smiled, teeth flashing white. "Chisos? Chisos did you say? Not the man who is hunting the Scorpion?"

"You seem to know," said Owens.

Don Santiago chuckled, a strange, secretive chuckle that irritated Owens somehow. Delcazar had taken the jaguar skin from the horse, and he spread it out beside the fire.

"Word gets around, *Señor* Owens," he said softly. "I heard it from more than one *peón*. So you really think you can find the Scorpion when so many others have failed?"

Owens shrugged, hunkered down across the fire from the man. The coffee made a soft gurgle, boiling in the blackened pot. Santiago looked out past Owens into the falling dusk. Delcazar caught the glance.

"The nighthawks have already eaten, *Don* Santiago," he said respectfully. "They will not be back in."

Santiago's sibilant voice might have held a different meaning than Delcazar had put into the words. "No. No, they will not be back in."

From under sun-bleached eyebrows Owens

had been studying the man, the horse, and now looked at the *don* again. Where had he seen them before? Santiago caught his eyes on him and began to chuckle in that secretive way again, voice mocking.

"Chisos. Chisos Owens. A thousand dollars for the Scorpion, dead or alive."

Owens felt that irritation again. His voice was harsh with it. "Is my story any funnier than yours?"

Santiago stopped laughing, and that change of mood swept him once more. He leaned forward, blood rising darkly in his face. His eyes dilated. For a moment his mouth worked around words that wouldn't come out. Finally he closed his lips into a thin line and sat there, fighting to control his hot anger.

"You don't believe in the Lost Santiago?" he said at last.

"I didn't say that," said Owens.

Santiago eyed him hotly. Delcazar stood to one side, eyes going in a fascinated way from Santiago to Owens. Then, sensing that whatever was going on between the two men was not for him, he withdrew to the far side of the fire. For the moment the coffee pot was the only sound, boiling a little higher.

"More than two hundred years ago," began Santiago finally, his voice heavy with control, "my ancestor, *Don* Simeón Santiago, held the title of *adelantado* and was entrusted with the visitation of mines in New Spain. Spain was having trouble with England during those times, you will remember, and one of *Don* Simeón's slaves was an English freebooter who had been captured while raiding our plate galleons in the Caribbean. Before turning to piracy, this Englishman had spent some time in the tin mines of Cornwall, and *Don* Santiago often took him along when he needed a man to help construct tunnels or sink mine shafts. In Sixteen Eighty-One rumor of a mine somewhere north of the Río Grande came to *Don* Simeón, and, leaving his only son to oversee their *rancho,* he took the Englishman and other retainers and set off northward into what is now Texas."

As he spoke, *Don* Veneno Santiago's breath came faster, and the excited dilation of his eyes was more pronounced. He looked out past Chisos Owens again, and Owens got the impression he was waiting for something.

"My ancestor discovered the mine," went on Santiago, "and sent back a *mozo* with an order for his son to send him a hundred *peónes,* a herd of his own cattle to feed them, and all the necessary equipment to dig. It is a matter of record that for six months *Don* Simeón shipped out of the Santiago Mine an average of two hundred and fifty thousand *reales* a month. Can you imagine, *señores,* how fabulously rich those diggings were? *Naturalmente,* the King got his royal fifth, and he granted *Don* Simeón all the land between the Río Grande and his mine. But the politics of New Spain at that time were so rotten that *Don* Simeón would have lost the Santiago had he not kept its location in the utmost secrecy. None of the *peónes* was allowed to leave, once they got there. And the chosen few who took the shipments south every month were sworn to secrecy, returning as soon as the gold reached the proper authorities. Then, suddenly, the shipments ceased, and the Santiago disappeared from sight of man as completely as if the earth had swallowed it."

It was just beyond the veil of memory for Owens now, and vainly he studied Santiago's face for the clue that would tell him where he had seen the man before. "The Englishman's a detail I never heard of."

"I suppose you don't believe it, either," hissed Santiago. "George Douglas was his name, a huge yellow-haired man. He was there at the mine along with *Don* Santiago when the shipments ceased. Neither of them was seen again. The *don*'s son searched, of course, but he hadn't seen his father since the old man set out to find the mine. To this day the Santiago has not been found. I can tell you that . . . I've devoted my life to hunting it."

"Douglas," almost whispered Delcazar. "That was the name of the *hombre* who was supposed to bring those *Circulo* S longhorns down here."

"Probably the same man," said Owens. "Must be a right spry *diablo* by now."

Santiago jerked forward. *"Señor . . . !"*

Lips still twisted over the hot word, Santiago looked out past Owens. First, Owens thought, it was the plunk of boiling coffee, then he realized it was the dull thunder of hoofs somewhere lower down in the Smoky Blue. As he recognized the sound, he remembered where he had seen that pinto before and where he had seen the man in shiny leggings. He had never been good at hiding his thoughts. The realization must have shown hard on his face, because Santiago's glance was suddenly drawn to him, and Santiago began to chuckle in that sly, secretive way.

"You have been trying to recall me ever since I first appeared," he said softly, "and now it has come to you, has it not? *Sí, Señor* Chisos Owens, it was I holding those two horses in front of the *cantina* in Boquillos, and one of them was mine, and the other was the Scorpion's palomino, and that is she out there now."

III

Santiago's gloved hand was stiffened above the ivory butt of his Navy revolver, and for that moment the three men were suspended there.

"She sent me up here to hold the old man," said Santiago, his breath beginning to come faster. "She didn't know you were here, *Señor* Owens. In the old days a Santiago would have spitted you on his blade for the way you insulted me. The only reason I controlled myself was to let her get those cattle running. They are going now, *señor*. Hear them? I don't have to wait any longer. Make your play, Chisos Owens, because you insulted the House of Santiago, and I'm not going to leave you here alive."

He leaned forward, face twisting like a man whipped, gloved hand trembling above his gun. Delcazar drew in a small, hissing breath. Owens kept his right hand well above his .44 as he turned it so the firelight revealed the bandage across the bullet-smashed fingers.

"With this?" he asked.

"With that or nothing, and right now!" Santiago almost screamed, all the anger he had held quivering within him suddenly exploding in his upward leap, his hand a blur that dipped for his Navy in the swiftest, smoothest slap-leather draw Owens had ever seen.

Without rising from where he sat, Owens shot his right leg out. His boot slammed into the fire and beneath the coffee pot, and he kicked violently upward, scattering the burning wood in every direction.

"*¡Diablo!*" shouted Santiago, and his shot went wild because he was lurching backward with the pot flying up at him and the scalding liquid casting its black spread across his face and upthrust arm.

The pot clanged off his shoulder. Then Owens was across the fire and on the man. One of his rope-scarred hands drove flat against Santiago's chest where the fancy braided jacket was soaked with coffee, and his hurtling weight carried Santiago over backward. Owens jumped on across the falling Mexican, going for the pinto that had taken a startled step away. He caught the ground-hitched reins and slapped a palm onto the big cactus-tree pommel, and, carrying the reins back over the horse's head, he vaulted into the saddle. His slamming into the leather like that caused the paint to wheel and break into a headlong gallop.

With stirrups snapping the scattered mesquite, Owens bent low, and whipped from side to side with the reins. Santiago's shots were a futile volley, passing into the dusk around him. Owens cut through the cottonwoods and down the outbank into the bed of the Smoky Blue, sand spurting from beneath the mount's pounding hoofs. Splashing through the thin trickle of brackish water that was all that remained of the creek, he urged the beast up the other bank and past the ghostly bulk of the creaking windmill. The Scorpion had gathered the herd on the side and was pointing them down the valley, and he struck the drag after a long, hard run.

Those mysterious *Circulo* S *ladinos* were all mixed in with the whitefaces, longhorns rising like huge, gleaming scimitars above the stubby spreads on Hawkman's steers. One of the girl's vaqueros was riding swing, popping his sombrero against his buckskin pants, whooping in Spanish. Owens bent over on the offside of the pinto as he went by the man, hidden but for his leg.

"*¡Viva Santiago!*" shouted the *vaquero*.

The pinto had run its heart out down the valley for Chisos Owens, and it was beginning to stumble beneath him when he sighted the girl. Once more he saw the blonde glory of her hair shimmering that way and the slim, tall roundness of her body, swaying to the gallop of her Morgan.

They threw a sixty-foot *lazo* down below the border, and Santiago's rope was lashed to his silver-mounted cactus tree. Owens freed it, and whipped the pinto into a final burst of speed. Then he slipped the hondo down the *lazo* until he had a community loop swinging in the air above his head. His target was that shining blonde hair, and he made his toss with a grunt.

With the *lazo* settling about her tall, slim body, the girl stiffened. Owens yanked backward. The hondo slid swiftly down until she was pinioned. Her hands still held the reins, and she sawed at her bit, bringing her Morgan to a rearing stop to keep from being pulled off. Owens skillfully walked his hands down the rope, nursing his quivering pinto along until he was up to her, the loop still tightly around her braided *charro* vest. The cattle continued to thunder on by, a rider passing in a cloud of dust. Owens was close enough then to see the flash of her blue eyes.

"You!" she exclaimed.

He grinned faintly. "*Buenas tardes, Señorita* Scorpion."

He had kept the rope taut, expecting her to try automatically to free herself by pulling away. She suddenly stood up in her stirrups and leaped out of her saddle directly at him. Desperately he tried to send another loop across the sudden short slack and snag her sideways so she wouldn't carry him off the pinto. But she hit him before he could do it, her body soft and warm against him for that moment, then both of them went on over the horse.

The ground jarred hard into him, and the girl's weight came down on top. With the breath knocked from his body, he was dimly aware of her straddling over him, fighting out of the rope. He lurched up after her, hands clawing around her slim waist. She fought savagely, striking, biting, kicking. One of her hard boot heels caught him in the chin. He slammed back against the ground, stunned for that instant.

Finally he groped to his hands and knees. She was already mounting the pinto, urging it into a jaded trot toward her Morgan. Shaking his head groggily, Owens lurched to his feet, took a few stumbling steps after her. Then he stopped, cursing the futility of that. The herd had passed and was nothing but dull thunder down the valley. A rider clattered past through the settling dust somewhere on Owens's left. He saw the girl change from Santiago's horse to her Morgan in the twilight, a dim blur of movement. Then she disappeared, leading the pinto, and the last thing he heard was that laugh, triumphant, wild, taunting.

Hiking back to the cabin took him an hour. On the way he found two of the nighthawks tied to an aspen where the Scorpion had taken them by surprise. Farther on was Ramón. He had tried resistance and had a slug through the shoulder for his trouble, and his horse had been run off along with all the others. The four men crossed the riverbed, and walked glumly through the cottonwoods to come up on the cabin from the lower side. Owens's buckskin was gone and his big Porter saddle. Santiago had undoubtedly taken the horse. Perhaps that last rider clattering after the herd had been he. Owens was the first to walk around the corner of the cabin. He stopped suddenly, and his blocky, rope-scarred hands closed into grief-tight fists.

"Ramón!" he called behind him. "You might as well come now as later."

Ramón Delcazar came around the corner, holding his shoulder. He stopped abruptly beside Chisos. For a long time he was silent. Then the grief crept into his face, and he closed his eyes.

"*Padre*," he said. "Father."

The two men stood there a long time in the silent darkness, looking at the sprawled dead body of Pedro Delcazar.

IV

Often, in the dry desolate badlands north and west of the Chisos Mountains, the only source of water was the occasional natural sink formed in the rocks to catch rain and hold it there. It was high on the rugged slope of the Rosillos, above one of these, that Chisos Owens hunkered in the meager shadow of a big boulder. A month had passed since the Scorpion's raid on the Smoky Blue. Cannily she had run off every one of the horses that night, and it had taken Owens three days to hike to Hawkman's Crown Mountain line camp and get a remount. By that time the girl had sold her wet cattle in Mexico and had disappeared.

It was useless to try and get anything from the *peónes*. Their sympathies lay with the blonde *bandida,* and, if they did know anything, they weren't telling. Thus Owens had turned to the *tinajas*. No matter how wild and nebulous the Scorpion was, she and her *vaqueros* would have to obtain water somewhere in these mountains. Owens had worked his way north up the ancient Comanche Trail, scouting out each rocky water hole as he came to it, patiently, stubbornly. Most of the tracks he found around the *tinajas* were those of wild animals. The few human prints were made by the bare feet of *peónes* who had *jacales* nearby. Then, at the end of the fourth week, he had come across the *tinaja* below him now.

About it were the usual prints, the trail of an ocelot that had come down the ridges to drink, the old marks of driven cattle. Then, across the face of rock that formed one side of the sink, he had caught the numerous scars made by shod hoofs. Some of them were old, indicating they had been made by horses that had drunk there more than once. Some were fresh, indicating the animals had passed recently. Where a narrow strip of sand spilled across the granite into the water were the distinct prints of more than one pair of high-heeled boots.

He had been waiting up here on the slope for two days, hidden from below by the uplift of granite in front of him and by the scraggly growth of scrub oak. It had been a long, weary search, through all the cruel heat of midsummer that lay over the badlands. He showed the effects of the pursuit. The weight had melted from him, and his ragged jumper fitted loosely about a torso that had lost some of its solid squareness. His face had a haggard, driven look, and his eyes burned deeply in their sockets like those of a man with a fever. *Well, maybe it is a kind of fever,* he thought heavily.

At first he hadn't been sure why he had gone out after the girl. He'd made so many false starts after the Smoky Blue, and a thousand dollars could set a man up once more. But he knew now it had never been that. No money could have driven him through all the hell of hunger and thirst and heat and exhaustion of the last weeks. He couldn't have said exactly whether it was the sight of her shimmering blonde hair, or the feel of her body warm against him when she knocked him off the paint horse, or the wild feminine taunt in her laughter. He only knew it was one of those things, or, maybe, all of them.

Behind him the stocky dun he had borrowed from the Crown Mountain camp cropped idly at some prickly pear. It was saddled and bridled, and, sitting there like a dusty statue, Owens could afford this last Indian patience. Few white men passed by here. The chances were in his favor.

The sun was low when he sighted the first spread of rising dust in the valley below him. His hands tightened in their clasp around his knees. It was the only sign he gave. From beneath the dust they appeared, a line of riders forcing flagging mounts. The blaze of the sun caught for a moment on the blonde head of their leader.

Owens remained motionless, watching them stop at the *tinaja*. He had made the same mistake twice before now, trying to get the girl. He wasn't going to make it again. He saw them allow their horses a short drink, then jerk their heads up to avoid foundering them. They were too far away to recognize individually. The only thing that marked the girl was her hair. Chisos saw one of the men suddenly stoop and hunker down, apparently studying the ground. He stood up finally, and another man came to him, and they seemed to be talking. Finally all of them mounted, rode toward a cut that led westward through the Rosillos, and disappeared.

Unhurriedly Owens stood and mounted the dun. He slid down through the talus and turned eastward into the cut. With night falling, he followed them through the mountains and out into the Rosillos Basin. Across the empty flats he kept out of sight behind them, following their fresh tracks by moonlight. Dawn was spreading its pink haze across the basin when Owens reached the first jagged uplift of the *Sierra del Caballo Muerto.* The Dead Horse Mountains. The range received its name from a party of Spaniards who had mistakenly tried to penetrate its vastness and whose horses had all died from lack of water. Anse Hawkman owned much of the land in and around the Dead Horses, but it was patently useless for cattle, and he had never seen it, and none of his line riders could be hired to go deeper than the first foothills after strays. Bick Bickford's Comanche trackers had quit on him when they reached these mountains on the trail out of Santa Helena.

Owens sat his sweat-caked dun there a moment and looked up at the dark bulk of mountains, rising infinitely desolate and mysterious ahead. Then a stubborn line thinned his mouth, and a dogged hump came into his shoulders, as he leaned forward in the saddle to put a boot against the dun's flank. Reluctantly the horse moved into the rising slope of the *Sierra del Caballo Muerto.* Already the horse was groaning beneath him with thirst, and Owens's tongue was swelling in his mouth. He knew the chance he took, following the riders any farther. Ahead of him lay the wildest, least known section of the Big Bend.

They were nightmare mountains, human in their malignancy, where giant buzzards circled on waiting wings above Owens as he rode over ridge after ridge that was covered with gaunt skeleton trees and dropped into valleys with riverbeds that had been bone dry before Texas was called Amichel. Finally he turned into a narrow cañon with walls of red rock so tall the sun reached its sandy bottom only at midday. It twisted and turned like a writhing snake, and Owens lost all sense of direction. Then rattling mesquite and prickly pear began growing in scattered clumps, and farther on the brush became thicker, and finally it choked the cañon from one wall to the other.

Catclaw ripping at his Levi's, nopal raking his face, he fought his way through. The stirrups on the dun had no *tapaderos,* and it was a constant battle to keep his boots from being torn out. His old apron chaps had been slung on the Porter saddle Santiago had taken, and a thousand times he had cursed the *don* for that.

The sand became covered with a thick mat of dried brush that had piled up there through the ages, and Owens lost the trail he had been following. But there was no way they could have gone except ahead, so he plunged on through the almost impenetrable thickets. Suddenly the jaded, thirst-crazed dun balked, and Owens was jerked forward

in the saddle. For a moment he stared un-
believingly at the cañon wall rising in front
of him. He realized then that this was a box
cañon, and that he had come to the end.

Desperately he wheeled his horse, hunting
for some sign of the riders he had trailed in
here. He came into an open patch finally,
and to his left some black chaparral grew up
the cañon wall, intertwined with mesquite to
form a dark, forbidding thicket. A lot of
branches had been knocked to the ground,
and the bush itself looked as if someone had
tried to ride his horse through it, and there
were even hoof prints all around the base.
Owens couldn't understand why anyone
would try to get through the thicket when all
they would meet on the other side was the
rock wall.

He had stopped the dun there and was
looking blankly at the brush when the shot
crashed out, its sound magnified to deafening
thunder by the narrow cañon. The horse
leaped forward in a startled way and
screamed with mortal agony. With the animal
twisting sideways and going down beneath
him, Owens kicked his boots free of the stirrups, and jumped.

He hit running and took two or three
steps, and then dove into the brush, rolling
over and over beneath the thickets, knocking
clumps of mesquite berries off, and before he
stopped his Bisley was in his hand. He lay

there like that with the sweat clammy on him, the gnats beginning to settle on his face and hands, and blood from the rips and scratches drying on his skin. He turned his head carefully so he could see the horse, lying on its side in the clearing, dead. His hat was dangling a foot off the ground on a nopal branch, caught there when he had taken the dive.

There was no sound but the maddening buzz of gnats and the mournful sigh of an afternoon breeze down the cañon. He tried to lick his lips, but there was no moisture in his mouth or on his swollen tongue, and he began to feel his terrible thirst. A last mesquite berry dropped off onto his face. The wind stopped, and utter silence settled down. He lay motionless, knowing that was the way it would have to be.

The man was an Indian. He made no noise coming through the brush. He walked into the opening with a Winchester held in dark hands across his spare belly. He stopped suddenly, head turned sharply toward the dead horse, surprise sliding into his face for that instant.

"That was the hoss screaming, not me," said Owens, "and, if you don't want to get shot out of your silver *conchas*, you better drop the rifle before you turn around."

The Winchester made a soft crackling sound against the carpet of brush that had piled up there through the centuries. Then the Indian turned to look through the mesquite to where Chisos Owens still lay on his back, Bisley .44 leveled across his belly. Owens rose. He got his hat from the nopal, and picked up the rifle, and all the time he kept the man covered. The Indian was barefooted, and the *conchas* he would have been shot out of if he hadn't dropped his rifle were sewn into a Navajo belt. For the first time Owens realized it was the same Apache who had been between those two hovels in Boquillos when the Scorpion had raided and who had stepped out to put a Winchester slug through Bick Bickford's thick leg.

Owens leaned forward slightly, his feverish eyes holding the Apache's glittering gaze while he spoke, and his slow, deliberate voice held a grim threat. "You better take me to the blonde gal now, or I'll wait till the sun goes down before I kill you."

The belief that a man who died at night would lose his soul eternally in hell was prevalent among most tribes, and the effect of Owens's words showed in the tightening of the Apache's skin across his high cheek bones, the flick of his eyes.

"Chisos Owens?" he asked.

"Chisos Owens."

The Indian shrugged, turned, and headed straight for the black chaparral where it grew up against the rock wall. Owens followed him, slipping his Bisley into leather, putting both hands around the Winchester. The Indian plunged into the thicket, and, wondering what the hell, Owens went on in behind, jamming the rifle up against the man's back. The Apache shoved a springy branch out ahead of him, then he ducked beneath it, and let it go suddenly. Owens tried to dodge, but it slapped across his face, stinging, blinding.

He went forward with the rifle held out in front of him. Instead of hitting the Indian or crashing into the rock wall, Owens burst through the last growth of chaparral and staggered on into empty blackness. He heard the Indian running ahead of him, and he lurched on forward, staggering two or three more paces before he regained his balance. His boots made a solid, thudding pound against the soft earth, and directly ahead of him he could hear the panting Apache. Dropping the rifle, he threw himself on the man.

They went rolling to the ground. Owens slugged blindly where he thought the back of the man's neck would be, and his fist hit flesh and bone with a solid, meaty sound, and the struggling body beneath him collapsed suddenly. Sprawled across the man, with his left hand out on the ground to brace himself, Owens felt a scattering of what seemed to be kindling wood beneath his fingers. With his knee in the small of the Apache's back, he picked one of the objects up, fishing for a match in the hip pocket of his Levi's. The flare of light showed him to be holding an *entraña* — the buckthorn cactus torch used by the *peónes* below the border for centuries. This one had been burned almost to its butt end, and he lit it with difficulty. Holding the torch high, he saw scattered around him more of the *entrañas,* the charred ends of them turned whitish as if they had been burned a long time ago.

Then the torchlight revealed the huge, hand-hewn rafters above his head. There was another farther down, and another, and each beam was supported by vertical timbers on either side. The Apache groaned and stirred.

"What is this?" asked Owens, but already he knew.

"That thicket of chaparral covers the mouth of it," said the Apache morosely. "We, *señor,* are in the Lost Santiago Mine."

V

Chisos Owens found the Winchester where he had dropped it and drove the Indian ahead of him through the ancient diggings. He had seen many examples of how the arid atmosphere of the Southwest preserved

things, but it gave him an eerie feeling to realize that, if this were actually the Lost Santiago, then these charred *entrañas* were the
torches Simeón Santiago's *peónes* had used to
light the workings over two hundred years
before.

He gathered up half a dozen of the
buckthorn torch butts, and the light lasted
them through the long tunnel, leading deeper
and deeper into the mountain. Finally they
came to a caved-in portion so narrow it
would barely allow the passage of a horse.
Beyond this daylight began to filter in, and
Owens snuffed out his *entraña*. They passed a
vertical shaft, sunk to one side of the tunnel,
the tops of a rawhide-lashed piñon ladder
poking over its crumbled lip.

"That is the shaft George Douglas was in
when the Indians raided," said the Apache.

"Douglas?"

"The Englishman Santiago brought up with
him to engineer the workings."

"Close your *boca*," said Owens, realizing
how loud the man was talking.

The Apache led on out, the silver *conchas*
on his belt gleaming as he stepped into the
sun. Owens waited a moment, then moved
after him, Winchester gripped in blocky fists.
He stood there, blinking his eyes for a moment at the large valley sweeping down the
slope beneath him. The Dead Horse Mountains rose, high and jagged and forbidding, in

a circle that enclosed the place completely. Juniper and scrub pine grew on the slope at Owens's feet, down to where shadowy bosques of cottonwoods marked a streambed. He realized this valley was not as dry as the rest of the Dead Horses. It would support cattle. Then there was a faint movement above that half turned him and a thin voice he knew well enough.

"Now that you have had your look at the Santiago Valley, did you think we wouldn't guard the entrance to it, *Señor* Chisos Owens?"

Owens realized then why the Apache had talked so loudly by that vertical shaft, and there wasn't much surprise in his voice as he turned around. "Santiago."

Don Veneno Santiago's shiny leggings were scarred and dusty with the long ride behind him, and his *charro* jacket was white with alkali from the Rosillos Basin. He smiled thinly as he waved the ivory-butted Navy slightly.

"Give the rifle back to Gitano."

Owens handed the Winchester back to the Apache named Gitano. A dull flush crept into Santiago's sharp cheeks, and he looked on past Owens to the Indian, something acrid in his voice.

"You *pendejo*, I told you, if it was Chisos Owens, you'd better make the first shot good!"

The Apache rubbed his rifle, face turned

down. "I heard the scream and saw him go out of his saddle. What would you have thought?"

"Stupid *burro!*" spat Santiago disgustedly, then he turned back to Owens. "You saw our tracks around the *tinaja?*"

"It took me a long time to find the sink you'd been using."

"Unfortunately, in reading our sign about the *tinaja,* you left some of your own and didn't succeed in blotting it all out," said Santiago. "When Gitano spotted the fresh prints, I supposed it was you. Nobody else would have gotten even that far. If you weren't such an insistent devil, *Señor* Owens, you wouldn't be dying now."

"Nobody's dying now, Santiago," said a *vaquero* who had come out of the juniper trees above the mouth of the mine.

Don Santiago jerked around toward him in a surprised way. He spoke hotly. "Address your betters correctly, Natividad, you *paisano.* I am *Don* Santiago, hear, *Don* Santiago."

Natividad wore a suit of soft red buckskin, and he had a gun, too, and the big single-action hammer was eared back under his thumb. He had jet black hair, and the angular cast of his face looked Mexican, yet his eyes were distinctly blue.

"The Scorpion wouldn't want the *hombre* killed," he said. "We'll take him to her."

Santiago's eyes began to dilate. Owens was

190

looking down the black bore of the Navy, and he saw Santiago's finger tremble against its trigger. Sweat broke out on Owens's palms, but the *don* wasn't unaware of Natividad's cocked gun. He drew in a hissing breath, speaking carefully.

"Listen, Natividad, this is *Señor* Chisos Owens. Anse Hawkman offered him a thousand dollars to bring back the Scorpion, dead or alive, and he is just the kind of *hombre* to do it. You see how much further than any of the others he has got. He is too dangerous to play with."

"I know he is Chisos Owens, and I know Hawkman offered him a thousand dollars for her, and I know he is dangerous," said Natividad. "But that isn't why you want him dead. You want to kill him because he kicked the coffee pot in your face back there on the Smoky Blue and because he almost ran that pinto of yours to death chasing the Scorpion."

"Just a show hoss," grunted Owens.

Santiago's head jerked back to him sharply. "What do you know about horses? That *caballo* of yours wasn't fit to skin for its dirty hide."

"You did take General, then," said Owens, anger creeping into his voice. "And it was you who killed Delcazar."

"You mean the old man?" Santiago shrugged. "He got in the way."

"You didn't need to kill him," said Owens.

Santiago bent forward, and his finger began trembling against the trigger again. "He got in my way, I tell you, just as you're in my way. . . ."

"You didn't need to kill him," repeated Owens with a dull bitterness.

"Gitano," said Natividad impatiently, "get us horses. And you, Santiago, put the *pistola* away."

"*Don* Santiago, you *pelado*," snarled Santiago, whirling back to him. Then he stopped, and that startling change of mood swept him, and suddenly he was smiling and chuckling. "*Por supuesto*, Natividad. You are right. We are all equals here in the valley. And we will take *Señor* Owens to the Scorpion. *Sí*, of course."

Gitano had gone up the slope to what was evidently the camp of the mine guard. He came back through the trees with three horses, one of them the pinto. Owens mounted and neck-reined the sorrel they had given him down the slope between Santiago and Natividad, leaving the Apache to stand there, watching them go. They came into an open meadow where several heifers browsed in the curly red grama. Their horns were huge and majestic and on their flanks was that *Circulo* S brand. Santiago caught Owens's look, and his smile was mocking.

"*Sí*, those longhorns you saw down in the

Smoky Blue came from this valley," he said. "The *Circulo* S is the ancient brand of the Santiagos, dating back to the time the Moors stamped *rúbricas* with their signet rings. These longhorn *ladinos* are a pure strain, descended directly from the steers *Don* Simeón Santiago brought into this valley from his *rancho* to feed the *peónes* working in the mine in Sixteen Eighty-One."

"And the Scorpion . . . ?"

"Also a pure strain," said Santiago. "Descended directly from the English freebooter, George Douglas, who was here with *Don* Simeón when the South Plains Indians came down the Comanche Trail in that year and raided this valley. That is how the mine disappeared, *señor*. You saw the caved-in portion of the tunnel? The Comanches and Apaches swept in here and committed their massacre and burned all the buildings and ran the cattle and horses off through the mine. On their way out, they pulled down a whole section of supporting timbers so the mine would cave in after them. But they had not killed quite everyone. Go ahead, Natividad, tell him the rest of it."

"You passed that vertical shaft on this side of the caved-in part," said Natividad. "George Douglas sank that shaft. You must remember that in the old days the women worked alongside the men in the fields and the mines. Douglas and a *peón* woman were in the very bottom level of that vertical shaft when the Indians raided. The Comanches missed them, and, when they came up, they found Simeón Santiago and all the others dead and the mine caved in, cutting them off completely from the outside world. There were a few cattle and sheep and a horse or two left in draws on the upper slopes where the Indians hadn't taken the time to look. From these Douglas and the woman made their start."

Owens rubbed his chin, speaking slowly. "And you mean to say . . . ?"

"That for two hundred years George Douglas and his descendants have lived in the Santiago Valley, cut off from the world," said Santiago impatiently. "They tried to dig out, naturally. But they had only crude tools, and you saw how long that cave-in extended. It was like trying to dig through the mountain all over again. Only fifteen years ago did they finally succeed."

"Delcazar said the *Circulo* S was registered about that long ago," said Owens.

"We kept the only Santiago brand, the *Circulo* S," said Natividad. "My father was the Douglas who finally dug through. It didn't take him long to learn how you register your brands and how you have to file a claim on property. He filed, and we have a deed, and our cattle are legal beef. But you had a deed too, *Señor* Owens, and yet Anse

194

Hawkman got your land. That's why we've kept the valley a secret, even after digging out. Hawkman's all around us. We're the last small spread in the Big Bend he hasn't seized."

"And the mine?"

They dropped down the slope past a split-rail corral. Owens saw his double-rigged Porter slung over the opera seat, and inside among other horses was the buckskin hide of General. Natividad shrugged.

"George Douglas was the only miner, and his knowledge died with him," he said. "Anyway, what good would gold have done us? What good would it do us now? All we want is to live here as we have been living here, left alone by men like Anse Hawkman."

Owens looked at him squint-eyed. "Natividad . . . ?"

"Is a Spanish name," said Natividad, reining his jughead around the corner of a sprawling adobe ranch house they had been approaching. "The woman George Douglas took was a Mexican *peón*, remember? We are of those two bloods, yet you couldn't call us half-breeds in the strictest sense. There have been so many generations in between that first union that we are a race apart, really. There are about two dozen of us in the valley now, young and old, all the same strain, all descended from George Douglas."

Natividad and Santiago dismounted before

the long portals that stretched across the whole front of the house, forming a roof for the flagstone porch. Owens swung his leg over the cantle, and stepped down. He was still standing with his face turned toward the horse that way and his back to the porch when he heard the light tap of boots across the flagstones. For a moment he was almost afraid to turn around. He had had only those two glimpses of her in Boquillos and on the Smoky Blue, and this would almost be like seeing her for the first time, and he had come so far for it and fought through so much. With a sudden jerky motion he turned.

She had removed her braided jacket. The pleated cotton *camisa* she wore beneath it was tucked into her tight leggings. The big Army Model Colt still hung heavily on her hip, cartridge belt hooked up to the last notch around the slim span of her waist. Chisos hadn't realized a woman's lips could be so red — like the scarlet of nopal after a spring rain. And the size of her blue eyes made him dizzy. Then he saw the hate in them.

"I might have known it would be you," she said bitterly, "Anse Hawkman's man!"

He felt his face flushing beneath the grime of dust. Then his shoulders humped forward a little, because he knew he should have expected it this way.

"Santiago and Gitano tried to kill Chisos Owens," said Natividad.

"I almost wish Gitano had succeeded," she said. "But I guess it would take more than that Apache to kill a man like this . . . this . . . ?"

"¿*Maldito*?" asked Santiago mockingly.

"From what Owens said, I gather Santiago killed the old man named Delcazar down on the Smoky Blue," said Natividad.

The girl turned sharply to Santiago. "Veneno, I told you not to, I told you! I only sent you up there to keep the *viejo* from getting into trouble. He worked for Hawkman, but he wasn't Hawkman's man, not like Bick Bickford or Chisos Owens."

"You seem to have something against Anse," said Owens.

Her blonde hair shimmered as she whirled back to him, and for a moment she seemed surprised. "Are you trying to tell me you don't know?"

Owens shrugged. She studied him for a moment, biting her lip, eyes clouded now, puzzled. Finally she turned toward the door.

"I can't believe you don't know," she said. "But come with me, anyway. I want you to see it!"

The living room covered the length of the house, thick wooden shutters open to let the afternoon light in through the few windows. It came to Owens that the ponderous oak center table and the crude chairs set against the adobe wall might have been pegged together by George Douglas two hundred years before, and the blackened *vigas* forming the rafters over the fireplace at one end had been hewn by the great, yellow-haired Englishman with the few ancient tools he had salvaged from the Indian raid.

The girl was going through the door into a hallway. She stopped suddenly, stepping back as a man lurched by her. His sandy hair was rumpled, his eyes bloodshot and bleary in a puffy, discolored face. He wore a dusty, tattered clawhammer coat over a soiled pinstriped vest. Putting one hand on the table to keep from falling, he raised his head with difficulty, taking a moment to focus his gaze on Chisos Owens.

"Ah," he said, "another hapless creature from the outer world. Pray, sir, what did they bring you in here for?"

"Go back to your room, Doctor Farris," said the girl stiffly.

The doctor's bloodshot eyes opened wider, shining with a sudden wild look as he saw Santiago behind Owens. He lurched away from the table, clutched at the lapels of Owens's jumper.

"You've got to get me out of here, please, got to," he babbled hysterically. "They brought me up to operate on the old man. Said they'd let me go if I was successful. But they'll kill me either way. I know. Nobody ever gets out of this valley, see? Help me, please, for . . . !"

Veneno Santiago took a swift step forward, one of his gloved hands closing around Farris's arm. The doctor winced, struggled feebly. Santiago whirled him sharply and shoved him abruptly through the opposite door into the hall. The girl followed, and, going in after her, Owens could hear Natividad's boots behind him. Santiago turned Farris down the hall, but the girl went straight across into a large bedroom.

She walked to the bottom end of the big bed, and stood there watching Owens with white-lipped intensity, her hands gripping the wooden-pegged bedstead desperately. The gaunt, still figure of an old man lay beneath the covers of coarsely woven lamb's wool, and the cast of his face bore the same wild aristocracy as the girl's, with its finely planed forehead, its aquiline nose.

"Your father?" Owens asked.

"Yes," she said bitterly. "John Douglas. Completely paralyzed since Anse Hawkman put a bullet through his back four months ago."

Owens turned sharply toward her. "Anse . . . ?"

"It's the way Hawkman works, isn't it?" she flared. "Our herds of *Circulo* S beef had grown so large the valley's browse wouldn't support them any longer. We'd kept the San-tiago a secret from Hawkman up to then. That's why Dad made the deal to drive the steers down the Smoky Blue. It happened on the ridge above Hawkman's line camp. Dad was riding point on the herd when Anse and his men started the stampede and shot him in the back. He would have been killed by the cattle except for Santiago."

"Oh," said Owens. "Santiago."

Natividad nodded. "Santiago came across us, driving the beef down the Comanche Trail. He was going south, anyway, and he and Gitano helped us with the beef."

"Gitano's his man?"

"Did you think he was a Douglas?" snapped Natividad. "I was riding drag below the ridge when I heard the first shot. By the time I galloped up to where Dad had been pointing the herd, there was more firing, and the cattle were stampeding. I found Santiago off his pinto, pulling Dad out of the cattle's path, shooting off down the ridge. He said Hawkman had his whole crew out, and we didn't have a chance."

"You hadn't seen Santiago before he met you driving the beef down the Comanche?" asked Owens.

"No," said Natividad. "He helped us bring Father back here. When he saw this was the Lost Santiago of his ancestor, he said he'd stay and help us fight Hawkman."

"Doesn't sound like Santiago . . . helping someone," muttered Owens. "Doesn't sound like Anse, either. He never had to do anything like that before when he wanted something."

"Don't you see?" said the girl hotly. "Somehow Hawkman found out about our valley squatting right in the middle of his holdings, the last piece of land in this section of the Big Bend that isn't his. He shot my father, I tell you . . . !"

"We tried to get a doctor," said Natividad. "We didn't have any money, and we got desperate finally and brought Farris in from Marathon at the point of a gun. You saw him. He said he wouldn't even attempt that kind of operation under ordinary circumstances, said it was a job for a specialist. We made him try, anyway, but his hands shook so much we were afraid he'd kill Dad."

"The next doctor's hands won't shake," said the girl. "When we bring him in, he'll be paid hard cash and won't know it's different from any other operation. Farris said there was a specialist in San Antone."

"Specialists cost real *dinero*," said Owens.

"Why do you think I've been running off Anse Hawkman's cattle and the cattle he stole from us and selling them wet?" she asked. "Why do you think I've robbed his bank and *cantinas*? He's the one who shot my father. He's the one who's paying. I swear, if

201

I ever meet him face to face again, it won't be his leg my slug hits."

"Too bad you didn't wait a minute longer in Boquillos."

"He was there?"

"You missed him by a hoss hair," said Owens.

"*Dios,* if I'd only known," she almost whispered. Then she straightened, eyes flashing, "And you . . . I should have done more than shoot you in the hand that day. It would have saved me this. Really, I don't know what to do with you, Chisos Owens. You claim you didn't know that Hawkman shot my father. Would you have come after me if you had known?"

"Do you really think I came all this way for Anse Hawkman's thousand dollars?" he asked her.

Some of the anger left her eyes, and once more that puzzled shadow darkened them. "I don't know what to think. I'm confused, puzzled. Hawkman made the same offer to other men, men who were stubborn or patient or who knew the country. They all gave up sooner or later."

"The kind of gun money Anse Hawkman offered carries an *hombre* so far, no further," Owens said. "It takes something more to drive a man through country like the Big Bend for months on end, hunting for what he isn't even sure is there."

"Then, what drove you?" she asked. "You don't look like a mining man."

"I didn't care about the Lost Santiago," he said, "and I guess from the first I didn't care about that thousand dollars. After I saw you in Boquillos, I would have come whether Anse asked me to or not. Maybe this isn't the right time to say it, but maybe it's the only time I'll get. I won't even try to tell you that you're the first one. There was a woman in San Antone, but I didn't stay there long, and I wouldn't have followed her through hell just because I saw the shine of her hair one evening down in the Smoky Blue. There were others, and I would have followed them. I followed you. That's how it is."

Her mouth opened slightly, revealing the shadowed line of her white teeth. Light from the window fell softly across the rich curve of her underlip. For a moment the spell held them like that, and Chisos saw a certain understanding begin to grow in her blue eyes. Then Santiago broke it, coming in through the door past Natividad with Dr. Farris. Farris had his black bag. His clawhammer was off, and his shirt sleeves were rolled to the elbow.

"I've sobered him up," said Santiago. "He's going to try once more, aren't you, Doctor?"

The girl turned sharply to him. "No, Santiago. I told you we were getting one from San Antone. I have the money."

Santiago glanced at the doctor, waved a gloved hand imperiously. Farris pulled the lamb's wool covers hesitantly down, and began unwrapping a cotton bandage from about John Douglas's gaunt waist. Reluctantly he turned the paralyzed man over on his belly.

"Santiago!" cried the girl. "Please! Wait till we can get to San Antone. Anything but this stupid fool, anything!"

Chisos Owens took a step forward, half turning to Santiago. The *don*'s gloved hand slid down till it hung above the ivory butt of his Navy .36.

"At the moment *Señor* Owens," he said softly, "I wouldn't say you were in a position to interfere, would you?"

Owens met his bright gaze, then he looked at Natividad. The Scorpion's blue-eyed brother was watching Santiago, and Chisos couldn't read the glance. He shrugged, feeling the knotty tension across his stomach relax. The girl's breath came heavier as the doctor opened his bag, took out a scalpel. He bent over Douglas. Owens saw the girl's eyes widen; her chin quivered. Then the doctor's hand began to shake.

"Stop it!" screamed the girl, lurching around toward him. "Stop!"

Owens had seen something on the strip of bandage still caught beneath John Douglas. He was around the doctor before the girl, and his rope-scarred hand closed over the small piece of lead, wet with the old man's blood.

"Must have lodged against his spine close to the surface," mumbled Farris. "I've seen bullets work free like that before. It was what paralyzed him, I guess."

"Anse Hawkman's bullet," half choked the girl.

"Anse Hawkman packs a Forty-Four," said Owens, wiping blood from the slug. "And none of his crew pack anything smaller in caliber. This bullet came from a gun you don't see much of nowadays. It came from a Navy Thirty-Six."

VI

As one, every person in the room turned to Santiago. He stood with his back to the open window, and, hanging above the ivory butt of his Navy that way, there was infinitely more threat in his gloved hand than if it had actually held the cocked gun. They all knew his unbelievable skill with that .36, and for a moment it held them.

"You told me . . . Hawkman," breathed the girl.

Chisos Owens's lips thinned then, and he began settling his weight forward, and his shoulders humped into a solid, dogged line.

Santiago took a step backward. He spoke to the girl, but he watched Owens.

"Of course, I told you Hawkman," said the *don*. "Did you think I'd let you know it was my bullet that paralyzed John Douglas?"

He took another step backward, toward the open window, hand stiffening. Owens took a slow breath. Santiago's eyes dilated suddenly, and he laughed.

"Go ahead, Chisos Owens. There isn't any coffee pot to kick in my face now. Go ahead and do it."

He took a third step backward, and Chisos Owens did it. He crouched and dove and drew with a hard-driving grunt. Before his gun was half out of leather, he saw Santiago slip the Navy clear with that blinding speed, and he knew he was bested. Santiago's slug caught Owens in the right shoulder and spun him back against the wall with his unfired Bisley clattering to the floor.

But it had given them their chance. Natividad fired from the hip almost before his gun was drawn, and the girl's Army was leaping out of its holster. Santiago made a difficult target in that half dark room. With Natividad's wild lead *plonking* into the earthen floor at his feet, the *don* jumped on backward and fired a last snap shot their way as he put his free hand on the window sill, and vaulted backward out through the open window.

It had taken Owens that long to get his gun, staggering away from the wall and scooping it up with his good hand. The girl caught at him, her weight dragging for a moment.

"You're wounded, Chisos," she panted. "You can't go out after him that way. He's loco. I never realized it before, but that's why he gets so excited talking about the mine. He's loco and he's a *diablo* with that gun, and you can't go after him left-handed."

"I never was so fast on the draw," said Owens, breaking free of her. "That part's over now."

He went through the window head first with his .44 held out in front of him and his finger whitened on the trigger ready to blast anything in the way. Santiago was already running upslope toward the corral. Another of the Douglas clan came from around behind the house. Santiago fired twice before the man went down, and slid on his face in the dirt.

The *don* glanced over his shoulder and saw Owens coming up after him in that dogged, forward-leaning stride. Santiago turned and broke into a run again, bent over his gun, reloading. Natividad was behind Chisos, and farther back was the lighter sound of the girl's boots.

Santiago stopped at the corral a moment, fumbled with one of the bars. Owens closed the gap between them. He threw a shot at Santiago, and the man quit trying to let down the bar and turned uphill.

The afternoon sun was low, and it cast long shadows of the split-rail corral across Owens as he ran past. General whinnied at him; he grinned thinly and stumbled on. He was breathing heavily now. The pain in his shoulder had turned to a dull throbbing. His right arm swung at his side with each jerky step, useless.

Gitano had been left at the entrance to the mine, and the shots brought him out of the stunted trees above the tunnel mouth.

"Cut around through the junipers!" shouted Owens. "Gitano has that rifle!"

The girl quartered toward the motte of scrub oak and juniper, disappearing in their shadows. Gitano levered his Winchester, threw a shot at Owens. It kicked dirt in Owens's face. Then the girl and Natividad showed in the trees, and their fire drove Gitano back until he no longer commanded the section Owens would have to cross following Santiago. The *don* halted and turned in front of the tunnel.

"Do you think you can get me in my own mine, you stinking *ladrón?*" he shouted crazily back at Owens.

Chisos didn't answer. His boots made a steady, insistent pounding, coming on. With a shrill yell Santiago whirled and disappeared into the black maw. Halting there at the entrance a few moments later, Owens could hear him running farther in. Bisley gripped tightly, Chisos followed. He ran past the vertical shaft George Douglas had been in when the Indians raided. He stumbled across an ancient fallen *soporte*. Daylight passed behind, and for a few minutes it was utterly dark. Then a ghostly yellow glow flared up ahead, and *Don* Veneno Santiago laughed in a cracked, panting way.

"See, Chisos Owens, that's an *entraña*, a torch. I've stuck it in the wall. You'll have to come through the light to get me. I'll be behind it, in the dark. Did you think you could get me in my own Santiago?"

Owens halted, still in the dark portion, taking a deep breath. "Why'd you shoot Douglas, Santiago?"

"When I came across John Douglas, driving those old longhorns down the Comanche Trail, and saw the ancient Santiago brand on them, I knew I'd found a clue to the Lost Santiago!" shouted the *don*. "It didn't take me long to find out Douglas was going to sell the valley to Hawkman as well as the cattle. The old fool had his deed and a bill of sale already signed by him, and all it needed was the buyer's signature. . . ." He cut off, and another light flared beyond the first. "There you are, *Señor* Chisos Owens, a second *entraña* for you to come past."

Owens gathered himself and rushed into the light of the first torch.

"*¡Borrachón!*" screamed Santiago, and his gun blared.

With the slug thudding into the wall at his side, Owens threw himself forward and knocked the blazing buckthorn *entraña* down, rolling over on it and snuffing it out with his own body. He lay there in darkness for a moment. Finally Santiago's voice came mockingly.

"Are you there, *señor?*"

"You didn't finish about Douglas," said Owens grimly, rising to his knees and looking at that next blazing torch.

"Ah, I missed you *Señor* Chisos Owens, how unfortunate!" called Santiago. "And Douglas? I told you he was going to sell the valley. Do you think I'd let him do that? Do you think I'd ever see my mine if Anse Hawkman got his hands on this valley? We were on the ridge above the Smoky Blue when I tried to force the deed and bill of sale from Douglas. He wheeled his horse, and galloped away. I shot him, and the noise started the stampede. I wasn't pulling him from its path when Natividad found us. I was searching for the deed and bill of sale, and he didn't have them on him . . . ah, there you are, *señor*, another torch."

It flared up beyond that second burning *entraña*, and again there were two spots of light Owens would have to go through, and

Santiago was backing on into the cave, laughing. Chisos rose to his feet, and moved into the weird glow, running hard.

"*¡Maldito!*" screamed Santiago and shot, and shot again.

Owens heard the first slug whine past him. The second one hit him in the thigh like the kick of a mule. As he went down with his leg knocked from beneath him, he grabbed desperately at the torch ahead and knocked it out of the wall. It fell to the floor and sputtered and died.

In the darkness once more Owens crawled to the wall of the cave and twisted around so he could sit up, biting back pain. "Why bother with telling the Scorpion that Hawkman shot John Douglas and riding along on her raids that way? Seems to me your style would be more shooting them all in the back and being done with it."

"*Dios,* what a stubborn *burro* you are!" shouted Santiago, a touch of hysteria entering his voice. "I told you I wanted the deed and that bill of sale already signed by the old man. When a *hombre* starts working a mine as rich as the Santiago, he has to have legal possession of the property, even up in this *malpais*. I was just as anxious to get a doctor for John Douglas as Elgera was. The old man couldn't exactly tell me where he'd hidden the deed as long as he was paralyzed, could he?"

Owens could hear him fumbling to light another torch. There was only one spot of light now, only one *entraña* burning. Chisos knew it was the last one he could reach. He was finished if the *don* got another lit. He dug his hands into the wall, clawed up till he was standing, then he lurched away from the wall.

Every time he took a step, his staggering weight almost went down on the side of his wounded leg, and he grunted sickly with each dull pound of his boot into the ground. Then the solid, blocky squareness of his figure burst into that last light, and the sudden racket of Santiago's Navy was all the sound in the world to him. He felt a slug burn across his ribs. Another clipped at his flapping denim jumper. He slammed into the wall, grabbing at the torch stuck there.

"Go down, you stubborn *patata*, go down!" screamed Santiago, and his gun drowned his voice.

With the same hand that held his Bisley, Owens tore the blazing *entraña* from the earthen wall and half knocked, half threw it out ahead of him. For that moment its light flared across the whole tunnel, flickering over Santiago. He was backing up with his face flushed excitedly and his eyes dilating, and he jerked his smoking Navy up to fire again.

Owens held his .44 out, and the light burned long enough for him to see his single, deliberate shot take Santiago squarely in the chest. Chisos leaned up against the wall with his weight on his good leg, feeling dully for the wound in his ribs, knowing he would fall over if he moved. Then he heard them moving down the cave behind him.

"Chisos . . . ?"

"Back here!" he called. "It's all over. Back here."

"*Dios,*" said Natividad, stumbling through the darkness, "that Gitano was a tough *hombre* to smoke out. You got Santiago?"

"Did you think he wouldn't?" asked the girl.

They were helping him back out then, and with one arm across Natividad's shoulder Owens spoke wearily: "Santiago said your dad had a deed and a signed bill of sale all ready for Anse."

"I should have known that was what Santiago wanted," muttered Natividad. "Before Santiago cut our trail on the Comanche, I found out Dad was selling the valley, and I took the deed and bill from him. I have them now."

"Natividad!" flamed Elgera. "Dad would never sell our valley."

"He's an old man," said Natividad heavily, "and, during the fifteen years we have been in contact with the outside, he saw all the small *rancheros* lose their land to Hawkman, no matter how bitterly they fought him. He didn't want to cause us the pain and blood-shed and heartbreak that would come with bucking Anse Hawkman. He hadn't brought himself to telling us about it yet when he left with the cattle."

"Santiago may have been loco," said Owens, "but he'd been hunting mines all his life. It seems to me he'd be able to tell one with yellow in it when he saw it. If the Santiago's as rich as he claimed, you won't have to worry about bucking Hawkman. You can buy and sell him every month."

"There'll still be some trouble," said the girl. "The only one killed in my raids was Delcazar, and Santiago did that. But I ran off a lot of Anse's cattle, and robbed his bank, and clipped him and some of his crew."

"When you get your diggings going good, you can ride down to Boquillos and pay Anse a visit, and I reckon the kind of man he is, he will be right glad to forget any worry you caused him when you plunk down a pack saddle full of solid gold bars in repay-ment," said Owens. Then he took his arm off Natividad's shoulder and turned to the girl. "Why did you try to stop me down at the house?"

"Because I saw you going out after San-tiago with your wounded shoulder and your gun left-handed, and I suddenly realized how I felt about you," she said, and it was natural for her arms to slip around him. "Remember how you tried to explain it to me . . . all about the woman in San Antone you wouldn't have followed and the other women you didn't follow, and me you followed because you saw the shine on my hair down in the Smoky Blue. That's how it hit me, Chisos, just as fast. You came a long way to find me. Will you stay?"

Chisos's head raised sharply, and he could feel his hands tighten on her suddenly.

"What would I be," he asked her with an effort, "if I did stay? A foreman in your mine maybe, or ramrod for your spread, or one of your waddies?"

She looked up at him, and in semi-gloom he could see the darkness creep into her eyes. Perhaps she was beginning to understand.

"You wouldn't have to . . . ," she began.

"Then what?" he said. "If I didn't work for you, I'd just stay and live off you, is that it? I couldn't do it either way, you know that. I couldn't take a job from you. I didn't come in here to be your ramrod or your waddy. And I couldn't let you keep me. Call it pride, call it whatever you like, it just doesn't seem right. When a man comes to a woman feeling the way I do about you, he doesn't come asking her for a job, asking her for anything. He should come with something to offer. But I haven't even that. And still, I'd almost ask you to come away with me. . . ."

"This is my valley, Chisos," she said. "I couldn't go away now. The trouble with Hawkman isn't over. The mine has to be worked, whether we want to work it or not, if we're to keep the valley. Dad has to be taken care of. . . ."

She trailed off, and Owens stood there, half supported by her, breathing heavily. He could see there was no use in further argument. He was too proud to stay and take anything from her that way. She was too stubborn to go. A man had no right, anyway, asking a woman to give up what the Santiago had to offer. He shrugged, and with his arm across Natividad's shoulder the three of them stumbled out into the open.

A week later two of them rode silently up through the shadowy bosques of juniper to the mouth of the cave. They halted there, saddles creaking as each turned to look at the other.

"Once more," almost whispered the girl, "won't you stay?"

"Once more," he said heavily, "won't you come with me?"

She shook her head, lips thinning.

"All right," he said. "It's *adiós* for now. But don't think this ends it. The Big Bend's my country as much as yours. I'll give you odds we meet again."

Then Chisos Owens neck-reined General

into the maw of the cave, and the darkness closed around him. He knew he would never forget the picture of her sitting the Morgan there with her blue eyes glistening and the sun shining on the blonde glory of her hair.

The Devil's Corral

The author's original title for this story was "Drifting Guns." It was sold to Fiction House, and the author was paid $350.00 on acceptance, the payment being received on October 17, 1944. The title was changed to "Blood Brand of the Devil's Corral" upon publication in *Lariat Story Magazine* (5/45). For the first book appearance of this short novel, the magazine title has been retained in somewhat modified form.

I

Ed Ketland dropped off the buckboard, trying to hide the faint bite of pain it caused him, because Danny Dekker was in the door of the Pothook's bunk shack. He was the same Dekker, his slightly sway-backed stance giving his broad shoulders a hard, youthful swagger beneath a denim shirt, faded blue Levi's accentuating the long, straight line to his legs. His flashing, black eyes showed faint weather wrinkles at the corners, the way they always did when he grinned, and he ran the tip of his tongue across his upper lip.

218

Ketland remembered that, too.

"Glad to see you back, Ketland. How're the legs?"

Ketland felt all the force of the man's strength in the grip of his brown, strong hand. "My legs are all right, Dekker. You rodding the Pothook now?"

"Been foreman since you left," said Dekker. "How're the legs?"

Ketland's pale face tightened. "You asked me that."

"I mean . . . really."

"I told you." Ketland's voice had an edge. "They're all right."

"Well," — Dekker's tone was smoothly patronizing — "we won't give you the toughest broomtail to ride right off, eh?"

Ketland felt himself stiffen and was suddenly conscious of his age, standing there beside all the grinning youth in Danny Dekker. He wasn't actually old. Things should just be starting for a man at thirty-one. Maybe he was through topping the roughest bronchos in the string, but he could still ride circles around any man half his age on all the other work. He was shorter than Dekker, more compact, with a leathery look to his face, and lines beneath his chin that deepened into furrows whenever he put his head down. His unbelted Levi's were tight around the heavy block of his waist, and that showed his age in a way, too, although it didn't necessarily mean fat, because he had always been that way more or less. Ketland turned to get his war sack from beneath the seat of the buckboard. The driver who had come to get him off the train was new to Ketland, sitting with a dirty shirt and shaggy brows and horse droppings on the boot he had against the rig's brake lever.

"I guess you already met Rock," said Dekker, grinning. "This is Ed Ketland, Rock. He used to be foreman here. Bronc' smashed him up a bit last year."

Rock curled a sensuous lip off yellowed teeth to spit. "That right?"

Ketland heard the thin, harsh sound of his own breathing coming out as he looked from Dekker to Rock. Now why had he done that? Rock knew who he was. Ketland turned abruptly to lift his war sack off the wagon.

The inside of the bunk shack was close and dirty, tin cans and cigarette butts littering its unpainted floor. Three men were sitting around the rickety plank table at the rear between bunks on either wall. The oil lamp cast its feeble, yellow light across a deck of cards, caught the glint of a half empty pint bottle, gleamed on the handful of coins in the poker pot. The skinny cowpoke facing Ketland jumped to his feet.

"Ed Ketland!" he shouted. "Tie my dally! If you ain't a sight for a sick dogie's peepers!"

"How're things, Highwoods?" said Ketland, feeling a warmth creep into him for the first time. "You and Uncle Harry still shooting biscuits for the boys?"

Maybe he was forty, Highwoods, and the smile left his face and his jowls settled back into their hangdog sag around the mournful line of his mouth. "Uncle Harry isn't cooking for the boys any more, Ket. He disappeared about three months ago."

Ketland looked around at Dekker. "Sorry to hear that. Just disappeared?"

"Hit us all pretty hard," said Dekker. "He was Midge's blood kin, of course, and only my uncle by marriage, but we all felt the same way about old Uncle Harry." Dekker nodded sadly, then turned to the other men. "This is Ed Ketland, boys. Used to 'rod the Pothook. Bronc' smashed him up a while back."

Ketland felt himself go rigid again. What was Dekker doing? Both these men were new to Ketland, but patently they would know of him, and what had happened. He looked at Highwoods for an answer. The sorrowful man had suddenly become very interested in the bare side wall.

"The gentleman with the beard is Oley Fanning," said Dekker. "Best roper this spread ever saw. Maybe even give you some pointers on a dally, Ketland. The boy with the fancy Colts is Jerry Poke. We're breaking him in around the barns. Should make a top hand someday."

Oley Fanning ran a slender hand through his luxurious brown beard. "Bronc' smashed you, Ketland? Too bad. I guess you won't be doing much riding."

Ketland inhaled carefully, trying to understand the speculation in Fanning's soft, brown eyes, beginning to sense something here. "I'll be riding."

Jerry Poke hitched at one of his silver-mounted Colts, voice high and womanish. "Forty a month and found will sort of stick in your craw after a foreman's wages, won't it, Ketland?"

Ketland looked at Poke's thin face for a moment and saw the same speculation that had been in Fanning's eyes. He turned to Dekker. It was there, too, in Dekker's grin. Maybe it had been there all the time, and maybe he should have seen it from the first.

"Got a spare bunk?" he asked carefully.

Dekker nodded toward the rear of the shack. "I'll see you out at the barns later on maybe."

Oley Fanning caressed his beard thoughtfully, watching Ketland move past him to the rear. Highwoods stood aside, still studying the wall. Ketland dropped his war sack onto the bottom bunk at the end. A loose board popped as Rock appeared in the doorway and stepped across the threshold. He turned to spit, then came deliberately back to the rear, big and heavy in his Mackinaw, battered Stetson flapping over his black brow.

"Don't put your truck in my bunk," he said, and tossed Ketland's war sack out on the floor, and sat down on the sideboard.

Ketland looked at him a moment, then he bent and lifted the war sack. It caused him that pain, more biting this time. He dropped the bag onto the bunk across the way. Jerry Poke shifted in his chair.

"You got mine there," he said.

Ketland felt his breath begin to come faster. He started to lift the bag to the bunk above, but Fanning stood up, shaking his head.

"That's Pedro's. He wouldn't like it."

"Where," said Ketland, and his palms were damp with sweat against the denim sack, "would you suggest I put it?"

"This room's full," said Rock sullenly. "Shed out back."

"Isn't that where they used to keep the old blind mule?" asked Ketland.

Fanning spoke softly. "They still do."

Ketland was swept with the first heat of his anger, starting way down in his loins, it seemed. This was what Dekker had started, out at the wagon. "This is Ed Ketland, Rock, a bronc' smashed him up a while back." Ketland hadn't known what it meant then. He knew now. "This is Ed Ketland, boys, a bronc' smashed him up." Dekker had raised the issue and brought it in here and had left it with the men like this.

Ketland's mouth closed flatly across his teeth. He saw how it stood and he didn't have to know why and it would be a mistake to let it get any further without showing them how his saddle was cinched on. There was only one way to do that, with men like this.

"I don't sleep with mules," said Ketland. "Get up, Rock."

Rock's brows raised, and he opened his mouth to speak. Then, without saying anything, he stood up. Ketland dropped the war sack back on the bunk.

"You can take your duffel somewhere else," he said.

Rock's heavy-boned face showed his surprise plainly enough. Maybe he hadn't expected Ketland to carry it back to them this way. Ketland made a square, solid block in the dim room, shorter than Rock by half a head, jaw tucked in until the leathery creases ran deeply beneath his chin. He knew he couldn't hope to last anything out. He knew he had to carry the whole thing to them now. Rock made a sudden, shifting move toward Ketland.

"You. . . ."

"Hold it!" Ketland's voice caught Rock's ponderous body like a hand. "Don't start anything you don't mean for sure, Rock. I know what you're after, all of you. I didn't come here to throw anybody out of his bunk. You forced it."

"I told you to take it easy," said Highwoods, standing back against the wall with his palms flat on the warped boards. "That's Ed Ketland!"

"Take the sack off my bunk," snarled Rock, and grabbed the bag.

Ketland caught his arm, and yanked it up. Jerry Poke got out of the chair like a snake sliding from a bush and his right hand gun was already out. Ketland swung Rock around, using that arm as a lever, and spun him into Jerry. The gun went off at the roof, and both men smashed back against the table. Oley Fanning jumped away from the table before it could fall over and pin him, and twisted around with the bottle in his hand, ready to throw.

Ketland went into him, doubled over, and heard the tossed bottle break against the wall behind. He had his fist hard against Fanning's middle, and carried him back to the wall that way. He put another set of knuckles into Fanning's beard, and the wall shook with Fanning's head smashing against it. Ketland drove his knee into Fanning's groin, and the man stiffened against the boards. Ketland was whirling as Fanning doubled over and fell sideways to the floor.

Poke was up on his hands and knees, one fist clutching the overturned table to support him while he grabbed his other gun. Ketland jumped feet first and caught the gun with one boot and knocked it upward to go off harmlessly. He caught Poke's face with the other boot. Poke went over onto his back, and Ketland let himself go on with all his weight, and felt that boot grind into the flesh and bone of the youth's face. Then all Rock's heft came onto him from behind, and a blow across the back of his neck sprawled him across Poke's body. He clawed for the silver-mounted Colt in the young man's hand, flopping over beneath Rock's next blow. The man's twisted face was above him. He caught Rock's arm, hauling himself to a knee by it, jerking back the gun.

"No," gasped Rock and tried to pull free — "No." — and then stiffened from the first blow. Ketland got on up, slashing at the man's face with the gun barrel again, deliberately now, wanting it that way. He kept Rock in close, holding his arm, and drove him to the other side of the shack, pistol-whipping him mercilessly until the big man sagged in his grip, sat down with his back against the wall with his legs spread out, holding his face in his hands and making small, strangled sounds.

Oley Fanning was crouched across the overturned table, holding his belly and groaning, and Ketland swayed above Rock, panting, feeling the pain through his legs that the violence had caused him. "I told you, Rock," he said gustily, "I told you not to start anything unless you really meant it. I guess you understand now. *I* really meant it."

II

It must have weighed twelve hundred pounds, with well let down hind legs that could mean plenty of speed and ribs that were sprung out into a barrel chest that gave a good indication of its endurance. Ed Ketland leaned on the corral fence, a strange, uncontrollable tension knotting his stomach muscles as he watched them work it across the yard.

Oley Fanning roped the animal with a skillful underhand throw, and ran in with a pigging string to hog-tie its kicking legs. Jerry Poke put the blindfold on, and they let the horse up, and Rock heaved a big, double-rigged Nelson with bucking rolls onto its back. Danny Dekker was topping off this coal-black stallion. He must have been working it for some time, because its heavy chest was briny with lather. Ketland, however, had come from the bunk shack only a few moments before, in time to see them changing a Cheyenne rig for this heavier

Nelson broncho saddle. He was so engrossed with watching that he didn't hear the woman come up behind him.

"I hear you had some trouble in the bunk shack yesterday, Ket."

Ketland turned sharply, and all the old emotion rose in him suddenly. Her eyes were deep and blue as the pool above Aspen Rock. Her high-heeled boots brought her wind-blown red hair up to his chin, and the curving white line of her throat was accentuated by the dark red buckskin of her jacket.

"No trouble, Midge," he said. "They just didn't have something straight, that's all. Highwoods told me about Uncle Harry. I guess you know how I feel. I worked a lot of coulées with him."

Midge Forsythe's eyes darkened, and she nodded. Judge Forsythe, Midge's father, and Uncle Harry Forsythe had been brothers. Uncle Harry had been a crotchety, lovable old whang-hide who still insisted on living the hard, free, open life he had known as a youth, trapping this country. Nothing his brother, the judge, could do or say would make Uncle Harry take the respectable comfort of old age that he could have found in the Pothook house, and the worst Cabine blizzard invariably found him in some line shack, cooking for the snowbound hands, or spinning his windies over a Crow medicine pipe. When Judge Forsythe had died, three

228

years ago, Uncle Harry had divided his time between the line shacks and the home spread, helping Midge run the Pothook with the aid of Judge Forsythe's lawyer, Bixbee Riddle.

"The only thing we can figure out is that Uncle Harry got caught out in the big freeze we had last winter," said Midge, then her hand tightened warmly on Ketland's arm. "Sorry I couldn't meet your train yesterday. I was up at Riddle's seeing about an injunction against Jonas Napperhan, and didn't get through in time."

"Napperhan?" said Ketland. "Doesn't he own enough of Centerpine now?"

She shook her head. "Last January his Number Four shaft caved in beneath Centerpine and swallowed the courthouse and half the other buildings on Oglala Street. Now he claims a bunch of our cattle stampeded into a coulée on that government land below Indian Ridge and caved in a section of his Number Three. He's been shoving our cattle off Indian Ridge on the grounds they endanger his miners, and, whenever we try to stop him, it's a fight."

"That's free graze, isn't it?"

"Government land," she said, "except for the strip we got by having our men file homesteads down Crow River. Now Napperhan has got through a petition to obstruct our use of it. He's got the Western Foundation of Miners behind him, and they swing a lot of weight. If the petition goes through, most of the Cabines will be useless to us. To block him, Riddle is trying to get Judge Harcourt to issue an injunction against Napperhan, forcing his men to get out of the Cabines because it's government land. Until either Napperhan's petition or our injunction goes into effect, the Cabines are no man's land."

"Things have changed a lot since I've been gone," he said, turning slowly to look again at the black stallion within the corral. "That hasn't, though. Devil?"

She nodded somberly. "Yes, that's Devil. Nobody's been able to do anything with him since he smashed you up last year. He's been getting more vicious all the time. I wanted to sell him, but Dekker wouldn't let the beast go. He'll roll on Dekker some day, just like he did you."

"If I can't do it, Dekker can," said Ketland softly.

"I never thought of it that way," she murmured. "Maybe some men are that way, though. When they aren't confident within themselves that they're as good or better than another man, they have to keep proving it."

He glanced at her, then back into the corral. Her eyes were on his face, and he knew she must have seen it, as he watched the black stallion, the faint tightening of skin across the leathery plane of his cheek.

Dekker rowelled Devil suddenly, and the black began to hump experimentally, feeling for the man's weight. Suddenly Devil pinwheeled and charged down the corral, and spun again. Dekker was still on the Nelson with all his weight forward. The horse erupted with all four hoofs spreading out when it came back down, and Ketland saw Dekker take the awful jar and come out whooping. Young bones, and young flesh, and young sinew. Something Ketland would never have again, he thought sorrowfully. Ten years he had taken it like that, and now he was through with the rough string, and it gave him a bitter, weary feeling.

"There he goes," said the woman, and was up on the fence.

Ketland understood what Midge meant, and the pain stabbed up from his loins suddenly. He stood there, rigid with it, his face bathed in perspiration. The woman had turned to watch him now, and her eyes were wide. He could hear his own harsh breathing, and couldn't help it, damn it, couldn't help it. He tried to relax, but the pain held him stiffly, and he couldn't take his eyes off the horse, and there was something more than the pain that he tried not to define.

Devil had begun to roll. Dekker stepped off with a lithe swing of his lean shanks when the horse went down, and was on Devil again as the animal came over and up, jamming his feet into the stirrups and raking the caked flanks with his spurs. The stallion began rolling madly, cleverly, viciously, twisting around with a glass eye to see what Dekker was doing every time he went off. On his fourth roll, Devil twisted while he was still on his back, and switched ends before coming up, kicking at Dekker with his hind legs.

Dekker's gusty breathing had a driven, desperate sound as he slapped the black's rump and came up over the rear legs as they struck the ground, hitting the saddle with a jar that drew a sharp gasp from Ketland. The horse raced forward, halted abruptly, pivoted on one hind hoof like a roper. Dekker was thrown off balance by the pivot. While his weight was still on the offside, the black reared and fell back deliberately, and twisted so he would land rolling on a haunch. Dekker lost control and had to kick free instead of stepping off to one side. The ground shuddered to his fall, and Ketland closed his eyes as if it had been he taking the agony of that.

The black came up off its flank with a triumphant scream, turning to charge Dekker. Dekker tried to roll away, shouting hoarsely. The horse skidded to a halt, rearing up above the man.

Not many hands could have done it with

the rope, then. Oley Fanning threw from the rail, his forty-foot hemp hissing out and snaking its loop around the black's forelegs. Oley twisted away with the rope across his hip, and the horse crashed down at the same time, its weight snapping the hemp taut suddenly. The violent jerk threw the animal off balance, and it went over sideways while its forelegs were still up in the air above Dekker, pinned together by that loop. It gave Dekker a chance to roll free, and the black came down on its shoulder where the man had lain a moment before. Rock galloped out, off his big dun before it stopped, throwing a pigging string around the stallion's kicking legs in a swift hitch.

"What did I tell you," said Midge tensely. "That Devil's a killer. . . ."

She stopped, and looked at Ketland again. His shirt was soggy with sweat, and his own eyes were almost closed with the pain, subsiding gradually now. He leaned weakly against the rail, cursing himself in silent bitterness. Why? Just the sight of that. Why?

"Guess you're glad you don't have to top that kind any more, aren't you, Ketland?" Dekker had come heavily over to the rail, wiping his face, and his laugh was a trifle forced.

Ketland felt the probing mockery in Dekker's words and hardly heard himself speak, talking more to cover what was going on inside him than for any other reason. "Ever try it naked, Dekker?"

"Bareback?" Dekker looked at him closely. "That's the way you were doing it when Devil rolled you, wasn't it?"

"A year is a long time to punish yourself on a job like that," said Ketland. "If you can't break Devil with a saddle, why not try the other way? You can slide around, naked, and you don't have to kick your legs off getting free every time. You can walk right over their belly with them while they're rolling and be there when they come back up."

"And get your head kicked off," said Dekker. "Or your legs smashed. I can do it with a saddle, Ketland. I will. Can you?"

Still fighting himself, Ketland didn't answer. He saw how the woman was looking up at Danny, her mouth open slightly so the light glistened wetly across the wet curve of her underlip, and suddenly realized what it could mean. And why not, he thought bitterly. Standing there like that, with all their youth between them, they made Ketland feel very old.

"Won't you let Devil go," said Midge tremulously. "I'm afraid for you, Danny."

She had never told Ketland that when he had worked the black. Ketland turned away suddenly as Dekker put his big, brown hand on the woman's, purposely softening his voice.

"I'm through with it for today, cousin. I sort of wanted that stallion broke for the fall roundup, but I guess I'll have to give it up for a while. We're starting branding today. Ketland, you might as well pitch in. I told Rock to find you a horse."

"I'm going with you," said Midge. "I'll get Baldy."

Dekker had stepped through the pack pole fence, and he watched Midge go for a moment, then turned to Ketland. "You'll be teaming with Oley Fanning. One thing. Stay clear of the Cabines. Napperhan's got his men thrown over Indian Ridge, and you're liable to get your head shot off. Here's your horse."

The slashes showed lividly on Rock's face as he led the saddled animal from the barns, and his heavy-lidded eyes smoldered with hate toward Ketland. The horse was a spavined, old paint with rheumy eyes and rope scars over its gaunted shoulders and a saddle back the shape of a hickory bow. Yet, just standing near it, with the heat of its body spreading around him and its smell in his face, Ketland could feel the breathlessness begin to rise again. He tried to cover it, speaking up harshly.

"What kind of crow-bait is this anyway, Dekker?"

Oley Fanning had led his gelding up with Highwoods, standing on the other side of the paint, running a hand through his luxuriant brown beard and watching Ketland with veiled eyes. Two more hands trotted up and reined in their horses.

"Why, we didn't think you'd want a bronc' right off, Ketland," said Dekker, and glanced at Oley Fanning. "After all, your legs. . . ."

"Is this what you were trying to do yesterday?" said Ketland.

Dekker's big chest swelled against his denim shirt when he took a breath. "What do you mean?"

"The same thing you were doing in the bunk shack," said Ketland. "They all knew I was coming and who I was and what had happened to me. You didn't need to keep telling them like that. Were you riding me? Did you think it would humiliate me in front of them? Like this?"

Dekker laughed thinly. "You're sitting a pretty tall horse, Ketland, and I'd hold the reins tight."

"What's your game Dekker?" said Ketland. "Don't you want me back? You certainly don't think I constitute a threat to your job. Are you doing something here?"

Dekker flushed, taking a step toward Ketland. "I told you to watch yourself, Ketland. Come down off that high horse before you fall off."

"No," said Ketland. "*You* watch *yourself*, Dekker. If you're trying to get rid of me this way, just remember that what I did in the bunk shack yesterday I can do again, any time, anywhere!"

Dekker's spike heels made a soft, scraping sound against the hard-packed earth. "Did you think marking up Rock's face like that so everybody would know what happened would do any good? The men don't like you any better for it, Ketland. You can't come in here and throw a hand out of his bunk and expect. . . ."

"Oh, stow that in your poke," said Ketland. "Everybody knows what you were trying to do in the bunk shack yesterday, and everybody who knows that, knows why I marked up Rock and threw him out. I wanted things plain from the first, Dekker. I don't sleep with any mules. Rock disputed that, and now every time anybody looks at him, they'll know what he got. I don't ride any stove-up windsuckers like this paint, either. Anybody wants to dispute *that,* I'm willing. Now, you'd better get out of my way."

"Where do you think you're going?"

"To get a decent horse," said Ketland.

He was sweating again. It was a sorrel with a running walk, so relaxed Ketland could hear the teeth pop at every step, like a Tennessee Walker, and a rocking chair would have been harder on a man. Yet he was sweating again. It was hard to breathe and the muscles of his stomach were tight as a stretched dally and he could feel the pain spreading from his hips. The horse shifted its weight to hit a rise, and Ketland's hand pulled up hard, and the sorrel shied into Midge's bald-faced bay.

"Sorry," he said.

"Ket," she said, "maybe you shouldn't be riding . . . maybe you aren't entirely well."

Ketland kept a moment's silence.

Ahead of them rode Dekker and the bearded Oley Fanning and the other two hands, rising out of the Poplar Bottoms to a low hill. The sorrel tossed its head, and Ketland slacked the reins, trying desperately to relax.

"I'm all right," he said. "Doc Haskell told me I'm well."

She looked at the rigid line of his torso. "What's the matter, then? At the corral, when Dekker was working the black. The same thing. You looked sick. You were pale and perspiring and stiff as a snubbing post."

His knees were like vises against the sorrel's hide. "Forget it, will you? Just a little tight, topping a horse after over a year, that's all. Where do you graze your two-year-olds if Napperhan's been shoving them out of the Cabines?"

"North of Poplar Bottoms," she told him, shoving a strand of red hair back under her flat-topped Mormon. "Fact is, we hadn't been using our strip in the Cabines anyway, since the last big freeze. Only that government land on the farther slopes, past Indian Ridge. The snow ruined our pasture flanking Crow River, and nobody's been to the Indian Ridge line shack since you left."

Dekker reined his roan in beside Ketland, pointing to the badlands between this ridge and the Cabines farther northward. "You and Oley cut down there and clean out the brush land in those dry bottoms. We've got our fires in the south turn of Aspen Creek. Drive the bunch there. Anything that runs toward the Cabines, you let Oley tail it, understand? Stay clear of those mountains."

Oley Fanning lined out ahead, and the woman flanked Ketland, dropping downslope, still looking at his seat in the saddle. They spotted their first bunch of Pothook steers in a coulée about a mile north of Poplar Bottoms, and Oley spurred ahead to cut around them. Ketland's face twisted with the effort it cost him to put his boot heel into the sorrel's flank. The animal broke into its gallop raggedly, feeling the indecision in its rider. With the run jarring him, Ketland began to breathe faster, and then the trembling started. He cursed himself bitterly, trying to relax and find his seat. But he was cantle boarding and grabbing the apple like a greenhorn. The stragglers began to drop back, and Fanning was soon out of sight, pushing them into the main bunch again, leaving Ketland to point the leaders. Yet Ketland could do no more than cling to his saddle horn, fighting his horse and himself, sweating, cursing. The leaders began lining out toward a butte, and Fanning came quirting his gelding up from behind.

"I can't watch drag and point too, Ketland." He coughed in the dust. "If you don't stop those leaders from splitting around that butte ahead, we'll have the whole bunch scattered again."

Drawing in a choked breath, Ketland let go of the horn with one hand, trying to put the sorrel in closer to the cattle. Trained for this work, the animal responded like a hair-trigger, leaping toward the cattle eagerly. Rigid and off balance, Ketland was thrown backward. The panic swept him again, and he yanked desperately on the reins, using them to keep from going off. The sorrel squatted like a jack rabbit. Ketland was almost pitched over the waving mane. The cattle thundered by, half obscured by their curtain of alkali. Fanning pounded leather, riding like a bunch quitter. He looked at Ketland, then jerked an angry arm up to where the leaders were already splitting around the yellow butte.

"If you can't sit a horse well enough to work cattle, why didn't you say so?"

The Herefords were scattering, and Fanning whirled his gelding after a cut of heavy whitefaces that had headed for a wash. Panting, sweating, filled with a bitter frustration, Ketland fought his sorrel around, trying to head it after the steers that had scattered the other way. The horse was shying and pitching now with Ketland's heavy hand on the reins, and he couldn't do anything with it. The steers were far northward of him, running into the first foothills, when Midge caught up with Ketland.

"Ket," she called, "what is it?"

He couldn't answer. With another look at his twisted face and rigid body, she galloped out ahead of him after the Pothook steers. He lay almost flat on the sorrel, chest banging the horn, sobbing now, letting the animal follow Midge as best it could, unable to control it at all, unable to separate his panic from his pain. They swept down a winding cut that penetrated the first hills, and, by the time they topped the first ridge, Ketland had lost all sense of direction, following Midge's dust down the opposite slope and into another twisted coulée and out of that and into a belt of sighing pines. He didn't realize how far into the mountains he was until, topping another ridge, he was almost thrown over the sorrel's head as it shied from talus striking its flanks. The shale had been kicked up by the front hoofs of Fanning's gelding as he drove it down, stiff-legged, from above and behind. The man must have left his own cattle, and his face was white with anger above the dusty curl of his beard.

"Didn't Dekker tell you to stay out of the Cabines!" he shouted, and had his six-gun out. "Now, get back there in the buttes before I blow you off that greenhorn seat of yours . . . !"

At first, Ketland thought it had been Fanning's shot. The sorrel screamed and reared and slid off sideways. In that moment, losing all his balance, Ketland saw Midge turn her bay in the shallow valley below and break into a hard gallop back upslope, and saw Fanning rein his gelding to a sliding stop down the talus, looking upward with surprise stamped on his face. Then Ketland lost sight of them, fighting to stay aboard the spooked sorrel.

Any experienced waddy could have rolled off at the first pitch instead of trying to stay on and unbalancing the horse and taking a chance of falling with it or under it, but Ketland was all panic now and hanging onto the horn like a crazed tenderfoot. The sorrel stumbled on down the coulée in a mad, lopsided run until another shot sent it into a frenzy of bucking and whinnying, and finally Ketland's weight carried the animal off its footing, and he went over its head. Even then, any experienced cowpoke could have taken the fall without too much damage, dropping limply, but Ketland couldn't loosen up, and he hit as stiffly as a split rail, feeling the stunning pain, and then feeling nothing.

He came out of that, hearing his own harsh breathing. His arms and legs were numb, and he couldn't move them. A shadow fell across him, and someone was lifting his shoulders. Midge? Feeling began to return, tingling pain. He heard someone groan, and realized it was he.

"Are you hurt badly, Ket?" asked the woman. "You're shaking like a blown horse."

He was on his knees now, trembling. He clamped his teeth shut, trying to stop. Why? It wasn't the pain. Even as hard as he had fallen, it wasn't the pain. He had taken harder falls. *Stop heaving like a spooked filly, damn you!* Another shot from the higher, yonder ridge kicked shale into his face.

"Just stunned," he said. "Let's get out of here."

They stumbled down the slippery talus, passing Fanning's gelding where it lay dead on its side and, reaching the bearded man, crouched among the scattered boulders in the dry streambed.

"Guess you should have taken that old paint, after all," said Fanning thinly.

"Oh, be quiet," said Midge hotly. "Can't you see he's hurt?"

"Not hurt," said Ketland savagely. "That Napperhan on the ridge above?"

"Who else?" said Fanning. "Dekker told you to stay clear of the Cabines. You had to play the fool clear up to the hilt, didn't you? Not enough you couldn't ride your horse. Now you've got us in a trap we'll never get out of. They'll dust us whichever way we move."

"You keep Midge here," said Ketland.

"You ain't going up there," snarled Fanning, raising his gun.

Ketland watched him a moment, then deliberately turned around and started crawling back toward the dead gelding, hearing the woman call after him — "Ket!" — and hearing Fanning's sharp, scraping move, and then nothing more.

He reached the animal, and hauled a Winchester from its boot under the double-barreled roping rig. He untied the saddle roll from behind the cantle and spilled out a handful of .45-90s Fanning had there, stuffing them into his Levi's pocket. He cocked the gun, and worked across through the boulders, passing Fanning and the woman a little to the right. Where the rocks thinned, he halted for a moment. He caught movement above him, and felt himself start to sweat again. His hand began to tremble on the gun.

Ketland bit his lips till the pain brought

tears. *That's all, damn you, that's all. Maybe on a horse, but not here, see.* He forced himself to rise, and broke into a hard, bent-over run for the scrubby juniper.

The first shot took dirt out from under his feet, and he answered it, shouting hoarsely, trying to blot out that spasm of fear with the violence of this. He cocked and fired again, from the hip, still running, and threw himself behind a gnarled trunk, breathing heavily. A vagrant breeze dried perspiration on his face and turned it to a caked mask. He saw that movement above him again, and decided it was one man moving back and forth and firing from different spots to make it appear there were several snipers. A bullet clipped alligator bark off a branch above his head. He moved out, firing above timberline, taking short dashes in between shots. At this height he could see how far he had really penetrated the Cabines after those steers. He finally worked out of timberline, failing to draw any fire, and struggled up harsh granite to the ridge, bellying down so as not to skyline himself. The thin air biting his lungs, he stared across at the yonder ridge, higher than this, its rugged granite forming the silhouette of a hawk-like face. An Indian's face. Indian Ridge.

III

It came to him like that. He hadn't been here for several years. It was one of the most inaccessible portions of the Pothook, and Uncle Harry Forsythe had been the only man who would take up permanent camp here in the line shack, the other hands putting in their hitch under protest. Ketland found Crow River finally, hidden beneath its furred mantle of pine until it wound into the yellow cottonwoods at the narrow bottom of Indian Coulée. The Pothook hands had filed homesteads along the river, which gave the Forsythes control of the water and the best graze, and left government land on either flank of the strip. The patches of meadow that showed on the opposite slopes were sere and brown, however, and Ketland remembered how Midge had said the freeze ruined this section for them. A movement on the slope below caught Ketland's attention. It took him a moment to make out the man, and then the horse, picketed in front of the Indian Ridge line shack in the bottom of the cañon. Ketland got up, and slid through shale to a cut that led down, hiding him from view in its bottom.

He stumbled through its talus and sand at a run, sliding on his hocks in the steep places. Once in timber, he climbed out of the cut and quartered toward the shack. The man had just reached his horse when Ketland made his appearance.

"Hold it!" called Ketland, and his lever made a metallic sound against the Winchester's oak stock.

The man had an old-fashioned Spencer sixteen-shot across his pommel, and one foot in the stirrup. He whirled that way, and his gun must have been cocked, because he pulled it around with his hand covering the trigger guard. Still going forward, Ketland fired. The man jerked, and the bullet he got out kicked dirt at Ketland's feet. He fell over on his face with his foot still in the stirrup.

The horse pulled him past the cabin before Ketland could stop it. Holding the spooked animal by its headstall, he kicked at the man's boot until it dropped from the stirrup, then toed the body onto its back. He didn't recognize the dirty, bloody, dead face.

The horse reared up, and, fighting it, Ketland began to pant, and it wasn't from his hard run. He cursed himself, and then quit trying to pull the animal down, and let it go, and stood there trembling, watching it gallop off into the timber. He drew a sobbing breath, turning bitterly toward the cabin.

The inside was typical of a line shack, bunks lining side walls. Uncle Harry's potbellied stove at the rear was flanked by a wash trough on one side and a few boards knocked together for a table on the other.

Jerry Poke lay just inside the door, one of his fancy Colts on the floor beside him. There was an overturned stool behind his body, as if he had knocked it over in getting up, and taken the step to the door before he had been shot. He was as dead as the man outside.

"Uncle Harry!" said Ketland.

The old man lay in the last bunk, and his gnarled face bore the signs of a beating. There was the stir of breathing beneath the tattered Army blanket covering him. Throwing it off, Ketland found Uncle Harry's hands tied to the sideboards with a length of hemp that looked as if it had been there for some time. He untied it, and got a tin dipper from a nail on the wall, sloshing it full from the water butt beside the wash trough. The old man came around after the second dipperful, coughing, sputtering. He looked up at Ketland with dazed eyes, not recognizing him at first.

"No," moaned Uncle Harry. "I won't. It belongs to the Pothook, and I won't. You can't do anything more to me. You done it all, and I . . ." — his eyes widened suddenly — "Ketland!"

Ketland could see now that some of the scars and bruises on Uncle Harry's face were old and partly healed, and others were fresh and raw. "What is it, Uncle Harry? What are they doing to you?"

"Ketland?" said the old man. "You come back? No. They said you wasn't. Oh, get me my teeth, Ket, will you?"

Ketland looked at the old man's puckered mouth, then glanced around the room. On the floor beneath the bunk was part of an upper plate, mashed and broken, and by the leg of the table was a white row of false lowers, covered with dirt. Harry Forsythe followed Ketland's glance, and shook his head.

"No, I should have remembered. They did that. So long ago. Broke my glasses, too. I been having headaches ever since. Have to get some more specs from Centerpine, I guess. Doc Haskell said I'd have trouble if I didn't wear them. Getting old, Ket. Yes, they did that. . . ."

Ketland realized that he was wandering. "Who did it, Uncle Harry? Napperhan? How long have you been here?"

"Napperhan?" said Uncle Harry. "I been here for years, Ket, you know that."

"I mean like this." Ketland shook him gently. "What is it, Uncle Harry?"

The old man stared emptily at the wall, then his toothless mouth spread in a vacant smile. "They think they could get it out of me like this? Why, this ain't nothing compared to what those Blackfeet did to me when I was traveling with Kit Carson. Law of apex, they said. What do I care about law of apex? They can't have it, see?" He broke into a violent fit of coughing, clawed at Ketland's arm. "Get me some water, Ket. I'm not far to go. . . ."

Drinking, he slopped it all over his face, and lay back, panting weakly. Ketland wiped his chin with a corner of the blanket. Then the horse snorted from outside, and saddle leather creaked. Ketland was turned toward the door when Danny Dekker came through. Dekker stopped just inside, holding his gun, and there were too many mingled emotions crossing his face for Ketland to define. But the rage shaking his voice was clear enough.

"I told you to stay out of these mountains, Ketland." Dekker glanced at Jerry Poke, then beyond Ketland. "Uncle Harry?"

"Yes," said Ketland. "Looks like he's been here quite a while. What made you come?"

Dekker was squatting beside the bunk, his hand on the old man's shoulder, and the anger wasn't yet gone from his voice. "Cutting a bunch of heifers in the badlands when I heard shots from the Cabines. Found Fanning and Midge in that coulée."

"You must have hit straight for this shack."

"I told you. We heard shots."

"But why this shack?" Ketland persisted. "You couldn't place the location that close on the other side of the ridge."

"Uncle Harry?" said Dekker, and the tone

of his voice made Ketland look. Dekker was shaking his uncle. He stopped, finally. Outside Ketland heard a horse snort, then there was no sound except for Dekker's heavy breathing. Finally Dekker stood up, still looking at Uncle Harry.

"Jerry?" he said.

Ketland glanced at Jerry Poke. "Dead when I came in. That man outside. . . ."

"You shot him?" said Dekker. "Clay Garr. One of Jonas Napperhan's men." Dekker turned on Ketland suddenly. His face was tight with strain now, and there was an odd speculation in his black eyes. He waved his hand at the old man. "Uncle Harry was alive when you got here?"

"Yes," said Ketland heavily.

"Say anything?" asked Dekker.

"Yes."

"Well?" said Dekker.

IV

Centerpine was in the Coeur d'Alene, south of the Pothook spread, its narrow streets twisting up the Montana hillside over a veritable honeycomb of mining shafts, its dusty, false-fronted buildings shuddering twenty-four hours a day to the constant roar of the stamping mills that stood at the foot of the hill, crushing ore.

Standing at the window on the second floor of the Napperhan Building, Ed Ketland could look down Oglala Street to the gigantic hole where Napperhan Three had caved in, swallowing the courthouse and half a dozen other structures. Behind Ketland, Dr. Roy Haskell's swivel chair creaked.

"Sorry to hear about Uncle Harry going that way," said Haskell, clearing his throat. "He disappeared about three, four months ago. Who would've thought he was up there at Indian Ridge all along. Why do you suppose, Ketland?"

"No telling," said Ketland moodily. "Even before the freeze, nobody went up to Indian Ridge unless they had to. They could have kept Uncle Harry there forever without anybody finding him. Just chance those steers stampeded into the Cabines like that. Whoever it was, they'd worked Uncle Harry over pretty completely."

"But why? An old man like that."

Ketland tucked his shirt tails in and buttoned his Levi's. "I don't know, Doc. They wanted something from him. You've been in this mining town all your life. What's the law of apex?"

Haskell's chair squeaked. "Didn't think anybody but Napperhan's corporation lawyers would know about the apex law. Where did you hear about it? Freddie Hintz used it in Butte some years back. Made his fortune by it. The law of apex provides that any miner who locates a vein surfacing on his property . . . apexing . . . can legally follow that vein through and under the property of another man, so long as the vein remains unbroken. This Freddie Hintz found an unstaked lot on Butte Hill, which flanked the old Hintz Healy Mines. Butte Hill was a lot like Centerpine here, all honeycombed with shafts, and it was only a matter of time before Hintz struck a vein which he could claim as apexing on his lot. It ran into one of the richest veins Amalgamated Mines had, and they took it to court, naturally. For six years they tried to loosen Hintz's claim on that vein. The courts put an injunction on the shaft and stopped work there till it was decided who owned it. Before he was finished, Hintz had caused so many of Amalgamated's stopes to be closed with those injunctions that Amalgamated finally paid him the tidy little sum of fourteen million dollars to drop his suit so they could get back to work again. In the end, the courts would undoubtedly have ruled against Hintz, but Amalgamated was losing so much money by having all those shafts idle that they figured it worth paying Hintz off. One of the biggest frauds perpetrated. All on the strength of an obscure little law like that."

Ketland put it in the back of his mind, nodding. "All right, Doc. Thanks. The other, now. You've been beating around the bush. You've examined me. What is it?"

Ketland turned to face Haskell. The doctor was a rotund little man whose white mop of hair accentuated the florid face that attested to his predilection for what he stoutly maintained was cold tonic. He leaned back in the chair, elbows on the arms, pressing plump fingertips together.

"It's like I said when you first came back from the Butte Hospital, Ket. You're mended. You're perfectly well. The jolting a bronc' would give you won't help none, but a man your age should quit the rough string anyway. Otherwise, you can do anything or ride anything you did before."

"But I told you," said Ketland tensely, "every time I get near a horse, it comes. The pain. All up and down my legs and back. And when I get on . . ." — he jerked his head from side to side, something desperate entering his voice — "what is it, then?"

Haskell pursed his lips above a snowy goatee. "That black stallion. Devil? Yeah, Devil. Rolled you pretty good, didn't he?"

"You know."

"And you had lots of time to think about it in the hospital. More than a year. Every night, maybe? Kept you awake. Not the pain, so much. Just remembering how it felt to go down under twelve hundred pounds of black devil, rolling and rolling."

Ketland's face tightened. "I guess so. What are you driving at?"

"This might be in your mind, Ket, this pain, this feeling. What is the feeling, really? Besides the pain, I mean. Breathlessness? Sweating? Skeery, maybe?"

Ketland didn't speak for a long moment. "You mean . . . fear?"

Haskell took his elbows off the chair, leaning forward. "No, I wouldn't call it that, Ket. It just gets in a man's mind this way. I've seen it in miners. They get caught in a cave-in, maybe, and ain't hurt much. Time comes to go back to work, they can't. Same symptoms. Sweating. Panic when they near a shaft. Maybe even a recurrence of the pain, without any logical stimuli to account for it, other than their proximity to what hurt them originally."

"You mean fear." It was a statement this time.

"No, Ket. I told you," said Haskell. "In your mind. Not really fear. . . ."

"All right," said Ketland. "You told me what I wanted to know. Maybe I knew it from the beginning. Office calls are three bucks, aren't they?"

Ketland stopped a moment at the bottom of the covered stairway that let out onto Tomonak Street, inhaling unsteadily. The air was foul and smoky. The shuddering pound

255

of the stamping mills at the bottom of the hill beat through his brain. *You're a coward, you're a coward. . . .*

Rigidly he moved across toward his mount hitched at the rack. The sorrel had been ruined, and this was the spavined old paint Dekker had ordered for him the first time. Even on this plug, his ride into town had been a nightmare, and he had never been able to force himself to gallop the animal.

" 'Morning, Ketland."

Jonas Napperhan stood on the sidewalk, his pale, heavy face outlined by a spade beard and long, black hair cut squarely across the back of his thick neck like a Crow Indian's. His torso filled out a black Prince Albert without being fat, and his thick legs were braced in their flat-heeled boots as if to thwart a Cabine blizzard.

"Hear you brought in Clay Garr this morning," he said.

"That's right," said Ketland. "I brought him to the sheriff's office an hour ago."

Standing beside Napperhan, Sheriff Gregory Arden pulled nervously at the mustache drooping raggedly over his slack, wet mouth. In the shadow cast by a battered John Stetson, his pale blue eyes shifted incessantly to Napperhan with a watery subservience.

"You killed Garr?" asked Napperhan. "That could mean trouble for you."

"Don't try to make it, Napperhan," said Ketland, conscious now of the miners gathering on the sidewalk behind Napperhan, and out in the street. "Sheriff Arden understands what will happen if you don't let things lay. I thought you would, too."

"I'm just here to talk with you, Ketland," said Napperhan heavily. "What things I let lay, and what things I don't, will be entirely up to you. You're one of Judge Forsythe's oldest hands, except for Highwoods, and you undoubtedly know more about the Pothook lands than anyone else. I'd like you to tell me about it now."

"Tell you about what?"

The plank walk creaked under Napperhan's weight as he shifted his feet. "I told you this depended on you. You *know* what."

"No, I don't," said Ketland. "What would you like me to tell you about the Pothook?"

Napperhan's breathing became heavier. "I'll put it another way. What else did you find in the Cabines beside Uncle Harry the other day?"

"What else should I find?" asked Ketland impatiently.

"You know." The mine owner waved a blocky hand. "Or maybe you didn't have to find it. Maybe you knew all along. Is Indian Ridge the place?"

Ketland's lips pulled back against his teeth. "What place?"

"Listen, Ketland," said Napperhan, looking at the men behind Ketland, "you're in no position to be stubborn. You know what I'm talking about. What land does Danny Dekker own in the Cabines?"

"I don't know Dekker's business," said Ketland. "If he has land in those mountains, I never heard about it."

Jonas Napperhan took a vicious step forward, grabbing Ketland by his shirt front, and the mine owner's hot breath slapped his words up against Ketland's face. "Quit stalling. I told you I'd let things lay if you acted right. You've picked them up yourself, now. You know more about the Pothook than anyone else, even Highwoods or Dekker or Midge. Now, you'll open that tight trap of yours here, or we'll open it for you in jail, and it won't be done so pleasantly there."

Ketland's voice came out from between his teeth. "Napperhan, I'm not one of your Centerpine stooges, and I don't care what you want to know, or why, and before this goes any further, you'd better take your hands off me."

For a moment, Napperhan's black eyes met Ketland's steady gray stare. Then the mine owner opened his fingers and stepped back, inhaling raggedly.

"All right, Ketland," he said. "I don't have to put my hands on you. Arden has a warrant for your arrest, for the murder of Clay

Garr. Take him into custody, Sheriff."

"Hold it!" Ketland's words struck Arden flatly, and the sheriff stopped with his body bent forward to take the first step. "I thought you understood, Arden?"

The lawman shrugged, waving his hand vaguely at Napperhan. "I know, Ketland, I know, but Jonas swore out a warrant for you. . . ."

"I thought you understood, too, Napperhan," said Ketland. "I brought Garr in and told the facts and didn't go any further because I thought things were rather plain. You can't hold me for murder. In the first place, Garr was on Pothook property. That's trespass. Whether he pulled a gun on me or whether he packed a gun at all doesn't signify. He was a trespasser and no court in Montana would call it murder. We don't have to go any further than that. But you seem to want it. You know I brought another body in with Garr's. One of the Pothook hands. Jerry Poke. We found him in the Indian Ridge line shack with a Spencer Fifty-Six in him. Clay Garr carried a Spencer Fifty-Six."

"Ketland. . . ."

"No," said Ketland. "Not yet. You try and hold me, and we'll publicize those facts. How would you like to be connected with Poke's murder? The ranchers of Sander County have been wanting something solid like that to fight you with for a long time. Armed trespass and murder, Napperhan. It was rather obvious to Arden, and he didn't push anything. I thought it would be plain to you, too."

Napperhan flushed hotly. "Ketland, I tell you. . . ."

Ketland was shoved forward by an uneasy shift of the growing crowd behind him, and he jumped onto the walk, forcing Napperhan to take a step backward. "We won't stop there, either. Neither will the ranchers. They'll want to know what Garr was doing there. They'll want to know what Uncle Harry was doing there. Whoever tortured him like that was directly responsible for his death. Was it you, Napperhan? Is that why you were trying to keep everybody out of the Cabines? Not because some Pothook cattle stampeded into a coulée and caved in your Number Three . . . because you had something at Indian Ridge you didn't want anybody to find? Clay Garr was holding Uncle Harry there for you, and, when Poke stumbled across it, Garr murdered him? It'll all come out if you want it that way, Napperhan. What did Uncle Harry have that you wanted so badly? The law of apex, Napperhan?"

Napperhan stiffened, then lurched up against Ketland, grabbing him again. "You *do* know, then, you *do* know. . . ."

"I told you to keep your hands off!" shouted Ketland, and brought his fist up between them and cracked it across Napperhan's heavy face in a short, vicious backhand blow that knocked the mine owner against the wall.

The shout from the miners behind Ketland was drowned by the shuddering of the plank walk as they jumped up after him. Arden took a step back to draw his gun. Ketland let himself be thrown forward by the weight of the first miner crashing into him from behind. He surged belly-up against Arden, cracking him across the wrist with the edge of his open hand. The sheriff cried out sharply with the pain, and Ketland got the Colt from his stiffened hand. He caught the sheriff by his gun belt, whirling him around into the miners, shoving him forward and sticking out a foot to trip him at the same time. Sheriff Arden's own momentum carried his falling body into the men, shoving one aside, knocking two more floundering out into the street. Ketland leaped forward into the hole Arden had created, slashing at a bearded face with the gun, twisting around to strike a second man before the first one had fallen away.

It left a free path to the paint for that moment, and he reached the horse, knocking the reins from the rack and pistol-whipping a last miner and vaulting onto the horse. He wheeled the animal with a vicious jerk, kicking at their clawing hands.

"Stop him!" It was Napperhan's voice from their midst. "Don't let him get out of town. Stop Ketland, you fools . . . !"

Ketland realized how it was now, and, when a man tried to grab his reins, Ketland shot him and saw him crash back into the hitch rack, breaking the pole beneath his weight and dropping through onto the curb. He reared the horse, bringing it down among them, forcing it screaming through the crowd. The animal surged forward, shuddering to the thud of a last man's body, then breaking free. Then he was galloping down the steep slope of Tomonak Street, crossing Oglala, hearing the first shot behind him, then others, crossing Lebarge and riding past the stamping mills, their thunder drowning all other sounds.

The excitement had carried him this far, but now that he was free, he once more became conscious of the horse beneath him. He began to feel the hard gallop and knew he was stiffening up. The dust swept into his face as he bent low, trying desperately to find his seat. The wind should have dried his perspiration, but somehow his shirt was soggy beneath the armpits and down his back. He tried to ride with his legs and couldn't, and began showing daylight between his hocks and the saddle like a greenhorn, clinging desperately to the horn with one hand, holding the reins taut with the other.

The paint began to fight his heavy hand, tossing its scarred old head. It shied to one side, trying to free the bit, and he almost went out of the saddle.

"Damn you, Ketland, damn you!"

He heard the hysterical curses, and realized they were his own. The wild look behind him almost cost him his seat again, and he saw the riders back there, and the panic flooded up in him, taking complete control. His breath had a hoarse, sobbing sound, and his face was twisted with the pain shooting through him, and the rising fear. The horse leaned into a curve, and he was thrown outward, all his weight on one stirrup, lying across the saddle now, with reins flapping loose and unheeded.

He managed to fight back onto the saddle, legs stiff and useless for any balance, body jerking like a stick with every hoof the paint put down. He knew there was only one thing to do now. He couldn't hope to escape them like this, even if he remained aboard. With a crazy, bawling curse, he fought savagely for the last vestige of control, and with the fear of what he intended to do clawing at him he forced himself to release the horn, and throw his body from the saddle.

That was all. No more control. No falling horse or rolling. He hit the slope beside the road, stiff as a corral post, and bounced down the embankment through a haze of jarring, thudding, spinning agony, with the chokeberry crackling all around him and the noise of the horse fading away above, and struck the bottom of the coulée, and stopped rolling, and lay still.

V

Danny Dekker stood sway-backed and broad-shouldered and young in the door of the barn, flat belly thrust out against hands stuffed in the pockets of his black Mackinaw, waiting for Ketland to limp across the compound. Midge was beside Dekker, stamping her fancy-topped boots to keep warm.

"Hear you had to hike it all the way from Centerpine last night." The black-haired ramrod grinned, running a sly tongue across his upper lip. "What's the matter, Ketland? Even that old paint too much for you?"

Ketland drew in the cold, morning air raggedly, still stiff and sore from the fall down the coulée and the long walk to the Pothook. He had laid there half stunned, while Napperhan's men had galloped past on the road above, tailing his riderless horse. Then he had cut off through timber, reaching the bunk shack about four in the morning.

"I'm not putting you on roundup today, Ketland," said Dekker. "That's why I told

Fanning I wanted to see you out here. You made a mess of it the other day, losing those cattle and ruining the sorrel and all. Jerry Poke was working the barns. Maybe you can take his place."

Ketland felt the dull flush of humiliation creeping into his leathery face and was unable to meet Midge's eyes. He rubbed a hand across his shirt, dirty and torn from the fall. Dekker deliberately let the stiff silence lengthen, and Ketland finally had to speak.

"Jerry Poke." He cleared his throat. "What was he doing up on Indian Ridge, Dekker?"

Dekker leaned back on long legs. "I figure Jerry had trailed some cattle into the Cabines, same as you, maybe a little farther north, and came across Clay Garr there at the line shack with Uncle Harry. We might be able to prove it was Garr who killed Jerry, but that wouldn't do us any good unless we could also prove Garr's connection with Napperhan. We know he worked for Jonas, but he wouldn't be on any of Napperhan's books."

"What did they want from Uncle Harry?" asked Ketland.

Dekker couldn't hide his surprise. "You said you talked with Uncle Harry before he died?"

"A minute."

"Well," said Dekker.

"What do you mean, Danny?" asked

Midge. "You think Uncle Harry said something. Did he, Ket? The tin box?"

Dekker turned slowly to her. "What tin box?"

Midge frowned. "It may not mean anything, of course, and I only remembered it yesterday, but about five years ago Uncle Harry gave Dad a tin box to keep for him. A few personals, he said. Maybe something in there would throw light on this."

There was an edge to Dekker's voice. "Where is it now?"

"I don't know exactly," said Midge. "Dad's things are in the house, but I've gone through them and couldn't find the box. When Dad died, Bixbee Riddle, as executor, took a lot of Dad's papers and things to help clear up his probate business and to go on running the Pothook. Maybe Riddle knows about the box."

Dekker took his hands from his pockets, and blew on them, breath steaming milky against the brown skin. He looked at Midge, weather creases wrinkling the corners of his black eyes. Then he shrugged, turning to Ketland.

"I guess you better get at the horses. The animals in the south stalls that open into the corral are range fed. Just give them water, and then turn them into the pasture above the house to graze. The ones on the north side are grain fed. Give Baldy an extra measure. Midge wants to fatten him. You weren't here when we built those special stalls for the wild ones, were you? Devil's in one. Show you."

The sawdust was soggy with morning dew beneath their feet, going down the aisle to the west end. Dekker stopped before the black stallion's stall. It was in two sections, with a slatted partition between, the door in the partition closed with a heavy drop bar. The outer doors of each side were high and solid, with slats only in the top quarter. The drop bars locking them were low and on the outside, and Dekker stooped to lift the one on the empty section.

"That's so the horse can't muzzle it out of its sockets," he said, opening the door. "Some of these broncs are too smart. It used to take three or four men to clean a wild one's stall, if you remember, having to blindfold it and hold it while one of them worked inside. This way, one man can do it. You clean the empty side first. Then you fill the water bucket and feedbag. That middle door works automatically. It has a bar and a latch for safety's sake. You raise the bar. Then you come out and close this outside door and lock it. From here, you pull this cord. It releases the latch, and the middle door swings open. The horse knows what's waiting on this side. It'll come through after the feed and water. The middle door's weighted to swing back as soon as the animal pushes through. Shutting, it hits a release that drops the bar back into its sockets. Then you're free to clean the other side. Got it?"

Ketland nodded. "Will Piper had some like it in his barns a couple of years back for stallions in rutting."

Dekker looked at him, running his tongue across his upper lip. Then he laughed and turned to swagger out of the barn, spur chains rattling. Midge watched without saying much while Ketland fed her bald-faced bay. In the narrow stall, the fetid heat of the animal enveloped him, and he felt the first insidious fear rise in his loins. He came out of the stall with a white line around his compressed lips. Midge put her hand on his arm.

"Ket, what is it? You're beginning to tremble again. Like the other day when the sorrel threw you. What happened to you?"

He pulled away, all the frustration and humiliation of the past days bursting from him. "You know what's the matter. All of them do. I'm yellow. I'm afraid to top the oldest, weakest, sickest plug in Montana. I'm afraid to get within fifty feet of a horse. I'm yellow, and you all know it." He saw the look in her big eyes, and his voice took on a bitter intensity. "Don't give me pity, Midge. A man doesn't want that. Anything else. Despise me. You should. The men do. I despise myself. I'm old, and stove-up and yellow and I haven't got the guts to top that old, blind mule. . . ."

He turned away sharply, breathing heavily, and moved down toward the west end. Perhaps she sensed that her seeing him like this was what hurt most, and she didn't follow. Dully he picked up the shovel and fork, and unlocked the door on the empty side of Devil's stall.

The black began whinnying shrilly, kicking at the slatted partition. Ketland felt his breath coming faster, and stooped suddenly and began shoveling out the manure with swift, vicious strokes. At first, the violent work seemed to dissipate the panic in him. But the black kept moving restlessly in its closed side, and with every move Ketland felt a new catch in his breath, and knew the sweat dribbling off his brow didn't all come from his exertion. It wasn't till he had shoveled the old hay out and walked into the aisle for the clean stuff that he realized he was trembling.

Breathing hoarsely, he clipped the wire and began forking the fresh hay from its bale into the stall, fighting himself with every move. His shaking hands slopped water all over the fresh bed when he filled the bucket. The horse began kicking viciously at the slatted partition between them again, and all Ketland's bitter concentration was on forcing himself to do this, and he wasn't aware of anything besides the horse's clatter and his own rising fear.

He moved to lift the bar on the middle door that was set in the partition separating the two sides. The sockets shook a little as he lifted the heavy two-by-four from them. He looked at one, pulled at the oaken piece. The socket came off in his hand. He stood a long, empty moment, staring at it. There had been no nuts holding it on the bolts. It had merely been resting there like that. He reached for the other socket. There were no nuts holding it on, either. A push from the other side of the door would have knocked the bar off. In that last moment Ketland's eyes went to where the latch should have been — and wasn't.

With him standing close, the black had gone into a veritable frenzy of bucking and screaming, the partition shuddering under its wild kicks. A sudden, animal panic swept Ketland, and his whole body shook with it. *Cut it out, Ketland, cut it out. Come on, Ketland. . . .*

He could hardly hold himself there long enough to replace the socket on its headless bolts. Then he let the bar down into place gingerly, so as not to knock the sockets off, jerking his hands away, whirling to the outer door. The black stallion threw itself bodily against the slats, whinnying crazily. Ketland halted, sweat streaming down his face, and with a terrible effort of will forced himself to move across the fresh hay at a slow walk. The black quieted some, snorting, watching him through the slats.

He reached the front door, shoving on it. The portal rattled under his hands. He shoved again, harder, panic in his harsh breath. It was a solid door, and he couldn't see through, but he felt it rattle loosely again, and jam against something, and stop rattling, and he knew with a sudden, sick dread what had happened.

The bar had dropped back into place outside. He was locked in.

Ketland tried to make his voice soft when he called, so as not to startle the horse. "Dekker? The bar's dropped on this door. Dekker, come and let me out."

There was no sound from outside. He tried to climb the door and reach the quarter at the top where it was slatted, but the inside was smooth, and the openings between the slats weren't large enough for his body anyway. The black began stomping around its stall, and the panic in Ketland gripped his vitals like a giant hand.

"Dekker, come and let me out. The bar's dropped, and I can't reach it from the inside . . ." — his voice raised and he began beating at the gate with both hands — "someone, hear me. I'm locked in Devil's stall . . ." — he was screaming now, throwing himself

bodily at the door like a frenzied animal —
"damn you, come and get me out. Damn
you, Dekker. You dropped that bar. Someone come and let me out, let me out. . . ."

He stopped suddenly, huddled against the
door, sobbing uncontrollably, realizing his
own screams had set the black off again. The
horse was thrashing about inside its section,
the slatted partition cracking and shuddering
as it threw twelve hundred pounds of vicious,
black dynamite against the walls. Ketland
turned, shaking, too far gone now to realize
clearly what he was doing or to fight himself
any more. The black whirled away from the
side, and kicked insanely at the middle door.
Ketland saw the door crash against the bar,
and the sockets jerk out on the headless
bolts. One more kick. . . .

"Damn you, Dekker, come and let me out!
Dekker, Dekker, Dekker . . . !"

The stallion threw itself against the middle
door again. The sockets slid off, the bar
dropped, the door crashed open. Devil stumbled on through and brought up against the
opposite wall.

The horse whirled on Ketland, little eyes
bloodshot and gleaming, nostrils flaring.
Ketland leaped to one side, and the stallion
smashed into the outer door where the man
had been crouching a moment before. The
animal turned, streaming blood from head
and shoulders, whinnying shrilly. Huddled

there in the corner on his hands and knees, Ketland felt a burning rage sweep up through his terror.

They thought he was through? They thought he was finished? They thought they could end it like this, putting him in a stall with a man-killer, and locking the door? The hell. . . .

He dove aside again as the black charged, feeling no pain in his legs, feeling no panic or fear, feeling only utter rage, scalding and cleansing. Where his movements before had been the blind frenzy of animal terror, they took on a swift, calculated deliberation. Maybe another man couldn't have done it. Maybe a younger man couldn't have done it. There had to be years of experience behind it, and innate horse savvy, and that only came to a man who had handled animals a long time. Ketland had handled them almost all his life.

He moved in front of the outer door, shouting hoarsely at the stallion. "Come on, you devil, here I am, come on . . . !"

The hay spurted beneath churning hoofs as the horse charged and reared above the man. Ketland waited until the last moment, then jumped aside. The outer door cracked as twelve hundred pounds of horseflesh came down against it, hoofs smashing the panels. The horse staggered off, whirled back at Ketland.

Gasping, Ketland pawed sweat from his eyes, dodged aside. The black caught itself before plunging into the back wall, whirling on one hind hoof like a trained roper. Ketland had put himself in front of the outer door again.

Once more it was the horse's wild scream and the leap aside and the maddened animal's shaking the whole barn as it crashed into the door. Another panel cracked, hinges creaked, and the door sagged outward. Blood covering its head, the black whirled and came at Ketland sideways. It didn't give Ketland enough room on either side, and the black's shoulder caught him as he tired to jump away from the rear wall. He went down, rolling up against the side partition with a force that stunned him.

The horse had smashed into the rear wall, and it backed away, shaking its head. Sensing Ketland at its side, the animal turned, shifting its weight to kick.

Ketland saw the movement and knew what it meant, and not even hearing his own shout he clawed up the slats and threw himself directly at the horse's rump. His weight struck the black hocks, and without leverage all the kick did was throw him bodily back against the partition. With a human cunning, Devil jumped forward to clear the space between them so it could catch Ketland with the full force of its kick. He rolled under the hoofs as they lashed out. One of them caught his shoulder, and he screamed in agony. Then he was up against the outer door again.

He didn't know how many more times he drew the black into that door before the portal collapsed. It was all a wild haze of choking hay and soggy sweat and salty blood and lashing hoofs. He could have escaped through the middle door into the other side, but the horse would have come in after him, and it would have been the same thing there. Time and time again he waited at the front gate till the last moment, and then jumped free, allowing the horse to batter on into the door, and finally, with the whole barn shuddering to the impact, the black crashed through the portal, tearing its lower half clear out and carrying the upper portion of the gate about its head and neck as it stumbled on out into the aisle.

It was logical that Midge should have taken this long to hear the racket from up at the house, but the men from the bunk shack or corrals should have reached the barns long ago. Highwoods was at the fence with Midge, and Dekker appeared just to have come from the bunk shack, followed by Oley Fanning and Rock.

"Ket," cried Midge, "get out between the bars! You can do it now, while Devil's still fighting that door. Ket, are you crazy? You can get away now."

"No," he gasped, "no," and ran on toward the horse where it had dragged the stall door clear out into the middle of the corral. He wasn't finished yet. He knew he had to do it now or never, while the anger in him still blotted out his fear. Exhausted and battered as he was, he knew he could never again ride another horse if he didn't do this now.

He worked the black into a corner, and got close enough to yank the shattered stall door off its neck. The horse tried to break away, but Ketland threw himself in front of it, getting the frenzied, lathered animal back against the fence. One of the hands was belatedly climbing the bars with a rope. Ketland couldn't wait. He moved in toward the horse.

Screaming like a woman, Devil opened up straight at Ketland. There hadn't been enough room between them for the beast to gain much momentum, however, and Ketland met it almost head-on, only throwing himself partly aside at the last moment, grabbing the long mane with one hand and hooking his other arm around beneath the neck and letting the horse's shoulder slam into his hip, knocking him up and over. Then he was on the bare, black hide, legs gripping like an Indian's, hand twisting hard into the mane.

"Ket," he heard the woman scream, "oh, you fool, Ket!"

He didn't hear any more, then, except the

horse's wild, frenzied sounds and the horse's drumming hoofs. He didn't see any more except the black devil beneath him, doing everything within the scope of its vicious cunning to get him off.

It bucked, and he took every jarring drop, screaming triumphantly at the agony it caused him. It rolled, and instead of stepping off like a man in a saddle would and waiting till the horse came up again, he rode it on around, eyes wide open, dodging the death in its flailing legs. There was an insane frustration in the black's eyes as it gained footing again and found the man had never left it. The horse rolled again, directing its kicks this time. Still Ketland was on when it came up.

He rolled it from one side of the corral to the other, until it had enough of that, and began going over backward. A man in the middle would have been forced to step off then, too, and ultimately lose his touch with the horse. But Ketland rode its neck when it twisted onto its hips and rode its head when it put its rump into the ground and rode its belly while it was upside down.

The horse became a veritable organism of mad bucking, pin-wheeling, sunfishing, humping up and coming down with all four hoofs planted and knocking most of the consciousness from Ketland each time it landed. Ketland was bleeding at the nose and ears, face covered with blood and sweat, clothes dark with dirt. His whole world was one of shocking, jarring pain, and a grim, terrible concentration on finishing this.

The horse began rolling again, trying desperately to get the man under its black body, and Ketland went with it, crying openly now, pawing blindly for holds, head rocking as a hoof caught him, laying over the animal's back with his nose streaming blood on its dirty hide.

Finally he felt the animal come to a stop beneath him, legs trembling, barrel heaving, lather dripping off it white as snow. Ketland slumped over, hearing his own sobbing, not knowing whether the wet on his face was sweat or blood, or both. He waited for the animal to gather itself again. It didn't! At last Ketland slid off, and his legs collapsed beneath him. He grabbed the horse's cannon bone and pulled himself to his knees, then the mane and pulled himself erect. He bent over and was sick. Choking weakly, he saw them coming from the corral.

"Stay away. I'm taking this horse back in. You wanted him for cow work? You got him." Dekker swam into his vision, and he spat out blood before he could speak again. "And maybe you don't know it, Dekker, but you did me a big favor. Yeah. A big favor."

VI

Ketland woke the next morning too sick to eat his breakfast. He had never packed a gun consistently, and his own weapon had been mislaid sometime during his year in the hospital. The first thing he did after getting up was ask the cook up at the house to lend him one of Judge Forsythe's ivory-handled Remingtons. Although its weight was an irritation to his battered torso, he strapped it on and meant to wear it from here on out, because he saw it stood that way now. He forced himself to do his duties at the barn, and finally sweated a little of the stiffness from his aching body.

The first horse he fed was one of the blooded Arabians the judge had ridden. He watched his hands as he dumped oats into its bag, and they weren't trembling. There was a grim smile on his face as he came from the stall and saw Highwoods riding in.

"Thought you were branding?"

"Not much going on down at the fires," said Highwoods. "Danny and Rock didn't show up this morning, and Fanning brought one bunch in and no more. Thought I'd come back for some shut-eye."

"High," said Ketland, "I want to know something square. I know where Dekker stands now, and Rock and the others. Where do you stand?"

Highwoods wouldn't meet his eyes. "What do you mean, Ket?"

"You know," said Ketland. "I examined that middle door in Devil's stall this morning. There's two bolts in each one of those oak sockets. I found the four nuts in the hay. It's possible that the horse, kicking constantly at the door, could have worked those nuts off the bolts, but not probable. The latch on the door was gone entirely."

Highwoods shuffled nervous boots in the dust. "Ket, you don't think . . . ?"

"You know what I think," said Ketland. "Now tell me straight. Are you with Dekker in this?"

"Ket, you know I'm not." Highwoods looked around almost fearfully. "It's just that so many of the old hands are gone. Tebo drifted south with his pal. And now, Uncle Harry like that. I've really been the only one left here at the house. I've been alone in that bunk shack for so long with all the new ones Dekker brought in. What could I do with Rock and Fanning and Poke and the rest? I'm not you, Ket. I couldn't take them all on in the bunk shack."

"Tell me what's going on around here, then," said Ketland. "Why does Dekker want me out? From the very first day. He put Rock and the others on me in that bunk

280

shack. Has it got something to do with Indian Ridge?"

Highwoods looked around that way again. "I don't know, Ket."

"Napperhan seems to think *I* know, and so does Dekker," said Ketland, leaning on the shovel. "You've been here longer than I have, High. When Judge Forsythe had his cowpokes file under the Homestead Act to get that strip across Indian Ridge, which man took the quarter section containing the line shack?"

"Uncle Harry, I believe."

"I suppose Uncle Harry signed his claim over to the judge?"

"That's customary," said Highwoods. "I know I signed over the quarter section I filed on. I wasn't no granger. I suppose Uncle Harry did, too."

"Suppose the other way," said Ketland, straightening. "Uncle Harry was always mighty fond of that god-forsaken hole, and he was the judge's brother. Suppose he didn't want to sign over. Who would inherit his property now that he's gone?"

Highwoods shrugged impatiently. "The only kin of his I know are Midge and Danny Dekker. Midge'd have first claim on anything, being Uncle Harry's blood kin. Danny was only his nephew by marriage."

"They wanted something from Uncle Harry pretty bad, whoever it was holding him up there," said Ketland. "Bad enough to kill him. If it had to do with Uncle Harry's homestead, do you think they'd stop with him? Where does that leave Midge and Danny? Where *is* Midge?"

"She left this morning for Centerpine. I was up when she got her horse. Heard her tell Dekker she'd be gone all day. Something about a tin box. . . ." He stopped suddenly, grabbing at Ketland. "If you're right, Ket, if she's in on this because she's kin of Uncle Harry, she's all alone. She's gone into Napperhan's town all alone. You'll never catch her in time. . . ."

Ketland pulled free of him, dropping the shovel and whirling toward the barns. "I got a horse that will make a damn' good try!"

Bixbee Riddle jumped out of his chair with a surprised grunt. "My Lord, Ketland, what have you been doing?"

"I've been riding," gasped Ketland, slamming the door of the lawyer's office behind him. "This has got to be fast, Riddle. I came into Centerpine by Tomonak Street, and Napperhan's boys spotted me before I hit Oglala. They'll be up here with Sheriff Arden and all the rest. Midge hit for town this morning. I have an idea she meant to see you."

Bixbee Riddle had handled Judge Forsythe's legal matters for many years, a thin, stooped man with a pronounced acquisitiveness in his beaked nose and bony hands, yet a capacity for kindness in soft, gray eyes. "You just missed Midge. She came to get some things I had of the judge's. Said she didn't trust them in Napperhan's town. I can't understand. . . ."

"Things?" Ketland wiped sweat from his face, drawing a shuddering breath, still filled with the wild exaltation of a ride like that. "What kind of things, Riddle? Quick!"

The bent lawyer glanced irritably at the sound of the stamping mills that swept through the open back window, raising his voice a little. "I brought a lot of the judge's personal effects here when he died. Midge wasn't of age then, and, as executor, I had to have them to take care of Pothook. There was an old tin box Uncle Harry had left with the judge. I asked Uncle Harry about it, and he said to keep it for him. That was almost three years ago. I hadn't remembered it until Midge came. . . ."

He broke off as Ketland grabbed him by his padded lapels. "Where is she now, Riddle? Her horse wasn't out front. Did she head back to the Pothook already?"

"Out front?" gasped Riddle. "Let go, Ketland. No, she didn't hitch up out front. Afraid of being seen by Napperhan or something. Came up past the mills into the compound behind. What is all this?"

Then, through the open rear window, over the incessant thunder of the stamping mills, Ketland heard the single word, a woman's voice speaking it, sharp, surprised. "Danny!"

Ketland released the lawyer, and whirled to the door. The front stairs shook beneath Sheriff Arden, followed by a crowd of Napperhan's miners, filling the lower hall. "Ketland," shouted Arden, "stop! You're under arrest. I'll shoot you if you don't. . . ."

Ketland was already turning the corner of the hall and running past Dr. Haskell's office to the covered stairway leading down the rear. He took the steps three at a time, tripping on high boot heels halfway down, and almost going headlong. An alley ran behind the buildings on this side of Tomonak, opening into a compound with hitch racks on the side directly below Riddle's office window. Dust was rising, kicked up by the blot of struggling figures over there. Danny Dekker must have realized how it was as soon as Ketland plunged out the back doorway, because the tall young ramrod whirled Midge around in front of him, grabbing for his gun.

"Don't do it, Ketland. You'll hit Midge!"

Ketland ran another stumbling step forward with his Remington held out in front of him, and stopped. "You?" he said.

"I guess you know now," said Dekker. "Did you have Napperhan pegged?"

He began shooting, and his second shot caught Ketland in the arm. Ketland tried to stay on his feet, but the pain and the heavy slug made him twist around and fall against the wall. He slid to the ground, pawing for his gun in the dust. Danny whirled to his roan, shouting at Rock.

"Help me get this wildcat on! Make sure of Ketland, Oley!"

Oley Fanning began coming toward Ketland. Ketland had found the Remington he'd dropped. Fanning saw the move he made to raise the gun, and stopped, and Fanning's own weapon blared red. Sprawled in the dust, Ketland heard the bullet hit the wall above him. Then the ivory-handled Remington bucked hard against his grimy left palm, and the jerk of Fanning's body made the man's beard pop up and down, and he fell with a soft, fleshy *thud*.

The woman was fighting madly with Rock and Dekker, and she tore free, twisting forward on the horse, screaming: "Ket, Ket . . . !"

Ketland couldn't fire at the men for fear of hitting her, but he understood their intent now. With the woman away from Dekker's horse for that moment, he threw his gun down on the animal. The mount screamed and lurched over against Rock's horse, then turned and broke into a wild, stumbling gallop back down the alley. Ketland had already put two more shots into Rock's mount.

The second horse went up against the wall, whinnying in pain, and kicked wildly at the boards, then went to its knees.

"Damn you, Ketland!" shouted Dekker, and began pulling Midge down the alley, firing at the closed end of the compound. "Get him, Rock. There's some more horses hitched in Lebarge. Get him."

The door of the back stairway creaked open, and someone began shooting from there, and it must have been Arden with Napperhan's men, because it was his crotchety voice. "Ketland! Quit shooting at me and I'll give you a chance to come in alive. Quit shooting and come in with your hands up."

Ketland was already moving down toward the alley. He saw the shift of Rock's figure, and shot. Rock cursed, returning fire at Ketland. The bullet whined past and clacked into the wall across the compound. Sheriff Arden shouted from the door and opened fire again. Rock sent two more Ketland's way, and that must have emptied his gun, because he backed down the alley at a stumbling run before Ketland's advance, not shooting again.

The stamping mills beat in on Ketland with a deafening thunder as he came out into Lebarge Street. The stamps were water-powered, and the overflow from the pumping system had sunk the north end of Lebarge into a veritable bog. It was an empty back street, brick mills lining its far walk, with rear windows of the business offices fronting on Tomonak frowning blankly down from this side. Ketland made a hollow rattle coming out of the passageway onto the plank walk. The high walls had cast the narrow alley into gloom in the late afternoon light, but out here it was still bright enough to see Rock clearly out in the middle of the street, reloading his gun, with Dekker farther on, struggling to haul Midge toward the three horses hitched at a rack in front of an open door in one of the mills. Ketland turned down the walk on this side.

"Get him, Rock!" shouted Dekker. "He's after those horses. What happened in the alley? Get him!"

"Somebody came out of that back door in the compound," said Rock, and raised his gun. "I had to clear out before they recognized me, didn't I?" He fired.

With the bullet chipping brick off the wall of the building behind him, Ketland turned, still running, and the Remington made a dull boom over the incessant beat of the stamps. Rock's heavy brows raised in a surprised way. It was the only expression Ketland could see on the man's face. Then Rock sank to his knees in the viscid mud of the street, and stayed that way, bent over, hands across his belly.

Ketland had passed Dekker, who was on

the other side and hampered by the woman, slogging through the muck. Dekker saw Ketland would reach the animals first, and quit moving toward them. Midge struggled feebly in his arms, and he whipped the gun across her head. She sagged forward with a sharp cry. Dekker began to back toward the mill door behind him.

Sweaty face twisted with rage, Ketland turned after him. The thunder of the stamps was so loud he had to scream.

"Let Midge go, Dekker! She can't do you any good now! You're through with it! She can't possibly help you get hold of that homestead now!"

"You know then!" shouted Dekker. "All right, Ketland! I wanted to get you out of it from the first! You know too much of the Pothook! I figured you'd find it if you stayed! And you did find it, didn't you, up at Indian Ridge?"

"That's why you locked me in with Devil?" called Ketland. "You thought Uncle Harry told me at Indian Ridge? He didn't! I know now, but Uncle Harry didn't tell me! Up till five minutes ago, I thought it was Napperhan! Let Midge go, Dekker! You're through! She can't be any good to you now!"

Ketland was within range, and Dekker began to shoot again, laughing crazily, backing into the huge open door. "You're wrong, Ketland! She's still good to me! She got those papers, didn't she? Had them all the time! I'm not through! Nobody's seen me in town! Nobody'll be able to figure out what really happened here! That was Arden back in the compound? All he'll see is that you had a gunfight with Oley and Rock! Nothing else to see, Ketland! I'll be out of here before they come down! I was going to do it different than this, but I guess we have something here just as good as I planned! They'll never find her, Ketland! Come on! They'll never even find you!"

His voice was drowned out as he backed into the mill. Ketland reached the door a moment later, the sound from within striking him like a physical blow. The stamps were huge beams, two rows of them rising in unison like one gigantic pestle in a titanic mortar, and crashing back down to crush the ore in the cement pans below with a roar that shook the building to its foundations. The only workers on this floor were those at the fire retorts and amalgamating pans at the other end, half hidden by the stamps. This end of the building was quite dark, hiding Ketland and Dekker to the men down there. Ketland stumbled through the gloom past a quivering row of rusty settling tanks, searching the confused pattern of pipes and catwalks and platforms for Dekker as his eyes became accustomed to the low light.

They'll never find her, Ketland. Dekker's

meaning hadn't struck Ketland at first, but now, with the roar of the stamps beating into his brain, Ketland understood Dekker's intent. *They'll never find her, Ketland.* It strangled his breath in his throat and made his stomach retch as he staggered through the shuddering obscurity, the floor shaking beneath him, the building echoing about him, the stamps crashing into their cement beds constantly, inexorably.

Finally he saw them. Dekker had dragged Midge up onto the iron-railed walk around the second cement pan, near the mouth of a chute down which the ore was dumped from above to be crushed by the stamps. Ketland tripped on the iron stairway going up.

Dekker's first bullet clanged off the guardrail near Ketland's head. Midge made her last feeble struggle, and Dekker gave her a vicious, backhand blow that sent her gasping to the floor. He straightened above her again, firing. It was all Ketland had left. Still going up the stairs, he heaved the empty Remington. It struck Dekker in the head, and the ramrod staggered back against the shaking steel housing of the stamp. Ketland tore off a boot heel on the top step as he threw himself into Dekker. They rolled across Midge, struggling and kicking, and brought up against the rail with Dekker on top.

Ketland felt all the surging strength of the man above him, as wild and tameless as that of the black stallion. His head thudded against the cement as Dekker's fist crashed into his mouth. With the thunderous roar of the stamps spinning about him crazily, Ketland tried to roll from beneath, but the powerful Dekker caught him and put a knee in his stomach.

Gasping quickly, Ketland clutched the rail, and twisted to haul himself up. Dekker clawed one of his hands off, slugging him on the back of the neck. Ketland's face struck the railing, and he sobbed, and fought on up to his knees, knowing his only chance was to get free. He lashed out backward with a boot, heard Dekker's gasp. He rolled down the railing till the weight on his back was off balance, then twisted around, striking blindly with an elbow. He felt Dekker knocked partly off him by the blow, and surged on up, and was free.

Ketland reeled backward, dodging the younger man's lunge. The deafening thunder of the stamp was right behind him. Ore crashed down the chute from above with a clattering rush. Dekker jumped across Midge's body with his mouth twisted in a soundless scream.

Ketland deliberately let the man come into him, driving him backward toward the open chute. Dekker got one arm around the small of Ketland's back and put his other in Ketland's face, arching the older man back like a bow. Pain shot through Ketland with a snapping crackle of popped ribs. He let himself go utterly limp.

Dekker shifted his weight against the cement to heave Ketland backward into the chute. Dekker was unbalanced for just that moment. Ketland stiffened with a grunt and veered sideways. He tore free from Dekker's arm around his back and twisted violently away from the hand in his face. In that instant, he was out from beneath Dekker and the chute. He whirled around and snaked a leg out in front of Dekker and caught Dekker's shoulder, heaving forward with all his weight. The man went head foremost down the quivering chute.

Ketland fell to his knees from the force of that shove, head hanging into the mouth of the chute. The ore clattered down in front of him with an eager rush, and the beam fell from above and struck the cement pan with a deafening roar that crushed the ore to pulp. *They'll never find her, Ketland? They'll never find you, Dekker.*

Sheriff Arden and half a dozen miners were in Lebarge when Ketland brought out Midge. Napperhan came running down the hill from above followed by more men, and slowed down suddenly when he saw Ketland, as if he sensed his defeat already.

"He was going to do that to me," sobbed

the woman, trembling in Ketland's arms. "Danny Dekker, my own cousin. He must have followed me from the Pothook, Ket! I told him I was coming after the tin box. I thought it was Napperhan!"

"Ketland," said Bixbee Riddle, helping Rock up out of the muddy street, "what is this? Dekker?"

"Where's Doc Haskell, Midge needs attention," said Ketland, and began walking her up the hill. "Dekker? Yes, Riddle. Danny was after the original patent to Uncle Harry's quarter section up on Indian Ridge. It was Dekker holding Uncle Harry hostage up there, trying to force the old man to tell where his deed was. That right, Rock?"

Rock nodded sickly, clutching his bullet wound. "Yeah. We took turns guarding Uncle Harry. Jerry Poke left to take his turn the day after that fight with you in the bunk shack. That's why you found Poke in the Indian Ridge cabin. Clay Garr must have stumbled onto it and had it out with Jerry. After Garr nailed Jerry, I guess he climbed the ridge to see if anybody'd heard the shots. That's how he spotted you, and tried to keep you off."

"But what would they want Uncle Harry's claim for?" asked Riddle.

Ketland looked at Napperhan, and the black-haired mine owner shrugged wearily. "All right. About three months ago, Danny

293

Dekker came to me saying he owned land in the Cabines upon which a vein of my copper apexed. He offered to sell out to me for a cool million dollars. I knew all the trouble Freddie Hintz had caused Amalgamated down on Butte Hill using that apex law to close up their shafts until they finally had to pay him off, and I was willing to talk business with Dekker, if he could show me the spot and prove ownership. He must have thought he was pretty close to forcing the whereabouts of that deed from Uncle Harry, or he wouldn't have come to me. I didn't know about that part of it, then. Dekker said he'd be back in a few days to close the deal. Things strung along, and he kept putting me off till I got suspicious. If he did have an apex, I was afraid somebody else would discover it, and I didn't want that to happen until I had control. I sent my boys into the Cabines on their own."

"Then no cattle stampeded into a coulée and caved in your Number Three," said Ketland. "You just used that as an excuse to keep everybody out of the Cabines. And when Danny told me not to go near the Cabines, he wasn't worried about your men shooting me up. He was afraid I'd find Uncle Harry there. I guess Uncle Harry's original patent was the only proof of ownership, right, Rock?"

"Yes," muttered Rock. "When the cave-in

here on Oglala swallowed the courthouse, all county records were lost. If Dekker fixed it so he'd inherit the homestead from Uncle Harry, he had to have the deed to prove his claim. Otherwise, not being able to check on county records, the sale and transfer to Napperhan would have to be done by litigation, and Danny couldn't risk the time that would take, or the investigations it would mean. Danny had to get rid of Uncle Harry and any kin of the old man's in order to have full title. Folks were already beginning to say Uncle Harry had probably got caught out in our last freeze, and Dekker planned on making Midge's death seem as natural."

"A million dollars," said Ketland. "An apex worth that much, on the cattleman's side, will do a lot toward cleaning the Napperhan stain off this town. You still want to contest it, Jonas? You want to try and rope me in on that murder charge?"

"Wouldn't hold water." Bixbee Riddle grinned. "Clear case of armed trespass on Clay Garr's part. Napperhan knows it."

They had reached the top of the hill, and turned into Tomonak Street now. Dr. Haskell was waddling down from the Napperhan Building. Midge suddenly saw the black stallion standing hipshot and lathered with its reins dropping on the curb in front of Bixbee Riddle's office.

"Ket!" she said. "You came in *that* way?"

"Yes." He smiled. "Riding Devil. And I didn't fall off once. I told Dekker he did me a favor when he locked me in that stall. It was what I needed to take my fear away. I'm getting old and I'm not as spry as I used to be, but there isn't a horse on Pothook I won't top now."

"An old man couldn't have ridden Devil, or beaten Dekker," said Midge. "You're still young enough to 'rod the Pothook, Ket . . . you're still young enough to do anything you want to do, or be anything you want to be."

"There's only one thing I want to do," he said, "or be." He saw in her eyes that she knew what he meant, and that she wanted it that way, too. Suddenly he did feel younger.

About the Author

Les Savage, Jr. was born in Alhambra, California and grew up in Los Angeles. His first published story was "Bullets and Bullwhips" accepted by the prestigious magazine, Street & Smith's *Western Story*. Almost ninety more magazine stories followed, all set on the American frontier, many of them published in Fiction House magazines such as *Frontier Stories* and *Lariat Story Magazine* where Savage became a superstar with his name on many covers. His first novel, *Treasure of the Brasada*, appeared from Simon & Schuster in 1947. Due to his preference for historical accuracy, Savage often ran into problems with book editors in the 1950s who were concerned about marriages between his protagonists and women of different races — a commonplace on the real frontier but not in much Western fiction in that decade. Savage died young, at thirty-five, from complications arising out of hereditary diabetes and elevated cholesterol. However, as a result of the censorship imposed on many of his works, only now are they being fully restored by returning to the author's original manuscripts. Among Savage's finest Western stories are

Fire Dance at Spider Rock (Five Star Westerns, 1995), *Medicine Wheel* (Five Star Westerns, 1996), *Coffin Gap* (Five Star Westerns, 1997), *Phantoms in the Night* (Five Star Westerns, 1998), *The Bloody Quarter* (Five Star Westerns, 1999), *In the Land of Little Sticks* (Five Star Westerns, 2000), and *The Cavan Breed* (Five Star Westerns, 2001). Much as Stephen Crane before him, while he wrote, the shadow of his imminent death grew longer and longer across his young life, and he knew that, if he was going to do it at all, he would have to do it quickly. He did it well, and, now that his novels and stories are being restored to what he had intended them to be, his achievement irradiated by his powerful and profoundly sensitive imagination will be with us always, as he had wanted it to be, as he had so rushed against time and mortality that it might be.

The employees of Thorndike Press hope you have enjoyed this Large Print book. All our Thorndike and Wheeler Large Print titles are designed for easy reading, and all our books are made to last. Other Thorndike Press Large Print books are available at your library, through selected bookstores, or directly from us.

For information about titles, please call:

(800) 223-1244

or visit our Web site at:

www.gale.com/thorndike
www.gale.com/wheeler

To share your comments, please write:

Publisher
Thorndike Press
295 Kennedy Memorial Drive
Waterville, ME   04901

15ω
1 X
2/28/06